TELL me no LIES

BOOKS BY RACHEL BRANTON

Finding Home Series
Take Me Home
All That I Love
Then I Found You

Lily's House Series
House Without Lies
Tell Me No Lies
Your Eyes Don't Lie
Hearts Never Lie
Broken Lies
Cowboys Can't Lie

Noble Hearts
Royal Quest
Royal Dance

Picture Books
I Don't Want To Eat
Bugs
I Don't Want to Have
Hot Toes

UNDER THE NAME TEYLA BRANTON

Unbounded Series
The Change
The Cure
The Escape
The Reckoning
The Takeover

Unbounded Novellas
Ava's Revenge
Mortal Brother
Lethal Engagement
Set Ablaze

Imprints Series
Touch of Rain
On The Hunt
Upstaged
Under Fire
Blinded

Colony Six Series
Sketches

Other
Times Nine

RACHEL BRANTON

WHITE
STAR
PRESS

This is a work of fiction, and the views expressed herein are the sole responsibility of the author. Likewise, certain characters, places, and incidents are the product of the author's imagination, and any resemblance to actual persons, living or dead, or actual events or locales, is entirely coincidental.

Tell Me No Lies (Lily's House Book 2)

Published by White Star Press
P.O. Box 353
American Fork, Utah 84003

Printed in the United States of America
ISBN: 978-1-939203-03-8
Year of first printing: 2012

For my daughter Cátia.
Thanks for always being there, and
for reading yet one more manuscript.

1

I blinked to hold back the tears, stunned by what I was hearing. No! I don't believe it. But I did.

Hurt followed the disbelief, growing to an agony that urged me to physically lash out at Sadie, my best friend and bearer of the terrible news, but I was frozen in place, as though my heart had stopped pumping blood to my suddenly useless limbs.

Besides, it wasn't Sadie's fault.

Oh, Julian. How could you?

Sadie put a hand on my shoulder, but the sympathy in her eyes did little to comfort me. "I'm sorry, Tessa. I really am. I didn't want to tell you, but . . . " She sighed and continued in a whisper, "I would want to know if it were me."

Her words released me from my mute state. "I need to be alone."

"Of course. I understand. Call me if you need me." Sadie stepped close and hugged me while I stood without moving. I barely noticed her departure.

My eyes wandered the room of my childhood, only

recently familiar again since I'd come home to Flagstaff to prepare for the wedding. Mother had insisted on dinners and celebrations, and because Julian and I planned to live in Flagstaff, where he would work in his family business, it only made sense for me to leave the job at my father's factory in Phoenix several weeks early. I missed the job and my friends the minute I'd left, but Julian and I were ready to take the plunge into matrimony—or so I'd thought.

The door to my walk-in closet was open, and I could see the wedding dress I was to have worn in just over forty-eight hours. Bile rose in my throat, and a tear skidded down my cheek. I brushed it impatiently away. I wouldn't cry for a man who had betrayed me.

Since tonight we were having the rehearsal dinner, last night had been Julian's bachelor party. Sadie's brother had been at the party and had told her all about Julian disappearing early with a woman whose hands had been altogether too familiar with a man who was about to be married.

I slumped on my bed, covered with the homemade quilt my grandmother had made, my eyes still locked on the white satin dress. Drenched in lace and small pearls, it had a sweetheart neckline and a gorgeous chapel train. The dress cost seventeen hundred dollars and had taken three weeks of daily shopping to find. My mother had been with me every one of those days, which had been a torture in itself.

I bit my lip until I tasted blood.

I'd met Julian Willis when I'd come home to visit for the Christmas holiday, though if the truth be told, my visit had more to do with my horse, Serenity, than seeing my parents. At my mother's insistence, I'd tagged along on their invitation to attend a party thrown by the Willises. I hadn't minded going, once I met Julian. If his blond good looks and toned physique hadn't won me over, his attentiveness and charm would have. After countless trips to Phoenix on his part and numerous weekends home on mine, the inevitable had happened: we'd fallen in love. He asked me to marry him, and I said yes.

Two weeks later, my father and Julian's had negotiated a business arrangement to take effect after the wedding. The Willis family owned a huge frozen food conglomerate, and my father produced a line of breakfast cereals, where I managed the swing shift. With the help of the Willises, our business would expand to new markets my father had never before reached. I wasn't sure what the Willises were getting out of the deal since our business was stable but not growing. Maybe they would simply have in-laws who were up to their standard of living.

Not that we'd ever been poor in my lifetime—thanks to my grandpa who'd worked himself into an early grave to create that first bowl of sugar-coated cereal. I still missed him terribly.

What am I going to do?

The awful thing was that a part of me wasn't all that surprised. Julian was attractive, thoughtful, and a big flirt—a hit with ladies of every age. Half of the marriageable women in Flagstaff had chased him at one time or another, and before we'd met he'd had a bit of a reputation—one he'd assured me was complete fabrication.

I won't marry a liar and a cheat. Every woman deserved better than that. I wondered if I'd purposely been blind or if he'd been good at hiding things. Perhaps his betrayal had been a momentary lapse, but if so, what did that say about our future? If I couldn't trust him now, how could I trust him for the next sixty or more years?

Maybe it's all a mistake. I latched onto the idea. Yet in the next minute I had to discard it. Sadie had been my best friend since kindergarten, and I'd trust her with my life. There was no way she would have spoken unless she was certain it was true. More likely she hadn't told me everything she knew, not wanting to hurt me further.

A knock on the door startled me from my thoughts. "Who is it?"

"Your mother."

"Come in."

Elaine Crawford didn't so much as enter a room as sweep into it. She was the epitome of grace and elegance. Even at eight o'clock on a Thursday morning, her hair was styled in an elaborate twist that was both attractive and left her beautiful neck bare.

"My, Sadie was in such a hurry this morning. I've never seen her run off so quickly. Did you two have a disagreement?"

I shook my head, unwilling to trust my voice.

My mother's eyes didn't leave my face. "What happened? We can't be losing your maid of honor at this late date." She smiled to show she was teasing, but there was a warning under the words.

"Sadie and I are fine."

"Wonderful." She walked to the closet and peered

inside. "You're going to look like a princess in this dress. Even without you in it, I could stare at it all day. Julian won't be able to take his eyes off you."

I gave her a weak smile. I did love the dress—a good thing, since it had taken so much time to find one we both agreed on. My mother wasn't a woman to give up on any goal, and her goal had been to find a dress that not only would I agree to wear but that would make people sigh with admiration for years to come.

She rambled on, going over a last-minute menu change and reminding me we needed to pick up my father's tuxedo. "I hope Lily's man comes dressed appropriately," she said, almost as an afterthought.

"Mario's wearing a suit. Lily said he looks great."

"I wish you hadn't insisted on their coming."

"Lily's my sister. Of course she'll be at my wedding."

"You weren't at hers."

I didn't say anything. Lily had done what she felt she had to, and I'd been happy for her.

"He will never amount to anything," my mother added.

"And you think Julian will?" I couldn't hold it back any longer, though I knew my mother was the worst person to confide in. She'd never been the kind of mother to bake cookies, to take her kids to the park, or sit and discuss school and boyfriends. As teenagers, Lily and I had agreed that she was like Mary Lennox's mother in the *Secret Garden*—too occupied with her own life and goals to really care about her daughters. "Well, you're wrong. I just found out he cheated on me. Maybe more than once."

My mother didn't gasp. She didn't hug me and ask me

how I knew. She showed no sympathy for me or anger toward my fiancé. She simply stared, her arms folded tightly against her stomach.

"I can't marry him," I said.

That brought her to life. "Of course you'll marry him. It's you he loves, no matter what you've heard."

Something in her demeanor tipped me off. "Wait. What do you know about this?"

"I know that Julian is good for you. He'll take care of you. His family's business is doing well, and our contract with them will do wonders for our company as well. Your company someday."

"You knew? All this time, you knew?"

It was one thing for my mother to disown a daughter because she'd married a man she didn't approve of, but I couldn't believe she'd want me to commit my life to a man who cheated before he was even married.

"How long has it been going on?" I asked. "Does everyone in town know?" I could imagine it now, people wagging their tongues and in the end sympathizing with Julian because he was oh-so-handsome and exciting, as if that excused everything.

Not in my book.

"The truth is," my mother said, "marriage is little more than a business arrangement. Eventually you will realize that, and then you will understand this is a problem you can overcome. Besides, Julian will see the error of his ways. He'll always come back to you."

I hadn't even known he'd left me. I shifted on the bed, searching for something to make her see reason. "Would you have married Dad if he'd been cheating?"

"I would and I did."

I gaped at her. I knew my parents' marriage wasn't perfect. Growing up, Lily and I had often clung to each other at night as they'd argued loudly in their bedroom. I'd been glad to escape to college, though it had hurt to leave Lily behind. But she was far more resilient and determined than I ever was, never wavering rom her dreams of leaving and building her own life. It was she who'd fallen in love and eloped in the middle of the night a year ago when she was only twenty-two.

We'd both come home for the Fourth of July, and telling our parents about her engagement to Mario hadn't gone well. I'd helped Lily pack the rest of what was in her old room, and she'd left during the night while our parents lay sleeping. I'd never forget how happy she looked.

"I love him so much!" She'd told me. "He's like the air that I breathe. He's a hard worker, and I know we'll make it. You don't have to worry about me anymore."

They had made it, at first, while both were working. They'd even bought a big, old, run-down house to fix up. Then a leaky water heater and a small fire set them back, and they'd cut their work hours at the beginning of summer semester to finish school. Now Lily was expecting and so sick she had to quit her job altogether.

Meanwhile, she'd filled every vacant space in their house with teenage girls who had nowhere else to go except the street or back to the unloving homes from which Lily had rescued them. In a few years, Mario would finish school and be able to support them, but for now they survived on love, money from the state for a few of the girls who'd been placed with them officially, the little money I could spare, and the funds I begged for them from my parents.

Now thinking of how Lily's face lit up every time she talked about Mario, or whenever he entered the room, and how careful he was of her, made me strong. I wanted that for myself.

"I can't go through with the wedding," I told my mother. "I'm sorry."

"At least talk to Julian. He'll make it right. I know it."

I knew it, too, and that was exactly why I didn't want to talk to him. When I was with Julian, he was all too persuasive. He should have been a televangelist, because he could convince anyone of just about anything. Since he'd been over sales in his father's company, he bragged that the business had doubled in profits.

My mother drew herself to her full height. "Think of the caterer. All our friends coming from out of town. I swear if you do this, you'll be making the biggest mistake of your life."

"The mistake would be marrying a man who doesn't love me!" Tears were coming, despite my effort to stop them.

"He does love you. Every bit as much as you love him. Please, Tessa, you must talk to Julian."

Would it be too much to ask to have her on my side for once?

I jumped to my feet and walked past her. "I'm going to see Serenity. Then I'm emailing Julian to tell him everything's off."

"What about Lily? She'll lose her house without our help."

I froze at the door. "What?" I turned, feeling stupid and slow.

"You heard me." My mother lifted her chin, and not for the first time did I notice her beauty. Lily took after her, with her blond hair, even-toned skin, and swan-like neck.

My hair was altogether something else, looking as though someone had upended a diluted bucket of orange paint on my head. Strawberry blond, they called it, though that was a big stretch of the word strawberry. A genetic gift from my grandmother, I'd been told. I didn't remember her myself, but when my grandfather had been alive, he'd touched the splotchy freckles that nearly covered all my face, and told me I looked exactly like her. I'd heard the love in his voice, and it was the only time I'd really felt beautiful.

"I'll give her my money," I said without thinking.

"You forget that if you aren't married, you won't have your trust fund. Not until five more years. And your father has already filled your place at the factory, so you can't help her out with a regular paycheck. Since Lily's married, she'll get her inheritance in two more years, but her house can't wait that long, which means all her foster girls are going to end up in the street."

She was talking about the trust fund my grandfather had set up—a half million dollars up front at age twenty-five if we were married or thirty if we weren't, and monthly payments of one thousand dollars thereafter. Lily was married, but too young at twenty-three to receive anything. Being twenty-five, I qualified if I married, and I'd planned to lend Lily my money to buy her house outright after my wedding. Now it looked as though she'd have to wait two more years.

I stared at my mother, fury racing through my body. "Are you saying you won't help Lily anymore if I don't get married? I don't believe this! Being angry at her because of Mario is one thing, but letting her lose her house because you're upset with me is—" I couldn't think of a word bad enough, not one I would say in my mother's presence, so I quit speaking.

My mother's eyes narrowed, and when she spoke her voice was as brittle as ice. "It's not for you to judge my relationship with your sister, but what I'm saying is that we're not in a position to help Lily further—that's why we're pushing for this merger. With the economy the way it is, you are the only one who can save your sister."

"Then I'll drive to Vegas and marry the first man I meet!"

She laughed. "Oh, Tessa. Stop this. You love Julian. Go talk to him. There's been a mistake, that's all. Go ride Serenity, or take a walk or whatever you need to do, and then get this taken care of. All the relatives will be here tonight. All your friends from Phoenix." She swept past me. "Or you can let Lily finally see what a big mistake she made marrying that boy."

She was gone before I could protest. Before I could remind her about the baby, who would be her grand-child, regardless of who his father was. Neither Lily nor I had ever discovered why our parents hated Mario so much, but it seemed to go much deeper than his race or his family's blue-collar status in society. I didn't under-stand their objection. Mario Jameson Perez came from good, hard-working parents—an American mother and a father from Spain—both of whom had taught him and his numerous siblings the meaning of love. Mario was fun and intelligent, and he loved Lily more than anything. That he was handsome was simply an added bonus. He was also good with the girls they fostered, helping them realize how special they each were by the courtesy he extended them. The example he was of an adoring husband changed the way many of them thought about love.

If I couldn't help Lily, and my parents couldn't or wouldn't, my little sister would lose everything she'd been working for. Except Mario, of course. And the baby.

I went out to see Serenity, putting a few sugar cubes in my pocket as I always did without thinking about it. I was on autopilot. What was I going to do? I couldn't marry Julian, not if what Sadie said was true, but neither could I leave Lily without help. I'd been mothering her since I was two and she so tiny that all she could do was suck at the bottle the nanny taught me to give her. After the nanny left when I was four, I became more of a mother to Lily than our own mother.

Serenity was out in the far pasture near the copse of trees that marked the border of our three-acre plot, almost as though she was trying to get as far away from the house as I was. When she saw me, she trotted over with a soft whinny, her brown coat glistening in the morning sunlight. She was beautiful, grace incarnate, and for a strange instant, she reminded me of my mother.

She put her face close to mine in greeting. I could feel the heat of her breath and the smell of freshly chewed grass. "I know what you want." I gave her a cube of sugar, which she ate greedily, her soft brown eyes begging for more. I gave her another before walking toward the trees. She hesitated a moment, as if confused about why I didn't head for the barn to get the tack so we could go for a ride, but I didn't feel like riding now. I felt like collapsing into a ball and crying my eyes out.

I wanted a mother to turn to for guidance.

Yeah, right.

There was a gate at the end of the pasture, which bordered a wide path on the other side of the fence line. The city had built the path before selling the land beyond it to a developer, who had promptly put up a myriad of tract houses that had infuriated my mother and the other neighbors. Thus the thick row of fast-growing trees that almost hid the abomination from our sight.

I, on the other hand, had been the one to put in the gate. I loved riding Serenity on the path that extended for several miles. I liked seeing mothers jogging behind strollers, children on bicycles, runners stopping for breath after their runs.

Today none of that mattered. I slumped down at the base of a tree and let my head drop into my hands.

What was I going to do?

Lily. I was calling her cell before I'd thought twice about it.

"Hello," she asked, a little breathlessly.

"It's me," I said.

"Of course it's you, or I wouldn't have answered. I would have stayed hugging the toilet."

"That bad, huh?"

"Worse than bad. On top of all this sickness and the house problems, I'm spotting, and the doctor told me I'm going to have to drop out of school to stay in bed. I don't mind, except that means I'll soon have to start paying on those student loans I took out. Not exactly what we need right now with the mortgage three months overdue. It's all we can do to get food in the house at this point. If not for you, the food I get from WIC, and what Mario and the girls make, I wouldn't know what to do."

She heaved a sigh before continuing, "The worst is all the phone calls from the mortgage company. I tell you, I will be so relieved when the house is paid for, and I can tell them to bug off. You can't know how much you are saving our lives. Well, I guess you know exactly how much, but I will be forever grateful. You've always been there for me."

I shut my eyes for a moment. What was I going to tell my sister? I couldn't marry Julian, but I couldn't let her down, either.

"Don't worry," Lily added, as if suddenly figuring out the reason for my silence. "I have permission from the doctor to go to your wedding—just not the rehearsal dinner. Sorry about that. At least I'll be there for the real thing."

"That's good. We'll make sure you have a comfortable chair."

"Is Mom okay with us being there? I mean, I know you must have had to sacrifice a limb to get her to help with our last mortgage payment."

"She doesn't have a choice. You're my sister. I'm just really sorry things are so hard right now."

"We'll make it. I'm happy, Mario and I are still crazy in love, and I want to be helping those girls. They've had it so hard. For some of them, this is the only place they've ever felt safe." Lily sounded fierce and a little bit scared. As if to make up for that, she tried to make the next comment light. "Anyway, the hard times are almost over with. The real problem is going to be losing this weight after this baby comes. I was fat enough to begin with. So what's up, anyway? Why did you call?"

I hesitated, still unsure what to say. I twisted the engagement ring on my hand, which all of a sudden felt too tight. It was a beautiful ring, though in lesser circles the diamond might be considered ostentatious.

"Tell me," Lily urged. "Is it Julian? What's he done now?"

"What do you mean, *now?*"

"Well, he's always doing something." She paused before adding, "Are you sure you should be marrying him?" She'd asked me this a dozen times in the past two months. I usually got mad. "Look, it's not too late to call it off."

What about the catering, the flowers, the guests? I wanted to say. *What about your house and all those girls?*

"Tessa, we both promised ourselves that we'd never have the kind of marriage our parents have. They barely talk. They live separate lives. If you aren't sure, you can't go through with it."

I had the sense she was speaking to me as if I were one of the girls she was trying to save. "I love him," I said.

"Do you really? Do you love him so much that you feel like you'll die if he doesn't love you back?"

I imagined her holding a hand to her heart and gazing out the window as she spoke. "It certainly feels like it right now."

Yet I knew I wouldn't die because thickly layered over the hurt was a growing coat of anger that was urging me to *do* something. To act. To show Julian I didn't need him.

"Maybe this is a sign. I've told you before that he's not real. I can't tell when he's being truthful or making something up. The worst thing is that you're not yourself when he's around."

"Mom would be furious if I canceled the wedding."

"Then leave and come here. We'll make it work somehow. I hope you know that I'd rather have you happy than all the houses in the world."

I did know that whatever the cost to her, Lily wouldn't want me to sacrifice myself. But she was the one who needed help now, whether she admitted it or not. "Maybe it's just pre-wedding jitters," I said, faking a casualness I didn't feel. "I should talk to Julian."

"I don't know. That might not be a good idea. If you're having doubts, maybe you should delay things a few weeks and decide without him around. You only have one chance to do this right the first time."

I didn't know if delaying things would help. It certainly wouldn't change his infidelity. If Lily knew about that, she'd probably hunt him down herself. She'd think I was crazy for even considering going through with the wedding. But for all the young women she'd saved, she didn't know what it was like to protect a younger sister. I'd been doing it all my life.

"Everything is going to be fine," I said. "In a few months, when we're sitting inside your mortgage-free house playing with your little baby, we'll laugh about this."

"Oh, Tessa. Are you sure?" The tone in her voice told me she was smiling.

"I'm sure. Don't worry about a thing."

"I love you, Tessa."

"Love you, too."

I hung up but remained sitting in the tall weeds, my back against the tree, staring into nothingness. Serenity nuzzled my head in worry. "It's all right, girl."

But it wasn't.

I have to think. Why couldn't I think? I kept seeing my mother's face drawn in disapproval and my father's flushed with anger. Lily sick in bed, her girls sleeping in the streets. Julian's smile—mocking. I rubbed my face with my hands, and they came away wet. I hadn't even realized I was crying.

The creak of the back gate signaled someone's approach. "Tessa? Are you okay?" A man's voice, one I recognized.

I hurriedly dried my face with the hem of my shirt before he came into view around the trees.

"Oh, there you are." He was a tall, broad, scruffy-looking man with restful green eyes. I thought he was nearing forty, but it was hard to tell with the brown beard and the hair that fell to below his ears. He lived in one of the tract houses, and many times over the last year, I'd caught him petting Serenity over the fence. I didn't mind because, except for the groom who fed her after I moved away, she didn't have company.

"Hi, Gage." I knew little more than his name, though we'd talked on numerous occasions. The rumor around town said he was an ex-con, recently released from prison, though no one seemed to know what he might have been in prison for and were either too lazy or unbelieving to research it. My mother had at least checked with the local police to make sure he wasn't on any child predator list, which he wasn't, but she still would have taken up a petition to force him from the neighborhood, had it been possible. I was glad she'd deemed it a waste of time. Over the months of talking to him and observing his gentleness with Serenity, I doubted the rumors were true. I suspected only his shaggy appearance kept the gossip alive.

"I saw Serenity, and she was looking kind of nervous. Thought maybe you'd had a fall."

"Ah, Gage, she's not even wearing a saddle, and I don't ride bareback. Not usually."

He looked at the sorrel. "Oh, right." He gave me a tentative smile, which didn't have much effect on his face under all that hair. "Well, as long as you're okay. But shouldn't you be shopping or at the hairdresser or something? You're still getting married Saturday, aren't you?"

I closed my eyes for a painful moment. I wondered if he'd heard the rumors about Julian, and if he felt sorry for me. "I don't know."

An emotion I couldn't define passed over his face. In a swift movement, he squatted down beside me. "What happened?"

"What makes you think something happened?"

He gestured to the grass. "Because you're sitting on the ground in a bunch of weeds two days before your wedding, looking like you wished a hole would open up and swallow you."

A hole would be nice, except then how would I help Lily? My father had hundreds of applications for each job opening in his factory, and other companies were just as flooded. No one would pay me what I'd earned with my father, and my degree in liberal arts now seemed rather useless. Of course, I'd never thought I'd actually have to find a job outside the family business.

A burst of anger blotted out the despair. How could I have been so stupid? Lily had at least tried to become independent, while I'd stayed reliant on my family. Now they controlled my life—and they wanted me to marry Julian.

No!

For a moment the hurt and betrayal were too great to endure. Yet I didn't die, and after a moment the pain receded enough to breathe again, and I knew what I had to do. I arose, brushing my hands on my pants. "I'm getting married," I said, "but not to my fiancé."

Gage's eyes narrowed as he stood. "What are you talking about?" At that moment he looked hard, like a man who actually might have served time.

"He's a liar and a cheat, and I'm getting out, even if I have to hitchhike my way to Las Vegas and marry the first man I meet."

"That's crazy."

"So is marrying someone who doesn't love you."

"At least you know him. Don't you think marrying some stranger in Las Vegas would be even worse?"

"Not if it's a business arrangement. Temporary." *Take that, Mother.* I was a quick learner. I'd find a way around the trust fund requirements because I knew if my grandfather were alive, he'd be the first one to help Lily, and he certainly wouldn't see me married to a man who would betray me. He'd been faithful to my grandmother not only for all the time they were married, but for twenty years after she was gone.

I stuck out my hand to Gage. "It's been nice knowing you, Gage. I hope you have a wonderful life."

His hand swallowed mine with a strength that made me slightly uneasy. "What about Serenity?"

Serenity had been a constant in my life for seven years, but I couldn't see walking down the Las Vegas strip with a horse in tow, looking for a likely marriage candidate. If I managed to get the trust fund, I could move Serenity to wherever I ended up. Maybe I could buy the field next to Lily's house. That is, if my parents didn't sell the horse first.

I bit my lip, tears smarting in my eyes. "She'll be okay here for now." I turned to go, but Gage's hand shot out to grab my arm. I felt a momentary shiver of fear, and he must have seen it in my eyes because he dropped his hand instantly.

"Sorry. I just—are you in trouble? Is there something I can do to help?" He was uniquely appealing at the moment, a mix of little boy and wild-looking ex-con. I hadn't noticed how tall he was before or how broad his chest, and I wondered what he looked like under all that facial hair.

I forced a smile. "How about a ride to Las Vegas?" My old car had been sold, and the new one, a wedding gift from Julian's parents, wasn't scheduled to arrive until after Julian and I returned from our honeymoon. "I'm kidding. Look, thanks for your concern, but everything is fine. I'm not the first woman to have her heart broken."

He arched a brow, and I noticed he had nice ones. Expressive. "You look more mad than heartbroken."

He was wrong. My heart did hurt. I hated knowing that I wasn't enough for Julian, that he didn't love me the way I loved him. Yes, I was also furious at him, and at my parents, but most of all at myself. I was the reason I was in this mess, the reason Lily was in danger. I'd trusted the wrong man.

"Then you don't know me very well," I told Gage. "Good-bye. It really has been nice knowing you."

I could feel his eyes on me as I left. Grabbing Serenity's mane, I pulled myself up on her bare back and let her take me to the other side of the pasture.

"I'll miss you more than anyone here," I whispered, giving her the last cube of sugar in my pocket. "But I'll be back some day. I promise."

2

It took all of fifteen minutes to stuff several extra outfits in a backpack, and all my valuables—jewelry, cash, credit cards, small electronics that I could maybe pawn or sell on eBay. Most of my clothing was already at the apartment where I'd planned to live with Julian. I hoped I could get that later.

Going online, I transferred every dime I had in my two savings accounts to the personal checking I had opened as an adult, the only account on which my mother wasn't a joint signer. Two thousand dollars. Not a lot, but enough to get started. I took more time to locate important documents and to type up a contract on my laptop. I'd need to make sure I didn't get swindled out of my entire trust fund. I didn't email Julian because the hurting part of me wanted him to find out from someone else the way I had.

I should let Sadie know I was coming, but there wasn't time for that because her phone was busy, and I had to get away before my mother returned from wherever she had gone. She'd stop me from leaving and call Julian and my father. My bid for freedom would be over.

The last thing I did was to remove my engagement ring and set it on my desk where I knew my mother would see it. Pawning it might be wiser, but I couldn't resist the message it would send to Julian—and to my parents. I would not settle for half a marriage.

The house was quiet as I slipped outside and headed for the road. Already, I could tell it was going to be a long, long walk. With each step, the pack grew heavier. I could only pray my mother wouldn't drive down the road and see me. My thumb went automatically to the place on my third finger where I'd worn the ring, finding nothing but bare skin.

I hadn't walked a mile when I realized I was being followed by a motorcycle. Fear tingled at the base of my spine, and I forced myself to walk faster. Another two miles or so and I'd be at Sadie's, and I was hoping she would lend me a car. After that, I didn't know. I needed to find someone to help me get my trust fund, a temporary husband who wouldn't mind making a fast buck.

I ran over candidates in my mind, discarding one after the other. Either they were married, seeing someone, employees of my father, or friends of Julian. Maybe one of my college friends could help. Unfortunately, I'd been so wrapped up in Julian these past months that I hadn't kept in contact beyond the occasional text message.

The motorcycle moved closer, and I didn't relax when I saw who was on it. I came to a full stop and turned to face Gage.

"Why are you following me?" Maybe there was more to the ex-con rumor than I'd thought.

"Are you really planning to walk to Vegas?"

"Of course not. I'm going to a friend's to borrow her car."

"And then you're going to marry a stranger."

"Unless I can find someone I know to marry me instead."

He stared at me flatly without speaking.

"Look, it's complicated," I said, "but once I have access to my trust fund, everything will be fine."

"To do that you have to be married?"

"Yes."

"I see."

His eyes were greener than I'd ever realized, and I liked the way they crinkled at the sides, but it was hard to look past the scruffy exterior. I couldn't imagine kissing someone with all that hair—not that I wanted to kiss him. My face flushed at the thought. Hopefully, he'd think it was the heat. Late September was better for walking than August, but not much.

"Get on," he said. "I'll give you a ride."

I hesitated.

"Come on. That pack looks heavy. You can put it in here." He opened the hard compartment on the back of his motorcycle.

Sighing, I handed it over, and he placed it next to a small black duffel already inside. With a little moving around, it all fit.

"What are you carrying in there—rocks?"

I rolled my eyes. "Can we just go?"

He grinned, and again I wondered what he looked like under the facial hair. "Wait a minute. Isn't that your mother's car?"

I glanced up the road at the approaching blue sedan. Instantly, I squatted down by the motorcycle, ducking my head.

Gage laughed, a deep, resonate sound. "I take it you don't want her to see you."

"Just looking for more rocks to put in my pack."

He laughed again, and something warm grew inside me. I laughed with him, straightening once the car passed. As soon as she found out I was missing, she'd call in the troops, but for the moment I was safe. Only an hour ago, I doubted I'd ever laugh again, but here I was, already laughing with Gage.

"This will hide your hair," he said, handing me a helmet, "and it can't possibly make it look worse. Did you even comb it today?"

He had some nerve, though now that I thought about it, I hadn't washed or combed it. I'd been about to jump in the shower when Sadie arrived. I didn't have makeup on, either. Not a good way to start a search for a husband, even if it was only a business arrangement.

I silenced him with a hard look, but after I climbed onto the back of the bike, I found myself smiling again. My mother would be mortified to see me out and about with Gage. As for me, who did I have to impress? Julian was the only one, and I was running from him.

"Where to?" Gage asked.

I gave him directions to Sadie's, and he revved the engine, starting forward much more quickly than I expected. I clung to him. I could feel his muscles under the T-shirt. Plenty strong to have hurt someone. Did the ex-con rumor mention something about that?

I couldn't remember. Cold sweat broke over me. What was I thinking even being with him?

No, I knew him well enough, and this trip was only to Sadie's.

I enjoyed the wind in my face, the way Gage leaned when he took the turns. Julian had a motorcycle, but he didn't like wearing the helmet and usually picked me up in his green BMW. I didn't mind because the places we went generally required clothing not suitable for motorcycle riding.

"Turn here," I shouted in Gage's ear.

We turned the corner, and I felt my breath leave as I saw Julian's BMW sitting out front of the fourplex where Sadie shared an apartment with two roommates. My grip around Gage tightened. Why was Julian at Sadie's? After this morning, I would have thought she would barely talk to him.

I didn't tell Gage to stop, and he drove to the end of the street before realizing something was wrong. He pulled over and twisted to look at my face. "Did I turn the wrong way?"

"That's Julian's car."

He lifted his gaze. "Why, so it is. Are you going inside?"

"No. Let's go."

"Where?"

"I don't care. Please, just go." If I spoke to Julian now, my chance for escape would be over. I wasn't strong enough to withstand him. Not yet. Because I'd become exactly the type of society girl Lily and I despised—spineless, choiceless, weak.

Gage nodded and took off, faster than necessary. I laid

my head against his back and let the tears fall, knowing I wouldn't be recognized with the helmet. As we passed Sadie's, I saw Julian at the door with her, his blond hair gleaming in the sunlight that angled in despite the porch overhang. They seemed to be laughing.

Laughing? I didn't understand what I'd seen or why Julian had been there. Had Sadie called him over to confront him? Maybe he was there to convince her of his innocence. Or maybe Sadie hadn't told me the whole truth. The idea hurt almost as much as Julian's betrayal.

No, she was my friend, of that I was certain. She loved me. We had history together that was stronger than Julian's charm.

Closing my eyes, I hung onto Gage. We drove and drove until my legs began to ache and my stomach protested with hunger.

Had I eaten that morning? I couldn't remember.

As if hearing my unspoken thoughts, Gage turned off the freeway. The sign read Kingman. We'd come that far?

After several turns, he pulled up in front of a quaint older building painted bright baby blue with dark pink trim. Even the picnic tables outside were pink. A big sign atop the building read *Mr D'z Route 66 Diner.*

"Hungry?" he asked.

I nodded. I'd heard of this place, but I'd never been here before. Not the sort of joint my parents frequented when I'd lived at home, and I hadn't had much cause to be in the area.

"The burgers aren't all that great, but the onion rings and the root beer make up for it."

I didn't think I could down a greasy burger anyway.

Just thinking about it probably caused me to gain two pounds. My wedding dress would never fit.

My stomach heaved.

"You okay?" Gage asked. "You aren't going to puke or anything, are you?"

"No, I'm not." I stalked toward the door.

Inside the diner, blue and pink padded booths alternated along the walls. Stools at the bar were silver chrome with blue seats, the floor was black-and-white checks, and the walls were plastered with pictures and memorabilia of the past. "Interesting," I murmured.

"Garish." He smiled, but again it was lost in the facial hair. His green eyes, however, were sparkling. "Because Oprah came here, everyone stops in. Rather annoying, but I'm sure it's good for business."

We settled into a blue seat, and he ordered two cheese burgers, fries, and drinks.

"Wait, I just want a salad," I said.

He arched a brow. "You need more than a salad. You need protein. You're too thin. And you're pale."

"I'm always pale."

"Well, even your freckles are pale today."

Great. He just had to bring up my freckles. I hated them.

The waitress was hovering, waiting for the final word. Gage looked at her. "Bring a house salad, and all the rest as well—please."

I fumed. What right did he have to order for me? He was exactly like Julian, thinking he always knew what was best. I choked on the thought. No, he wasn't Julian. Julian would never wear that faded T-shirt and those scruffy boots or appear in public looking like a mountain man.

"Are you sure you're all right?" Gage asked.

"I'm fine," I said tightly. The pain inside was growing instead of diminishing. I was hurt, embarrassed, depressed, and desperate. Through all these emotions, I had only one thought: I had to show Julian and my parents that I didn't need any of them, that I didn't care. I would never let Julian know how much he'd hurt me.

Taking my iPhone from my pocket, I brought up the address book. There had to be someone in it from my past who could help me. Either that or I really would marry a complete stranger, get my trust fund, pay him off, and be on my way to Lily's. I'd send a picture of the wedding to Julian for good measure. That would show him.

Tears bit at my eyes, and it was all I could do to keep them from falling. I couldn't see the names on the screen.

Gage's hands covered mine. "Can I help? You're shaking."

I jerked away. "No." Then it occurred to me that he was only being nice, and I shouldn't be so rude. "Sorry."

"It's okay. You've had a rough morning."

I could see the names on the phone now, but as I scrolled down, I had the sinking feeling that none of them would solve my problem.

I lifted my gaze to Gage. "Will you take me to Vegas? I'll pay you for gas, and whatever more you feel is fair." He must be missing work by now.

"You want me to drive you to Vegas?"

"Yes."

"To get married?"

I nodded.

"To a total stranger?"

"Maybe." Surely something better would come to me.

He sighed. "Look, I'll do it."

"Thank you. It's only a few hours."

"No, I mean, I'll marry you. For however long you need. If it'll help you out."

Was he crazy? I wasn't going to marry a scruffy-looking mountain man rumored to have spent time behind bars, however untrue the rumors were. Wait. I had to remember it wasn't a real marriage. It was only to get around the trust fund issue and help Lily. Okay, and to get revenge on Julian.

"At least you know me."

"Not really."

He frowned. Or at least I thought he'd frowned. I was really beginning to hate overgrown facial hair. "Well, Serenity knows me. She'll vouch for me."

I laughed. I couldn't help it. Serenity did like him. A lot. I suspected he gave her pieces of apples and carrots regularly because whenever I came home to visit her and Gage appeared, she always hurried to greet him.

I pulled the pre-nuptial agreement from my pocket. It was rather worse for wear, but I could print more copies from the laptop stuffed in my backpack. "Fine. You'll have to sign this, first. You get fifty thousand after the annulment, no more. Nonnegotiable." Fifty thousand would hardly make a dent in my half million, but he didn't know how much I'd get or about the additional monthly allotment of a thousand dollars for the rest of my life.

His eyes narrowed and his lips tightened.

"It's all I can offer." I tucked the paper back inside my pack. "Take it or leave it. Otherwise, I'll have to find someone else." I was hoping he'd take it because if I couldn't entice him to do it for that amount, any alternative husband I'd find was likely to be a lot worse. As he'd said, at least I knew him. He had roots, a house, a job. He was a lot better than a complete stranger.

"I'll take it," he growled.

Well, excuse me. I didn't know what I'd done to offend him. *If he's looking for more money, too bad for him.*

The food came, the salad made of leaf lettuce and surprisingly good. The root beer was nothing short of miraculous, and one bite of the onion rings forced all thoughts of calories from my mind. Without thinking, I started in on the hamburger, too. I loved every wonderful bite, but then I probably hadn't eaten one since high school.

I felt Gage's eyes on me. He'd settled back on the seat and was watching me with an amused smile on his lips. "What?" I said.

"You have ketchup on your nose."

I reached for a napkin at the same time he did, our hands colliding. I laughed self-consciously as he dabbed at the spot with decided gentleness. Our eyes met, and for the first time I wondered who he really was. I knew he worked for a mining company, something to do with geology, field visits, and numerous reports, but that was about all I knew.

"How's Lily?" he asked, lowering his hand.

"Really sick—with the baby and all. She's had to quit school."

"Tough break. Maybe those girls she's helping can pitch in for a change."

"Maybe." If she could keep the house long enough. But I didn't feel like talking about that.

"Good thing she has Mario. He seems like a nice guy."

"So how come you know about my family?" I asked. "I can't remember you saying anything about yours."

"Everyone knows about your family."

Maybe everyone who'd been in town a long time, the older, more established families. Not someone who was new to the city and living in tract housing.

"I've been blabbing, haven't I?" Perhaps Serenity wasn't the only lonely one this past year. Yet I'd met Julian at Christmastime, so why would I have been lonely enough to spill my heart to a neighbor simply because he liked my horse?

Gage's smile widened. "You never blab. Serenity does. She tells all your secrets."

"Now I know you're insane."

"Probably. After all, I never planned on getting married, and look at me now."

"I really appreciate it."

His eyes narrowed again. "Fifty thousand is more than enough thanks."

Of course, the money. I should never forget it. "At least tell me where you're from."

"From here. Kingman."

That would explain his familiarity with the history of the diner.

"Another hamburger?" he asked.

I shook my head. "No, thanks. I'm full."

The waitress came to take our money, and Gage said to her, "Hey, we decided to get married. We're heading to Las Vegas."

"Congratulations!" she gushed. "You are like the third couple coming through this week. I'm so happy for you. Let me take your picture. Do you have a camera?"

Gage handed her my iPhone that was still on the table. He crawled into the seat next to me and put his arm around my shoulders. It was all I could do not to push him away.

"Smile!" she sang.

We smiled, my face a bit frozen. I was going to kill him.

"Now a kiss."

"That's okay," I said.

"Come on. It's for posterity, darling." Gage leaned over and planted a kiss on my mouth. His hair tickled my nostrils, but he smelled good. Clean. Not at all as I expected. His warm touch sent a shiver through me.

I pushed him firmly away. "Thanks," I told the waitress, not meaning it.

Gage riffled in his wallet and dug out a twenty and five.

"I can pay my share." I patted the back pocket of my jeans before remembering I'd stuffed my wallet in the backpack.

"Don't worry," he said. "I'll put it on your tab."

"Thanks." This was going to be a long day.

"No problem, darling."

When the waitress was gone, I glared at him. "Don't do that again."

"You mean the pictures? I thought they might come in handy. You know, to prove to your family or your lawyer or whatever."

"Oh, right." My grandfather's trust fund did have an attorney as executor, and I would rather work through him than my parents. I had a feeling that if she could, my mother would find me and force me somehow to marry Julian, even though I was an adult. That was illegal in this day and age, wasn't it?

"Come on," I said, "let's get this over with."

"You do have ID with you, don't you?"

"Yes. Do you?"

"Yep. I also have a friend who works at a hotel in Vegas, and they have a chapel there. I'll give him a call and see exactly what's required. Let him know we're coming." He took out his cell and pressed a few buttons. "Go ahead and make yourself comfortable on the bike. I'll be right there."

I don't know how I could be comfortable on a bike that was tilted over on its kickstand, but I took the hint. I leaned up against the bike and watched him pace, the phone against his ear. If one overlooked the scruffiness of his facial hair, he didn't cut too bad a figure. He was broad and well-proportioned, and his body hinted at coiled energy.

Had he really been to prison? If so, what for? Too many speeding tickets? A land deal gone wrong? No, it was all simple-minded gossip.

Of course, I'd imagined my response to him in the diner. I hadn't really felt anything when he kissed me. Well, not like I did with Julian.

It wasn't too late. I could go home, talk to Julian, work it out. I could figure out how to forgive him. Couldn't I?

Inside I rebelled. I'd trusted him, and he'd betrayed me. Going back meant committing myself to a relationship that had no future, or a lifetime of living together without being one, like my parents. No. Better to marry Gage temporarily.

Except first I had to know if he'd really gone to prison and why. If it was for embezzlement, well, I'd watch my funds carefully. If it was for drunk driving, I'd make sure to keep him from the booze if he was driving me anywhere. If it was for murder, well, I'd run for the hills.

He was coming toward me with a bit of swagger I recognized as his usual gait. There was a spring in his step. "We'll have to stop for a marriage license, but it's easy enough. My friend will have everything ready for us at his hotel. Do you have something to wear?" His eyes went to the compartment that hid my backpack.

"Uh, won't this do?" I looked down at my jeans. "I didn't pack a dress."

"Not if you want to convince anyone it's for real. But they have some dresses for rent, and my friend is saving us a room so we can clean up first and stay the night. By the time we get this all taken care of, it'll be too late to go elsewhere."

"We'll need two rooms then."

He gave me that placid stare, and this time it sent heat to my face. "I booked two. Isn't that what I said?" He climbed on the bike and started the engine.

"There's just one more thing." I wished I could see his

expression better. "People say, uh—did you really spend time in prison?"

His jaw tightened, and his eyes searched mine. "Yes, I did. Six years."

"What for?"

"That is none of your business."

O f course he was kidding—I could tell by the smirk on his lips. He'd heard the rumors and was getting me back for using him.

"Is my record a problem?" he asked.

"Well, uh, I . . ."

"I did my time. I paid my debt. You are in no danger from me. I would never hurt you or anyone."

Of course you'd say that, especially if you had plans to hurt me, I thought. Wait a minute—what was I thinking? He was joking about serving time, and that was the end of it.

Or was it? He seemed awfully grim, and a six-year sentence would mean a serious crime.

"Well?" he asked with a mocking smile. "Are we going?"

I climbed on the back of the motorcycle without saying a word. Lily would kill me if she could see me now. She'd want me to be absolutely sure of the truth before I went another mile. Yet I'd known Gage for months, and he'd never given me any reason to fear him. Aside from Sadie, he was the nearest thing I had to a friend in Flagstaff—which was really sad if I stopped to think about it.

Anyway, Serenity trusted him. She didn't like my dad or even Lily, and she didn't like Julian. Every time Julian came over with a mount from his father's stable to ride with us, her ears would go forward, a sure sign of wariness, and she would skitter away from his hand. It had become so bad lately that I'd quit asking him to ride with me at all. On the other hand, she liked Gage. That had to mean something. I hoped.

Besides, I couldn't deny that there was something strangely exhilarating about being on the back of a motorcycle with Gage, rumors or no.

The ride to Vegas went far too quickly, whether because Gage was driving fast or because of my fear, I couldn't say. My dread grew with every mile. I couldn't help feeling my whole life was about to change forever.

Obtaining a marriage license at the county building was ridiculously easy. Afterward, we drove to a hotel several blocks off the main drag. I combed a hand through my seriously tangled hair as I took in the place. Nice, not too run down, and the chapel Gage had spoken of was advertised as being inside. Lover's Lane Hotel and Chapel, the place was called, the gaudy neon sign over the door no doubt more visible by night.

Great.

We went inside, the bell over the door alerting the staff to our presence. The lobby wasn't large, but everything was decorated in gold and reds that screamed romance. Before I had time to grow more uncomfortable, a short, balding man dressed in a silvery blue shirt and casual black slacks burst from a back room behind the reception desk. He was stocky without being fat, and I got the sense from the way he came around the counter that he was proud of his physique.

"Welcome," he boomed. "Nice to see you again, Gage!" He pumped Gage's hand as his eyes ran over me. "So this is the beautiful woman. Why's a nice girl like you interested in this scruffy old dog? You're a lucky man, Gage, a lucky man. Are you sure you don't want me to make this a—" He broke off as Gage gave a quick shake of his head. "Ah, never mind."

What had he been about to say? How well did this man know Gage? I wondered if I could ask him about Gage's past so I could let Gage know I knew for sure he'd been joking about the prison thing.

"This is Calvin Sanchez," Gage said, placing a casual arm around my shoulders. It took all my effort not to flinch away. He'd better not try to kiss me again, or he'd learn how sharp the end of my elbow could be. "He's the one who's going to perform the ceremony."

Calvin raised his large hands. "I can only work you in at eleven tonight. I know it's late, but we got a full schedule. Tomorrow's even worse."

Gage looked at me, and I nodded. "That's fine," Gage said. "We'll clean up. Go out to dinner first."

"Good idea, good idea." Calvin was annoyingly affable, but his smile was engaging. "Lots to see in Vegas. In fact, I'll get you reservations for dinner and a show." His eyes ran over me, calculating now. "I got a girl. I'll send her up to your room. She'll help you pick out a wedding dress, and one for dinner tonight, too, if you want. Got a ton to choose from. Comes with the package." Calvin cast another glance at Gage and shook his head. "Gage, you gotta lot of work to do before you can even begin to look as good as she does. Fortunately, you've come to the right place. Follow me, please."

I bent to pick up my backpack, but Gage beat me to it. "Allow me. You're probably tired from our trip."

I let him play it up. If we were really in love, he'd probably do that and more for me. A lump of something heavy formed in the pit of my stomach, but I tried not to notice.

Calvin led us up a wide, slightly curving staircase with plush red carpet that matched the lobby. It was ostentatious rather than elegant, but it fit the purpose of the place. "Here are your rooms," Calvin said. "There's a door between them." I didn't see Gage's room, but mine had a heart-shaped tub in the corner of the room, surrounded by sheer pink drapes.

"Thanks, Calvin." Gage set down my backpack inside the door, and the men disappeared into the other room. I locked the connecting door and lay down on the bed.

Now that I was alone, more doubts assailed me. What was I doing? Gage was right—this was insane.

My phone vibrated, and I saw it was my mother—again. She'd called already five times during the past few hours. I'd have to text her and Lily both to let them know I was okay but still not going through with the wedding. The wedding to Julian anyway. I wouldn't add the part about Gage until after the deed was done.

I typed out the message, sent it, and shut off the phone. I sat staring at the ceiling, tears leaking from my eyes. *Julian,* I thought, *How could I have been so wrong about you?*

A knock on the door made me start. I jumped to my feet. "Who is it?"

"Avery. Calvin sent me. May I come in?"

I relaxed, and it was only then I realized I'd been expecting my mother or Julian. But even if they suspected I'd come to Vegas, they'd never be able to find me in a city this size.

I opened the door to an Asian woman whose sleek, exotic beauty made me feel colorless and frumpy. *Joy.*

She smiled. "You are exactly as Calvin described you. Come, I know just the right gown." She spoke perfect English, with the barest hint of an accent. I could speak a little French, but no way would my French ever be as good as her English, and I bet I couldn't even speak two words in whatever Asian language she'd been born to.

I followed her down the stairs and into an oblong room with two long rows of dresses. She went to the end on the right side. "I found this in Utah," she said, taking one from the rack. "I buy used dresses all over the States, but many aren't traditional. Most brides who come here think less is best. And sometimes it works for them, you know? Other times, well, you wouldn't believe some of the awful dresses we have here. But every now and then I find a dress too beautiful to pass up. Classical, elegant." She pulled off the plastic. "Do you like it?"

The white satin gown had lace and pearls only on the bodice, and the volume and length of the train were far less than the dress I'd chosen, but the cut was nearly identical. My mother would say that its plainness was beneath my status, but I knew this was a dress that wouldn't overshadow my pale features. I reached out to touch the bodice.

"Don't you like it?" A hint of disappointment tinged Avery's voice.

"It's exactly what I would have picked out."

She smiled. "I knew it. I have a matching veil, too. Calvin says you're here alone and that I'm to come up and help you dress when it's time. Is that right?"

Tears sprang to my eyes before I could stop them. Lily should be here.

No. None of this was real.

"I can do it myself, if it's too late."

"Oh, I don't get off until one. And that's early." Avery laughed, a glad sound.

"Then, yes. Thank you."

"We have other dresses, too. For a night out."

She led me to the other row where several feet of colored dresses hung in clear plastic sheaths. "Not as much call for bridesmaids' dresses, and even less for dinner dresses, but I have a few. Your hair is more blond than anything else, and with your coloring and blue eyes, I think this one will look the best. Many people think strawberry blondes shouldn't wear vibrant colors, but I think it's only a matter of knowing which color to wear."

She held up the dress. It was a simple thing, with a high, gathered neckline that I didn't much like and more gathering on the sides that caused the material across the stomach to fall in gentle folds. Probably going to make me look like a small cow. The only thing that attracted me was the vibrant blue, which made me think of a warm spring day at the beach.

"It'll make your eyes stand out—I promise," she assured me.

"It's fine," I said, because it really didn't matter. I wasn't here to impress Gage with this borrowed dress. The money would be enough.

"You go on up and bathe then. I'll come up with the dresses in a while. Will that be all right?"

I escaped without another word, glad to be away from the room of dresses, which to me radiated lost dreams. A wedding in Vegas without my sister or my friends—I'd truly reached bottom.

Not for long. Tomorrow I would be on my way as my own woman, able to take care of my little sister, the baby she carried, and all those young girls she'd picked up along the way. Those girls wouldn't have to marry to make ends meet or work dangerous or demoralizing jobs. Not if I did this right.

I took a long bath, soaking away the grime of the day and wishing I could shut off my mind. Strangely, I was thinking not of Julian but of Gage and how he'd come to my rescue. Who was he really?

When Avery knocked on the door, I wrapped myself in the plush pink robe the hotel had provided and let her in. My face was flushed from the heat of the water.

"All ready to do your hair?"

"I can do it." I'd planned to let it dry like it was. No need to go overboard.

"If I do it now, it'll be easier tonight for the ceremony."

"What will it cost?"

She shook her head. "Comes with the room and the full-service package."

I decided not to worry about how much that would set me back. "Great."

She gave me the dress and a pair of blue heels before going to the bathroom with two baskets of assorted hair care and facial products. Pulling out the stool under the vanity, she indicated that I should sit.

When I saw how deftly Avery styled my hair, coaxing the flatness into curls and sweeping it up on my head, I was glad to let her do it.

"You have a lovely neck," she said. "It's best to let it show on occasions like this."

I'd thought that family feature had completely skipped me, but the mirror confirmed her words.

The makeup she put on smoothed out the blotches of my freckles, but there was nothing really to do about them. Avery didn't seem upset but fell to my eyes with gusto. Blues and browns mixed together. Tiny false eye lashes that looked so natural when they were on that I was surprised. "Now a little bit of mascara to tie them in," she said. "Then we get you dressed. It's nearly five, and you'll need to hurry to make your dinner reservations and the show."

I hadn't realized it was so late, or that we'd be eating so early. Back in Flagstaff, our relatives would have arrived, and my mother would be furious. She would have told Julian by now, and I felt a sharp gladness. He wouldn't feel like laughing now. Even if a part of him were relieved, he'd be upset to have been jilted. Or at least that he'd been discovered.

Avery left the bathroom while I put on my under-clothes, but I had to call her back to help me with the dress so I didn't mess up my piled hair. Too bad I hadn't insisted on a better dress. It was a shame to let my hair and makeup go to waste.

"There." Avery finished adjusting the material. "A bit looser than I'd hoped, but still nice."

I let her push me out of the bathroom to stand in front of the full-length mirror on the wall, thinking that if the waist were any tighter I wouldn't be able to breathe.

"Well?" Avery asked.

I stared at myself in the mirror, definitely not breathing now. The dress narrowed my waist, while the gathered neckline, not as throat-smothering as I'd first assumed, actually lent me a bit of shape in the bust where I really needed it. Between the color of the dress and the eye shadow, I looked like someone I didn't know.

My mother's daughter.

"Thank you," I said.

Avery grinned. "You were easy. You should see some of the ladies I work with." We laughed together as Avery gathered up her products. "I'll be back at ten," she said. "And I promise you will look even better tonight. He won't be able to take his eyes off you."

I felt as though she'd kicked me in the gut. Of course he'd be able to take his eyes off me. Gage didn't love me. We were acquaintances. Or casual friends at the most.

"Do they take pictures?" I asked. "I want to send one to someone."

"As many as you like. Or want to pay for, rather," she said with a wink. "But if you want me to take one for free with your camera before you go out tonight, I'll be downstairs."

After she left, I went to sit in front of the vanity mirror and tried to dredge up the courage to leave the room. I hoped Gage didn't laugh, because I felt like an idiot. A nicely dressed, even pretty, idiot, but this was all fake. It would have been better to complete the ceremony in my jeans and drive to Lily's tonight. Actually, I probably shouldn't go right to Lily's. Disowned or not, that would be the first place after Sadie's that my mother and Julian would look for me.

I'm leaving now, I told myself. I marched to the bed, put on the heels that Avery had left, and made my way to the stairs. No one was in sight. *Good.*

My luck didn't hold. As I followed the curved staircase, a man came into view, hands linked together in front of him as if waiting. He was wearing black dress slacks and a brown blazer despite the heat. Probably another groom about to take the plunge into matrimony.

I felt an urge to tell him to go somewhere else for the ceremony, where they could be surrounded by loved ones.

Who was I kidding? He and his fiancée might have brought along their family and friends. Not everyone was here looking for a way around trust fund restrictions. He was probably madly in love.

The man was staring to the point of rudeness, and a flush crawled up my face. That's the really terrible thing about being a pale, strawberry blonde. It's hard to hide emotion.

He was handsome, with well-formed features—a square jaw that spoke of strength, a long straight nose, wide forehead, and longish brown hair combed back from his face. I could envision him equally at home in the mountains or at one of my mother's elegant dinners, where he'd be the focus of attention with those chiseled features. Julian would be annoyed to find me staring.

He smiled, and it transformed him, softening the jaw, and adding warmth to the green eyes. He had very nice teeth. I descended the last few steps, unable to look away. Something in my brain was screaming a warning, but I didn't understand what it said.

"Nice dress," he said with obvious appreciation. The deep voice sent a shiver through me. I knew that voice—and those green eyes.

This man was Gage.

"Thanks. You—you look different."

He rubbed his chin. "Calvin wouldn't leave me alone until I shaved."

"Well, it's not as if it's for real, but I guess he doesn't know that."

Gage frowned, and his face became cold, just as the smile had warmed it earlier. "I guess not."

I felt as if I'd hurt him somehow, but that was ridiculous. I wouldn't let either of us forget we were in this only for the money. "This is probably costing too much," I said.

He shrugged. "Not much. Calvin owes me a favor."

"Oh?"

"It's personal."

And we weren't. I took the hint. "Right. So where are we going?"

"Dinner first, and a show. Then dancing if you're up to it."

If he knew me better, he wouldn't have to ask. I was a night person in every sense of the word. I might feel tired now, but as dusk fell and night slid over the town, I would be wide awake and ready for anything. I could dance all night, or read, or go for a walk, or ride Serenity. I adored night.

Just don't try to wake me up in the morning. There was a reason I'd worked the swing shift at my father's factory.

"I'm up to it." I said. "I seem to be starving again." Stress was obviously good for the appetite.

He offered me his arm, and I took it, my eyes falling again over his face. So absolutely different from the scruffy mountain man who'd befriended Serenity. I'd wanted to see under the hair, and now that I had, I liked what I saw. He was much more attractive this way. He definitely didn't look like an ex-con.

The pit in my stomach was back, but I ignored it. This town was full of things to do, and I was going to enjoy myself. Having a handsome escort didn't hurt things one little bit.

The MGM Grand Hotel where we were heading was too far away for us to walk, and I couldn't exactly climb onto Gage's bike in the dress, so we called a taxi. The heels were remarkably comfortable, though, and I was already thinking about dancing later. I silently blessed Avery for her choice. I might even name my first child after her someday, provided I survived this adventure long enough to have one. Because my mother was going to kill me when she caught up with me.

"Is everything okay?" Gage asked as we watched for the taxi.

"Not at all. It's a beautiful man, isn't it? I mean night."
Great. I sighed internally.

Gage grinned at me as if he knew exactly what I'd been thinking. "Beautiful," he agreed. His grin grew wider as I flushed and looked away.

Thankfully, the taxi arrived, and we drove to the MGM in silence. The place was huge and elegant, and even I, who had run with the cream of Flagstaff society, felt a little awed.

At the Craftsteak restaurant there was a crowd waiting for seating, and when Gage gave his name, the hostess couldn't find our reservation. She wrote Gage's name on a sheet of paper and told us there would be an hour wait.

As we left the desk, I noticed two older ladies near the wall staring at Gage and poking each other. One had a round face, bright with blush, and stylish silver hair layered close to her head. The other wore a mournful expression on her thin, sagging cheeks and looked as if she'd forgotten to comb her brown hair after she'd removed her overnight curlers. They were whispering animatedly now behind raised hands, their eyes never leaving us. Maybe they thought Gage was a movie star.

"Wait here a moment," Gage said. "Maybe Calvin used his own name." He returned to talk to the hostess, and the eyes of every woman in the place followed him, including mine.

"Excuse me."

I looked up to see the silver-haired woman addressing me. Her companion was close behind. "Yes?" I prompted.

"Is that Gage Braxton?" Her voice was hoarse and nervous.

"Yes. Why? Do you know him?"

The woman looked as if she'd been sucking on a lemon. Her pale eyes were as sharp as toothpicks. "We know of him, don't we, sister?"

The other woman nodded, the tight brown curls bouncing slightly. She gave an exaggerated shiver and said in a breathy voice, "Everyone in Kingman knows him."

Oh, they were from his hometown.

"He has some nerve," the first woman said. "Showing up after all this time. Doesn't look a bit different, though it's got to have been at least five or six years. Isn't that right, Gretty?"

Her sister nodded. "He's a murderer, you know, and that's how long he's been in prison." They stared at me in expectation, as if hoping I would exclaim or faint from the knowledge.

"So you know about that," I said, the casualness in my tone belying the pounding of my heart. Murder. That couldn't be possible.

"My word, of course! Everyone knows. It was in all the papers. We were only too grateful that his mother was dead before it all happened. Her heart would have broken to pieces."

"You knew his mother?"

"Not personally, but we'd seen her around. Kingman isn't very big, you know."

"Yeah, I know."

The silver-haired woman leaned closer to me. "You must be careful, dear. Very careful. You have no idea how dangerous he is."

"Cold-blooded murderer," added the other.

"Premeditated."

"Took a poker from his own fireplace. Shoved it right into the poor fellow's head."

"Sneaked right up. Poor man didn't know what hit him."

"Cold blood. Must have planned it for months."

My head bobbed between the two sisters as they talked. A poker? They were saying Gage used a poker to commit murder? If Gage had committed murder, he'd surely have used a gun or knife, or even his broad hands—all in self-defense, of course, or sudden revenge. But a poker in cold blood? Premeditated? That was cowardly, and Gage did not strike me as a coward.

I'd run into women like this before during some of my mother's never-ending luncheons. Women who gossiped and changed the truth to suit themselves. Old broads who simply wanted to make trouble.

"Wait," I said, keeping my voice low. Already we were drawing interested stares from some of the people around us. "You're telling me he killed a man in cold blood with a poker? So did he carry the poker around as he searched for the guy? I mean, isn't that what premeditated means? Going out and getting a weapon and planning to use it? Seeking for an opportunity? It seems sort of odd, his walking around with a poker, if that's what he planned to use. Kind of noticeable. You'd think someone would come up and say, 'Hey, what are you doing walking around with that poker?'"

The women stared at me blankly for a moment and finally decided they didn't like my attitude.

"Well," silver hair humphed. "It was premeditated,

even if he didn't carry the poker around. It certainly made no difference to the man with the hole through his head if he carried it around or not, now did it?"

"There was a witness after all," added her sister in her obnoxious breathy voice that didn't match her hangdog appearance. "He had blood in his heart, and that's the honest truth. That handsome face can't hide the evil in his heart. If it hadn't been the poker, it would have been something else."

"And his poor fiancée. Sweet thing. Practically didn't talk for a whole year. I doubt she knows he's even out of prison. She's been waiting for him all this time. Writing him letters and such."

"Judy!" Brown hair blanched and nudged her sister, looking over her shoulder at Gage who was coming our way.

"You'll stay clear of him, if you've any sense," silver hair hissed.

"Well, that might be a little difficult," I said. "Seeing as how we're getting married tonight."

As one they gasped and held their wrinkled hands to their sagging chests. I watched them scoot away in a hurry.

4

"**P**roblem?" asked Gage, eyeing the retreating women.

I forced a smile and did what I always do when I was worried—I made a joke. "They thought I was a movie star. Wanted my autograph."

"I'm not surprised."

That warmed me so much my worry dissipated. No matter what those old vultures had said, I couldn't believe Gage had killed anyone with anything, much less a poker.

Unfortunately, that piece of lead was back in my stomach again.

"Calvin did put our reservation under his name, so they're ready to seat us now. Good thing because Cirque Du Soleil starts at seven."

I stopped walking. "We're seeing Cirque Du Soleil? I've always wanted to see that."

"I know. You told me."

Had I? I couldn't remember, but I suppose it could have come up during one of our conversations in the pasture.

"I've wanted to see it, too," he added. "So I asked Calvin to pull in some favors to get us the tickets. I hear some of the performers have trained since childhood."

Minutes later we were seated as far away from the bar as possible, in a corner that made me feel secluded, even in a room full of people. "Three courses?" I asked, eyeing the menu. "You really are trying to make me fat. Serenity won't be pleased."

He laughed. "If she can carry that boy who feeds her while you're gone, she can handle two of you."

"She has. That's the only way my sister could ride. Serenity wouldn't let her get on by herself, but maybe that's because Lily was always afraid she'd fall off and Serenity would step on her."

"Serenity wouldn't hurt a flea."

We ate soup with our first course, followed by grilled prawns for me and filet mignon for him. For dessert we both chose fresh fruit. "I didn't take you for a fruit kind of guy," I said.

"Oh, what kind of guy am I?"

How to answer that? I couldn't exactly say, "Well, not the kind to hit someone with a fireplace poker."

"I don't know," I said instead. "With your beard and mustache, I thought maybe you'd be more into slabs of Dutch oven cake or something. Why do you wear a beard, anyway?"

Even as I said it, I wondered if he was hiding. Hiding from people like the women who'd accosted me earlier. Yet wouldn't that mean he had something to hide? That maybe he hadn't been joking when he said he'd been in prison? Because for all its insidiousness, a rumor often began with a kernel of truth. A kernel, though, wasn't the full truth, and for whatever reason, I trusted Gage. Certainly I'd trust him over those biddies whose primary agenda seemed to be spreading hurtful gossip. I felt embarrassed for having asked about his beard at all.

"So I can fend off all the women," he said, winking at me.

"Right." He had a point there because I was finding it hard to remember we weren't on a real date. This was a business arrangement, nothing more.

Still, I was glad to have something to do before our eleven o'clock appointment in the hotel wedding chapel, or I'd be thinking about it too much.

My mother was going to disown me. My father, too. At least my actions wouldn't hurt Lily, and we would always have each other.

"What is it?" Gage asked. "You went quiet all of a sudden."

"It just hit me. What I'm doing."

His eyes were still kind, but he might as well have been wearing his beard for all the emotion I could see in his face. "It's not too late to change your mind."

"I don't have a choice."

"There are always choices. It's finding one you can live with that matters."

Why did I think he was talking more about his life than mine? "I can live with this."

"Okay, then. So, are you finished? The Cirque Du Soleil awaits."

The seats around the arena were packed, and a feeling of anticipation hung in the air. I barely sat back in my seat during the performances, my eyes pinned to the amazing feats of daring, dancing, and martial arts.

"Did you see that?" I leaned over and grasped Gage's arm for probably the hundredth time. "I can't believe it."

His warm hand closed over mine. "I don't know which is better—watching you or the performance."

I laughed and tried to sit still. After a moment, Gage's arm went around the back of my seat, and it felt natural to lean into him.

I found myself becoming increasingly curious about his life, his family, his friends. His likes and dislikes. While our association would end soon, I'd probably face a lot of questions from my family. They'd want to meet him, and if Gage wouldn't agree, I'd have to supply a lot of excuses until the trust fund was taken care of and I could announce a permanent dissolution of the marriage.

"Look," Gage said. "I could so see you doing that." He pointed to an acrobat who was leaping through a ring of fire.

I laughed and forgot my worries.

The show ended about nine, and we still had an hour to kill before I needed to start getting ready. As we left, he took my hand to guide me through the crowd, and I realized I hadn't thought of Julian all night. What did that say about me? Maybe Lily was right when she said Julian was all wrong for me.

A fresh wave of pain hit my chest, and I clung to Gage's hand with more force than necessary. He glanced at me with one eyebrow raised. I loved how he did that. So expressive. A question without speaking a word.

"It's early yet," I managed. "Let's go to a dance club."

"They have one right here. People dance until the wee hours of the morning. Maybe all night."

"Let's go."

"Aren't you a little tired?" He stifled a yawn.

"Not at all. You?"

"I'm fine."

The music in the club was loud, the beat exactly what I needed to drown my doubts and fears. I pulled Gage onto the floor and began to move. I didn't have a lot of talents, but I could dance. As a child, my mother had put me into every imaginable dance class available, more to keep me busy than for any other reason. I didn't mind. I'd loved every minute, every step, every routine learned. At one time, I'd imagined myself on the stage—a short-lived dream that died when I learned of the daily hours of practice involved. I still loved the beat, though, and freestyle was the best.

To my surprise, Gage matched me move for move. What he didn't know in theory, he made up for in effort. When a slow song came, he drew me into his arms.

"Tired yet?" he asked, his lips close to my ears so I could hear, his breath warm on my cheek.

"No." In fact, life was seeping into me. "I love staying out late. Tomorrow, though, I won't be able to get up. I'm not a morning person. You?"

"Mornings are my favorite time. I especially love watching the sunrise."

Something caught in my throat because I suddenly had a picture of us on the porch of a cabin somewhere, hot chocolate in hand, with me wearing one of his flannel shirts, as we sat and enjoyed the sunrise.

"I don't think I ever saw a sunrise," I admitted. "Plenty of sunsets. I love to watch them, especially over the ocean."

"Maybe you'll show me someday." The music ended as he yelled this in my ear. We stared at each other, and I knew that like me he was suddenly remembering that none of this was real.

"Sure," I lied.

The tension was thick between us. I didn't understand it, and I didn't want to. What I wanted was for him to put his arms around me again and dance until morning. Julian and I didn't often go dancing. He liked movies better, or playing golf, or hanging with stuffy business associates.

"Uh," I said, "Something seems to be vibrating in your pocket." We were still close enough for me to feel the movement, not to mention the hardness of his chest.

Gage released me and reached into his blazer pocket, drawing out his phone. "Someone's trying like mad to reach me. It's got to be at least the sixth phone call since we got here." He glanced at the number. "Oh, it's my sister."

Sister? I didn't even know he had a sister. Wait, yes. He'd mentioned her before. She was younger and married with a child. Maybe.

"Go ahead and call her," I said. "Might be important." I only hoped no one had seen me with Gage and tracked me down through him.

He nodded. "She's not usually this persistent. I'll go find someplace quiet to talk to her. Be right back."

In seconds he was swallowed by the noisy crowd. I swayed with the music, pondering Gage and his family. His mother was gone, according to the women at the restaurant, if they even had that right. What about his father? How close were he and his sister? He'd lived in Flagstaff nearly a year that I knew, but where was she?

Odd that I felt so alone without him. Alone and vulnerable in this huge city.

"Hey, sweetheart."

I looked around to see a man addressing me. The man was taller than Gage, but half his width. The thin, tennis player type. Unruly blond curls dominated his head as though he was trying hard to be a surfer. I smiled at him. Why shouldn't I? There was no telling how long Gage would be gone, and it wasn't as if we were engaged. Well, not really.

"I'm Eddie," he yelled over the music. His breath told me he'd been enjoying himself at the bar.

"Tessa."

He nodded and got into the dance. He was more practiced than Gage, but his movements were not as graceful. I smiled my encouragement.

The music ended, and we moved off the dance floor. "Can I buy you a drink?" Eddie asked.

"I don't think so. I'm waiting for a friend."

His eyes turned hard. "You didn't say anything about a friend a while ago. If you don't like me, you should just say so."

"I like you fine, but I really do have a friend. I need to wait here, or he won't know where to find me."

"He? You have a boyfriend?"

"Not a boyfriend. Look, it's complicated."

"Then come on. We'll only be a minute."

I was becoming angry at having to explain myself—for

feeling obligated to explain. We'd shared a dance, for crying out loud, not a contract. He had no claim on me. "No, thank you," I said, nearly shouting to be heard over the music. "Thank you for the dance, though. It really was fun."

He put his hand on my arm, pulling me close. "Let's do another. I can show you some moves." His body pressed against my side, sending a shudder of fear through me.

I tugged my arm but couldn't break free. "I don't want to dance. Please, leave me alone." Around us everyone went blithely about their business, not glancing our way or noticing my dilemma, and I realized he could do anything he wanted to me in this crowd. I jabbed my elbow hard into his stomach.

His face grew dark. "Why, you little—"

Whatever he'd been going to say was cut off as Gage stepped between us. "Sorry for taking so long."

Eddie glared at Gage, but Gage smiled blandly. "I'm Gage. Are you a friend of Tessa's?" Gage put a possessive arm around me.

With another black look, Eddie stalked away.

"Thanks," I said.

"You should choose your dance partners a little more carefully."

So he'd seen me dancing. "What I need is to learn self-defense."

He laughed. "That elbow thing was really good."

"Is your sister okay?"

The smile faded. "She's fine."

"Why'd she call?" I wondered if he'd even tell me.

Every time I asked a personal question, he somehow directed it back to me.

"She heard I was getting married."

"What? From whom?"

"I don't know. I haven't seen anyone I know except Calvin since we got here, and he wouldn't tell her."

Guilt struck me. That left only the little old vultures— ladies. No doubt they'd spent the past few hours on the phone spreading gossip. Which meant his sister probably still lived in Kingman.

"We'd better get out of here." Gage checked the time on his cell. "Not much time to get dressed."

My stomach did a flip-flop that left me feeling queasy. "Right."

"We should call a taxi."

"Let's walk instead. If we get tired, we'll stop and call. It really wasn't as far away as Calvin said." When he hesitated, I added, "Please."

"Okay."

We strolled along the brightly lit boulevard. Music, laughter, people all around. The Las Vegas Strip. We were two people in a crowd, enjoying the nightlife. Strangely, I didn't want to share this moment with anyone else.

"I think we need to turn here," Gage said.

As the lights and noise slowly died away, it happened. Running steps, a figure coming at us, the silver flash of a knife.

In a blur of limbs, Gage reacted. He stepped to the side, grabbed the attacker's arm, and twisted it behind him. He pushed, forcing the man down onto the sidewalk, holding him there with a hand and a foot. It all happened so fast I barely had time to become scared.

"Looks like your friend from the club doesn't want to take no for an answer." Gage pulled the guy's arm up farther and removed the switchblade from his hand, closing and pocketing it. "I'm going to let you up," he said, "but I'm keeping your knife. If you don't leave immediately, I'll use it. I promise you that."

Eddie grunted in pain. "Okay. I'll go."

Gage released him, but the minute Eddie was on his feet, he rushed Gage, murder in his eyes. In a blink, Gage slammed his fist into the taller man's stomach, followed by another punch to the face. When he whipped out the switchblade, Eddie fled.

Gage watched to make sure he was gone before turning back to me. "You all right?"

I nodded.

"Shut your mouth. The flies are getting in." He sounded amused.

I snapped my mouth shut, only to open it again. "Where'd you learn that?" A man who could fight like that could clearly do a lot of damage if he tried. He wouldn't even need a poker.

"A bit in the army. I was there a year or two. But mostly in prison." His smile was gone, and without it his face looked bleak and more youthful, unsure. Seeing my quickly blanked expression, he winked.

Stop with the joking! I wanted to yell, but I didn't feel I had the right. After all, he was the one doing me a favor.

"Well, it's a good thing you did," I said, purposely keeping my voice light. "He was a really bad dancer."

Gage laughed. "Just when I think I have you pegged, you surprise me."

"What's that supposed to mean?"

"Nothing. I had fun tonight—dancing, dinner. All of it."

"So did I." I put my hand in his, and he tightened his fingers over mine. I found myself wishing we didn't have to go back to the hotel at all, that we could keep on walking and walking. Or maybe find a park and swing and watch the stars. The night would never, ever end. I would never have to remember that I was a woman betrayed, a woman marrying without love for reasons that no longer seemed so important.

Lily, what should I do?

We kept on walking until we reached the hotel.

When Avery was finished with me, I looked like a real bride. My mother couldn't have done any better with all her high-priced hairdressers and seamstresses. Avery had fixed my hair again because it'd come loose at the night club, but she didn't pull it as tight. Curls softened my face, and in the light my hair looked almost blond instead of orange, which always put me in a good mood.

Downstairs a group of people loitered in the lobby. A few gave me admiring looks, and I felt so grateful that I almost invited them to the wedding. Fake friends were better than no friends. But Avery hustled me down the hall to the chapel, whose narrow double doors were wide open. Raised voices leaked out.

"I don't want her to know anything. I know what I'm doing."

"I could get in trouble."

"You owe me. I don't like it any more than you do, but I won't see her hurt. I may not ever be able to tell her, but I care about her a great deal."

The first voice was Gage's and he was talking to Calvin, but they couldn't possibly be discussing me. Nope. Not me. Because Gage couldn't hurt me. I didn't love him, and I wasn't about to love anyone else, either. If I ever did get married for real, the man would have to prove himself beyond any doubt. Like that could ever happen. A man was a man after all. His entire gender was suspect.

Thanks to Julian.

Here I was all dressed up for a wedding, and my real fiancé wasn't here. Funny how much it still hurt—like a fresh wound every time I thought about it.

"It wouldn't take much more adjusting after," Calvin said. "Just a few forms."

"My name is sullied, and I won't let that touch her." Gage's voice was devoid of expression now, except maybe a faint disgust.

Who were they talking about? Then I remembered the old women at the restaurant saying something about Gage once having a fiancée, the one who hadn't spoken for a year after his supposed conviction. I felt relief that the conversation had nothing to do with me.

Avery was staring at my face with a frightened look as though she believed what we'd heard would make me change my mind about marrying Gage, but I had the paper he'd signed earlier, and I was going through with it. Lifting my chin, I smiled at Avery before sweeping into the room.

The conversation cut off, and I heard Gage draw in a swift breath. A real smile hovered on his lips, and his green eyes were brilliant. "You look—" He stopped and cleared his voice, which had gone hoarse. "You look amazing."

No one had ever told me that before—especially not someone who was as drop-dead gorgeous as Gage was at that moment. The cut of the tux accentuated his broad shoulders and the squareness of his jaw. The black made him seem rich and mysterious.

"Do you have rings?" Calvin asked.

My eyes shot to Gage's in consternation. "Ah, no, we haven't had time."

"No worries," Calvin said. "We have these little bands we use in a pinch." He proffered a small box filled with cheap gold-painted metal rings, a far cry from the lovely ring I'd left at home. "Each of you choose your size and then trade so you can put them on during the ceremony."

Blindly, I did as he asked, passing the little band to Gage and taking his in return.

"Smile for the camera!" Avery had ducked behind a fancy digital camera standing on a tripod.

I smiled as Gage took my arm, a shiver sliding through me at his touch. This wasn't going to be hard. I could handle it.

I was wrong.

Before I was ready, Calvin pulled out a book, rattled

off a few words, and pronounced us man and wife. "You may kiss the bride."

I hadn't thought that far ahead, and now I tried not to panic. To my relief, we exchanged a chaste little peck that had Calvin smirking at me like he knew a secret.

Blame it on the late hour, the magic of the show we'd seen, the adrenaline from the dance and the subsequent attack—whatever the reason, I gave it another shot. Gage started in surprise, but he kissed me back. His lips were firm and yet molded perfectly to mine, and his arms wrapped around me like a familiar blanket. He smelled of spice and something uniquely his own. Emotion arrowed through my chest, though I'd been determined never to feel anything for a man again.

This close, I could see a pattern of thin scars covering his left cheek, the largest disappearing into his hairline. I wondered how they'd come about—but I couldn't wonder long because the kiss was taking most of my energy. My heart pounded so violently, I wondered if Avery could hear it across the room.

When at last we separated, I felt stunned. Is that what a kiss was supposed to feel like? If so, Julian and I weren't very good at it.

In a daze, I let Gage lead me to the door, where Avery handed me a CD of the pictures.

Then it was over and we were back in my room. No family, no wedding celebration, no exchanges of real vows, no more earth-shattering kisses or whispered endearments. I took shallow breaths so I wouldn't cry. This was not how it was supposed to be. I felt as if something inside me had died just when it had started to live.

"Well." Gage glanced at the door to his adjoining room, and I wondered if he wanted to escape.

"I'll call the attorney in the morning," I said.

"They have Internet here. You can send pictures to him and your family, if you'd like."

"Good idea. I'll do it right now." I'd send them to my mother, but not to Lily. I needed to decide how much I would tell her. She might worry herself into a miscarriage if I said I did it for her.

"Need help?" Gage asked.

My hands were shaking as I tugged my laptop from my backpack, so I let him put in the disk and bring up the pictures. Most were bad, but Avery had succeeded in taking a few exceptional ones.

"Do you care which pictures?"

I shook my head and then almost changed my mind when he chose one of us kissing. It was one of the better pictures; Avery had waited for exactly the right moment, and we looked as if we were in love.

He studied my face when we finished sending the email. He opened his mouth to say something, but all that came out was, "Well."

"Well," I repeated. A sort of hysterical laughter bubbled up inside me as I thought of us staring at each other all night saying, "Well."

"I guess we'd better change." He strode to the adjoining door, yawning. "Let me know if you need anything."

"Okay."

The minute I was alone, the tears started to fall. I hugged myself and cried until I was afraid I would ruin the wedding dress. Still sobbing, I went into the bathroom, and when I'd finally managed to unzip and rid myself of the gown, I stood staring into the mirror, crying.

I hate you, Julian! I hate you! I screamed in my head. *This is all your fault.* But in reality I hated myself. I'd been the one to trust him. I'd been the one to fall in so easily with what everyone had wanted for me.

What if now I'd made another huge mistake? Marriage wasn't something to fool around with, especially with someone I didn't know that well. What if he tore up our contract, and I disappeared in some remote place in the desert? How much money would he get then? I had no idea.

Oddly enough, the idea made me smile. Gage wouldn't hurt me. I knew that much.

The fact remained that I'd looked forward to my wedding my entire life, and now I felt as if I'd lost something infinitely precious. The cheap ring still on my finger mocked me.

Too late now. Tomorrow, I'd be okay, but tonight I was going to throw myself on my bed and cry myself to sleep. Ripping the ring from my finger, I aimed toward the trash but stopped at the last moment, placing it instead on the sink. I might need it yet.

No sooner was I in bed than a knock came from Gage's connecting door. "What?" I called, annoyed at the interruption in my pity fest.

"Can I come in?"

I knew my face was a red, blotchy mess, but it made little difference. I pulled on a pair of sweats and opened the door, leaving off the light in the hope that my grief wouldn't be too noticeable.

Gage took one look at me and pushed his way into the room, flipping on the lights, but when he spoke, he didn't mention my condition. "You said you were a night owl, so look what I found." He held out a pack of cards, and I noticed he still wore his cheap band. "Wanna play?"

Suddenly I did. I nodded, squinting at him. "Prepare to lose." My voice was low and unsteady, but maybe he didn't notice.

"In your dreams." He sat at the table and shuffled the cards like a pro. I was glad he'd looked away from my ruined face.

"I'll be back." I fled into the bathroom and gazed into the mirror. I looked worse than I'd thought, and I was glad Gage hadn't made any snide comments. Not only was my face red and blotchy, it was smeared with mascara, and the false eye lashes were half off. Turning on the water, I began washing my face. I felt a lot better when I emerged.

Playing cards wasn't exactly the way I had planned to spend my wedding night, but it beat crying alone in that huge bed—especially when I didn't feel a bit tired. Besides, by tomorrow or the next week, I wouldn't be married anymore. This would all be over as if it had never happened, and I would have the money my grandfather would have already given me if he hadn't died.

"It's your turn." There was a gentleness in Gage's expression, a kindness that took me by surprise though it somehow seemed natural on his rugged face.

My mind drifted to that fabulous kiss.

Not good. Definitely not good.

I was still in bed asleep when Gage knocked on our adjoining door the next morning. "Go away," I mumbled. Light came in from the curtained windows, but I solved that by smashing the pillow tightly over my head.

We'd played cards until he fell asleep at the table at around four, and I'd had to prod him awake enough to get him back to his room. Surely I couldn't have been asleep more than a couple hours. What was he thinking?

I heard footsteps into the room. "Tessa?"

He dragged the pillow off my face, and I moaned, pulling the blanket over my eyes instead. What kind of person was he to wake me up so early? No wonder they'd put him in prison.

That thought made me wake up in a hurry. I tentatively opened one eye. "What do you want? What time is it anyway? Five? Six?"

"Ten," he said dryly.

"Oh." I opened the other eye. "Checkout's probably at eleven, isn't it?"

"Don't worry, I arranged with Calvin to check out late. They're used to honeymooners."

I pulled up the blanket again to hide the flush that crawled over my face. For a blessed few hours I'd forgotten about the wedding fiasco and the tears that now embarrassed me.

"Look, I know you were planning on going to your sister's, but I have a favor to ask." His words came so hesitantly that I came out from under the blanket and sat up.

I was still dressed in my sweats from the night before. In fact, I hadn't even brought pajamas. My backpack wasn't very big, and I'd figured Lily could lend me a pair when I got to her place.

Gage looked like he'd been up for hours. His face was freshly shaved, his hair combed back, and he had on a red button-up shirt that was snug across the chest. Though he was standing near the edge of the bed, I could smell soap and aftershave.

"What favor?" Then I had a thought. "I can't give you more money."

"It's not about the money," he grated.

"Excuse me. And I thought you were a morning person."

He clenched his jaw briefly before forcing out, "I'm sorry. It's just that my sister wants to meet you."

"What?"

"My sister wants to meet you," he repeated. "She keeps calling and calling and calling. She's rather persistent."

"Didn't you tell her it's all fake?"

"What if the attorney asks her? We don't know what

we're really up against legally at this point, do we? Besides, Mia wouldn't approve of faking a marriage."

"She's not the only one." Lily would be worse than upset if I told her.

"So I thought we'd go to Mia's place in Kingman and stay a night. Let her see you. She has plenty of room, and her house is in a nice area. Peaceful. You'll like it. Then I could take you to Lily's in Phoenix, or get you a ride. I was able to take a few personal days off work, but I'll have to get back soon. Mia won't know we're not going to Flagstaff together. She doesn't visit me there. I usually go see her." He rubbed his chin, and I wondered if he was thinking about his lost beard. "Sorry about the inconvenience. It would have been better if Mia hadn't heard about this."

"Uh, that might be my fault. Remember those ladies at the restaurant? Well, they didn't want my autograph."

"No kidding."

"They were from Kingman. They recognized you."

His brow furrowed. "What'd they say?"

Oh, no. I wasn't going into that whole poker thing. If he didn't know the exact rumor going around, I wasn't going to be the one to enlightened him. "Nothing important, but I did mention we were getting married."

He stared at me as if trying to read my mind, and I shifted uncomfortably.

"Sorry. I bet if you hadn't shaved for the wedding, they wouldn't have recognized you."

"Probably not. My face is rather famous in Kingman."

"Why?"

"I told you already. I served time."

"You weren't joking?"

He sighed, and the sadness in his expression hurt my heart. "Believe me, it's not something I'd ever joke about. I've worked hard to put that all behind me, but some people won't let it go."

I was beginning to suspect he'd accidentally hurt someone in self-defense, and I wondered if he'd ever trust me enough to confide the details. Normally my mouth would ignore my brain and demand the whole story, but he was saved because I wasn't yet fully awake.

"Please come to my sister's with me," he said. "We won't see anyone else. I don't have any friends there."

"Okay."

He blinked at me. "Okay?"

"Yeah. I mean, why not. You did me a favor, so I'll do you one. I haven't talked to Lily yet, anyway. She doesn't know anything except what my mother may have told her." I reached over to the night stand and retrieved my phone, pressing the on button. "I'm sure she's called and emailed, and texted, and Facebooked, and probably even tweeted."

"All that?"

"She's bored since she had to quit her job. Yep, I have thirty-five missed calls. More than half are probably from her." My mother, Julian, Sadie, and even my father would make up the remainder.

"I see." There was a smile on his lips again, and I was glad.

Tossing down the phone, I stood and walked over to him. "I like you without the beard." The light was bright enough to see the scars on his cheek. "Bet it itches less."

"You got that right."

Though there was no change of tone, I sensed unhappiness in the words. Was he thinking of Kingman and everything he'd left behind? I wanted to ask about his fiancée, but the hard line of his mouth forbade me. *It's none of my business,* I told myself.

"What will we tell your sister?" I asked.

"I think sticking as close to the truth as possible will be best. You know, we were together with Serenity, and you realized you couldn't go through with your wedding, and one thing led to another, and here we are."

Somehow I didn't think it would be that easy in practice. "Okay, give me a few minutes, and I'll be ready."

Gage headed toward the door. "How about I get you breakfast while you dress? Don't worry about looking fancy. Mia's not big on fashion."

I hadn't been worried in the least until he'd said something. Did that mean he wanted me to look nice? Was there something he wasn't telling me? Did he have some secret rivalry with his sister? Why didn't the man just spit it out?

I glared at the door after it had closed. Well, I wasn't getting all dressed up—so there! I would have to wear my nice black pants because my comfortable jeans were dirty, and the blue top with the black pinstripes only because it matched the pants, not because it made my waist look smaller and my hair less orange.

After I changed, I called Mark Carson, the attorney, to talk about my inheritance. "I received your email a few hours ago," Mark said, sounding a little stiff. "Your mother called me as well to inform me of your marriage.

Needless to say, I was a little surprised that you, uh, changed course so abruptly."

"Me, too," I admitted. "But yesterday I realized Julian wasn't the right man for me. Better before marriage than after, I always say." The lump I'd felt in my stomach since the day before had turned bitter.

"Well, congratulations." His voice warmed considerably. "Your husband is a lucky man, and you seem to make a nice couple, though I would never tell that to your mother."

I laughed. Could it be this easy? "Thank you. What I need to know is how soon can I obtain my funds? I'd like to help my sister, and you know how my mother is. She's not at all happy right now."

"No, she isn't, but it was your choice, wasn't it? As for the trust fund, there are only a few formalities we have to go through. I'll need copies of the marriage license and certificate and all relevant information. I can obtain all that on my own, which will take longer, or you can send me what you have."

"No problem. I'll send it right away. There isn't a waiting period for the trust fund, is there?"

"Not unless someone contests the validity of the marriage, which is supposed to have been entered into in good faith. Your grandfather figured if you were old enough to get married, you'd be old enough to handle your own funds."

That made me feel guilty, though I would have come into the inheritance anyway if I married Julian tomorrow as planned. In my book, good faith could mean a lot of things. Thankfully, I wasn't required to produce an heir.

"Great. I'll send you what I have," I told Mark. I hadn't seen the marriage certificate, but Gage probably had it.

"You sure everything's okay?"

I laughed. "Of course. I'm actually heading over to Gage's sister's house right now. Lot of catching up to do. She's not happy about the eloping thing, but hopefully we won't have to stay too long and can leave for our honeymoon."

"Well, I'll keep you apprised of how it's going with the funds."

"Thanks." I hung up feeling happier than I had since Sadie had broken the news about Julian.

I'd almost repacked my few belongings when Gage came in with several Styrofoam take-out containers in a paper bag.

"How do you feel about pancakes with strawberries and whipped cream?" He smiled as he hefted a drink container. "And hot chocolate."

"My favorite!" I grabbed the containers, feeling ravenous. Truth was, I didn't often get up in time to eat breakfast, but pancakes were always at the top of my list when I did.

He watched me dig into the food.

"Aren't you having any?" I asked, my mouth full.

"I ate earlier."

"Pancakes?"

He grimaced. "Donuts, actually. But I remembered you saying you liked—" He broke off in mid-sentence. "Calvin says to leave the borrowed dresses in the closet, and they'll take care of them. Is there anything I can help you with?"

"I didn't bring much, I'm afraid. I'd better get my funds soon or I might get awfully sick of these clothes."

"Won't your mother send your things?"

"I don't know. I might have to appear on her doorstep during one of her parties so she'll have to let me in for the sake of saving face. Though with the embarrassment I've caused her this weekend, even that might not work. I should have planned better."

"You might be right about that." His eyes fell to my blouse, and I followed his gaze to see a large splotch of strawberries. I sighed and began to clean it up with the napkin, which promptly fell to pieces, leaving bits of paper on my blouse.

Why me?

Gage busied himself grabbing my backpack and didn't meet my gaze, but I could tell inside he was laughing. I peeked in the bathroom to make sure I hadn't left anything. The cheap band glinted on the sink counter, and after hesitating a few seconds, I slipped it on.

My phone rang as I rejoined Gage, and I reached for it, instinctively checking the caller ID. Lily again. "I'll meet you downstairs," I told Gage, clicking the answer button. He nodded and left the room, not closing the door after him.

"Tessa!" Lily screamed in my ear. "What are you doing? Mom emailed me some pictures—which goes to show how crazy she is right now. She has never returned any of my emails since I left home. Did you really elope? I can't believe it! I mean, you said you were having doubts about Julian, but who is this guy? Mom thinks he's some stranger you picked up to get at your trust fund, which she's blaming on me, by the way. If you can believe that. I—"

She rambled on, and I held the phone away from my ringing ear until the torrent of words ceased. "Yes, Lily, to all your questions, except Gage isn't a stranger. I met him months and months ago while riding Serenity."

"Oh, thank heaven! I couldn't live with myself if you married someone just for me. That would be worse than marrying Julian. You look so happy in that picture where he's kissing you. What a kiss! You can tell he's totally crazy about you. He's got that dazed look. And he's so hot! Makes Julian look like a prissy little school boy. I bet he loves the outdoors like you do. So where are you two going now?" She gasped. "Oh, you're on your honeymoon. I'm so sorry! Are you in some fabulous place?"

I was holding the phone away from my ear again, but not so far that I couldn't hear every word. Now what? Did I tell her the truth? An ache pulsed in my temples, and I rubbed the left one in an effort to alleviate the pain.

"Look, Lily. I'll have to call you back later. We're on our way somewhere right now. But I'll come see you soon, okay? I'll tell you everything."

"You'd better. I'm bored to death sitting here, but that's the only way I keep anything down. This baby had better appreciate all this sacrifice."

When she talked like that, it made me wonder how our mother had made it through two entire pregnancies. I remembered her being in bed while expecting Lily, so maybe I'd been adopted.

"I really have to go, Lily."

"Okay, okay, but I'm so happy for you! I have to say,

the guy looks like a keeper. And did I say he's hot? Plus, maybe you can be yourself around him."

"I love you, too," I said and hung up, feeling worse than I had before the call.

The phone rang again, and I answered it quickly. "Lily, I told you I—"

"It's Julian."

I froze.

"Is this true? Did you go and marry someone else? Tess, I don't understand." His use of my nickname made me feel faint. "Please, talk to me. Why are you doing this? Better yet, tell me where you are, and I'll come and get you. Whatever it is you've done, I love you, and we can work it out."

Whatever it was I had done? I would have laughed if it didn't feel as though he were stabbing me in the heart.

"Talk to Sadie," I said, having to force out each word. "She's the one who told me."

"I have talked to Sadie. Honey, you can't believe her. She's had it out for me since I didn't want you to go to that concert with her in San Diego earlier this year. She's jealous, that's all. I promise you."

My knees were feeling weak, so I sat abruptly in the chair behind me, nearly missing it altogether. I wanted to believe him. Tears squeezed from my eyes.

As if sensing my weakness, he rushed on. "Whatever Sadie imagined happened, it was in her own mind. Sure, women flirt with me, but there was never anything inappropriate. You have to believe me."

Gage appeared in the doorway. He took one look at my face and grabbed the phone from my hand. "Who is this!" he demanded. "Well, stop calling. Tessa is *my* wife now. *Mine.* You will leave her alone or deal with me." A pause and then, "Gage, Gage Braxton from Kingman. Google me and you'll know why you should stay far away from her." He shut the phone.

I rolled my eyes.

"What?" Gage handed me back the phone.

"You don't have to defend me. I can handle it myself."

"Oh?" He put one finger to my cheek and came away with a tear. His voice became so soft it was almost a whisper. "Should I call him back for you?"

"That's okay."

"Good. So are we getting out of here, or should I tell Calvin we love this place so much that we're staying another night?"

"I'm ready."

I wished I hadn't agreed to go with him to his sister's. I didn't like the anger in his voice or the look in his eyes when he'd told Julian that I was his wife, as though I was his property. I'd also begun thinking that if whatever had happened in Gage's past was serious enough to be on the Internet, I might have made a huge mistake.

We reached Kingman shortly after noon. I was feeling stiff and sleepy from the ride on the bike, but I'd enjoyed being close to Gage, even if I'd never admit it. There was something secure about him.

I noticed he didn't drive through town, but kept to the lonely back roads once we'd left the freeway. He probably didn't want to be recognized more than necessary. Behind us, I saw a white sedan that looked similar to one that had followed us on the freeway. An unease touched my mind, but I pushed it away. No one knew where I was, and no one had a reason to follow us.

After several more blocks, we turned down a narrow road that soon became dirt. The sedan didn't follow, and I breathed a sigh of relief. Now only the occasional house popped up awkwardly out of the desert, a bit of unexpected organization in the sprawling landscape. Dust rose in a cloud behind us, and I found myself yearning for a drink of water.

At last Gage stopped in front of a single-story house with a wide porch, surrounded by a grove of green trees. Like an oasis in the desert, the place was as different from its distant neighbors as if it had been transported from another place or time.

"It's so . . . refreshing," I said. Also surprising and quaint, but I didn't want to gush.

He grinned and helped me off the bike, slinging his duffel over his shoulder. "There's an underground river going through the property. One in a million. Our neighbors think our water bill is outrageous, but you can follow the line of the river if you try." Sure enough, a line of brush and trees stretched out behind the house, and ran alongside the road in front as well, where a thriving bunch of weeds were taking advantage of the moisture.

The house itself was a small, tan, stuccoed affair that looked on the new side. The porch had rough-cut beams for support, and hanging from the outer crossbeam were three large pots spilling an array of colorful flowers and greenery. More flowers lined the walkway and filled the narrow flowerbeds. There were even a few cacti.

"My sister has a green thumb." He paused before we began up the walkway. "Look, about Mia, she's . . . well, she's . . ." He ran out of words.

I took the fake gold ring from where I'd shoved it into my pocket at the hotel and put it on my finger. "Don't worry. I'll be nice."

He didn't even crack a smile, and suddenly he was a stranger, not the man who'd let me win at cards all night long. He reached for my backpack, but I took it myself.

We weren't even up the steps when the door pushed open and a woman appeared, dressed in jeans and a frilly apron. My first impression was one of innocent beauty. She had lively green eyes like Gage, but there the resemblance ended. Her hair was dark enough to be called black, and it was long and glossy and held in a careless ponytail. She was small, delicate, almost childlike, and her freckled nose turned up at the end. She flung herself at Gage, and he hugged her tightly.

The moment they separated, Mia's hands and arms were moving fast, almost a blur, betraying her excitement. Realization dawned on me—Mia was deaf.

Gage held up a hand. "Wait," he said, signing the words as he spoke. "Tessa doesn't know sign language."

Mia grinned at the expression on my face. "You didn't tell her," she said, the words awkward but recognizable. To me she added, "I am so pleased to meet you. I can't believe he didn't tell me you were getting married." She added something in sign to Gage and then laughed.

Gage looked at me. "She can read lips pretty well—and guesses at the rest."

"Nice to meet you," I said. I was of average height and on the slender side, but I towered over her and felt like a giant in comparison. "Sorry about the surprise. It was sort of . . . well . . . it surprised everyone, even us."

Mia smiled at me, and I smiled at her. Gage rocked on his heels and didn't meet my eyes. No one said anything until Mia finally waved us inside. "My husband is traveling," she said. "You will have to meet him another day. But my son will be home soon." Some of her pronunciations were odd, and her voice had a nasally sound, but it wasn't unpleasant.

"Dylan's a great kid. You'll like him," Gage assured me.

Mia said something I didn't understand, and she motioned to Gage to translate.

"She's made us lunch," he said.

"Thank you." I was starving. Something about being on the run had affected my appetite. At this rate, I'd end up as chubby as Lily, and without a baby to show for it.

"It's chicken noodle soup," Mia said. "Gage says you love it with the big noodles."

I glanced at Gage, who looked uncomfortable. This was the third time he'd remembered something I must have told him in the pasture. Either he had a good memory, or he'd been stalking me. "I do love it," I told Mia a little too loudly.

She smiled and then pointed at my backpack. "I'll show you where to put this."

We followed her to a guest room. It was smaller than my room at home, but bigger than the room at the hotel.

A plush couch sat in front of the bed and an armoire with a TV inside was opposite. There was a small dresser, but the closet looked more than large enough for the little we'd brought.

The little I'd brought, because there was no way Gage was sleeping in here with me. He'd have to tell his sister something.

"Gage added the bathroom when he did the stucco," Mia said. "I always keep this room for him. And for you now. I hope you'll make him visit more often."

Gage's face showed a fleeting remorse, but before he could speak, Mia turned to him. "Why don't you go pick up Dylan from school early? He won't want to miss you."

Features hardening, Gage signed something vigorously to Mia, and she signed back with equal fervor. A silent argument that went right over my head.

"I'm just going to wash my hands," I said. Good thing we were only staying here one night.

When I emerged from the bathroom, Gage was gone, and Mia was in the bedroom waiting for me on the couch, her eyes bright with unshed tears. "He's so angry," she said. "I'm sorry for making everything sad."

"Don't worry about it. He's worried about being here, cutting his beard. I don't think he wants to be recognized."

"That's why he doesn't come. Only when Aiden is out of town and I need him. He doesn't want the kids to torture Dylan about having an uncle who is a murderer."

"A murderer?" I said slowly, but she wasn't looking at me and couldn't read my lips. Thoughts raced through my head—Gage telling me about prison, the women in the restaurant, my own belief that he hadn't done anything serious. Of course it wouldn't be the first time I'd been wrong about a man.

"I never thought Gage would marry," Mia continued. "Not after what happened. I—" She broke off, hesitating a second before rushing on. "It was hard for us as kids living under that shadow, but more for him. I was a girl, and besides, I couldn't hear what the kids said."

I sat down next to her. "I don't understand." And not just because her words were garbled with tears.

Her watery eyes met mine. "Our father killed a man when I was a baby. He went to prison and died there. More than anything, Gage wanted to prove he was different."

I was beginning to understand. The son of a murderer would have carried that stigma all his life, and school in a small town would have been torture. But that didn't explain what Gage had done.

"No matter what he told you," Mia continued, "Gage didn't hurt anyone."

"But he was convicted of murder." I said the words without making them a question, made sure she saw my lips. My heart pounded in my ears.

Mia shook her head. "He didn't do it."

"How do you know?" If he'd been convicted, there had to be proof of some kind, didn't there? Forensic evidence?

"Because I was there." She took my hand, and her next words chilled me. "The only reason Gage went to prison was to save me."

G age came in at that moment, and we both started guiltily. "I'm sorry, Mia," he said, signing the words as he spoke. "I didn't sleep much last night, so I'm a little out of it."

Mia smiled at him, her tears already vanishing. She grabbed her brother's hand. "Come. You need to eat."

Her chicken noodle soup was better than what I usually made, but I'd lost my appetite. The pancakes I'd eaten that morning curled in a sodden mass in my stomach, and my unanswered questions weighed even more heavily inside my brain.

"So how long have you known each other?" Mia asked.

"Since Christmas," I said at the same time Gage said, "Thanksgiving."

Thankfully, she could only look at one person at a time, and she was looking at Gage.

"Thanksgiving," I repeated to myself thoughtfully. Maybe he was right.

"Yeah. The week I moved in." His eyes met mine, but I looked away. At the moment, Gage both fascinated and repelled me, and Mia . . . well, I didn't know what to make of her.

"When did you know she was the one?" Mia looked at her brother, then at me, and back again, as if to be certain she didn't miss anything.

"The first time I saw her on Serenity," Gage said.

Mia nodded and smiled at me. "Gage told me about your horse. I would like to see her someday."

I opened my mouth to agree, before I remembered that I wasn't likely to see her again, this childlike woman who was as quick to laughter as she was to tears. Was her anger just as volatile? Had Gage been protecting her or covering for her when he'd been sent to prison?

"And you?" Mia asked me. "When did you fall in love with my brother?"

The noodles in my mouth tasted like ash. I should have never agreed to come here.

Gage scooted his chair closer to mine. "Yes, tell her, sweetheart. When did you first know that you were in love with me?"

I was blushing, probably a bright red, but two could play at this game. I reached over and set my hand on his, my eyes on his face. "I knew the minute he ran into that light pole. Did he tell you about that? He couldn't keep his eyes off me, and he just ran into it." There had been no light pole, of course, but if he wanted Mia to have a story, I'd give her one.

Mia laughed. "Oh, so she was the woman that day. But I thought it was a fence you ran into, not a light pole. Wasn't it a fence?"

"I don't know what either of you are talking about,"

Gage muttered and went back to eating his soup. He didn't meet my gaze. Had he really run into a fence? I wondered if it had been my fence.

"So where are you going for your honeymoon?" Mia asked.

Neither of us answered, and then Mia was off and signing again, rapidly, in what I recognized as yelling in sign language. Her face was bright and indignant.

Gage turned to me. "Uh, she's saying it's thoughtless of me not to have thought of a honeymoon, or at least stopped and bought real wedding rings instead of the ones we're wearing, which she is sure are fake, and I told her she wasn't helping any by insisting that we come here right now, and she said I should have invited her to the wedding or had it here." He grimaced. "Apparently, I'm an unromantic, self-centered jerk."

There was an unspoken plea in the words, and I began to feel sorry for him, despite the fact that he hadn't exactly been forthcoming about the reason for his prison term.

I held my hand up for Mia to stop signing. "It was really all spur of the moment," I said. "He was lucky enough to get the day off work. But he took me out for a wonderful dinner last night in Vegas, and we saw a show I've always wanted to see." I told her everything we'd done that night before, including the dresses, the dancing, and the man who'd attacked us. By the time I was finished, Mia was beaming again.

"Okay," she said to Gage. "You're off the hook. But you will take her somewhere nice as soon as you can get off work. And get a real ring. Promise?"

Gage was saved from further examination when a

twelve-inch console on the wall near the kitchen doorway began blinking wildly, changing from color to color, casting a faint rainbow over the entire kitchen.

"Excuse me," Mia said. "I need to get the door."

I smirked at Gage when she was gone.

"What?" Gage said.

My grin dissolved into laughter. "This is nuts. Where are you sleeping tonight, anyway?"

"I think the better question is where are *you* sleeping?" He tried to leer but failed miserably, and we both burst into laughter.

Mia returned to the kitchen, her expression a little lost. She signed something to Gage.

"Let her come in," he said. All the laughter was gone now, and his muscles bunched beneath his shirt. "Maybe she'd like a bowl of soup."

"Who?" I asked, as Mia disappeared again.

He sighed. "A woman who was my fiancée once. A long time ago. Look, I know this is asking far too much, but could you pretend a little harder? She's really bright. It's been over between us a long time, but I think she doesn't believe that. It would do her a favor if we could help her go on with her life."

"Forty-five thousand, then, instead of fifty," I said.

"What?" He frowned and a deep crease spread over his brow.

"Playing newlywed for your ex wasn't in the deal. Take it or leave it." Five thousand would go a long way toward paying whatever expenses came from the Lover's Lane Hotel and Chapel.

"Fine! Whatever. I don't care about the money."

Sure he didn't. "I want it in writing."

"Later. You'll have to take my word for now."

"The word of a convict." My mouth took over for my brain, and I regretted the words the instant they left my mouth.

"I've never pretended to be anything I wasn't. You knew what I was." His face was expressionless, his eyes cold.

I shook my head. "No, I didn't." Somehow it hurt that I'd refused to believe the rumors, though they'd been true all along. Had the old ladies been telling the truth as well? In the face of what Mia had said, I didn't know what to believe.

Mia cleared her throat in the doorway.

We had been talking quietly, our faces close together. I drew away, my face as red as Gage's shirt.

"Sorry to interrupt." The woman standing next to Mia was almost as tall as Gage. She wasn't beautiful in the delicate way that Mia was, but she had classic features that turned heads—high cheek bones, large brown eyes, sculptured eyebrows, aquiline nose, and close-cropped, dark brown hair that followed the attractive curve of her skull. Arresting. Her face and exposed skin were deeply bronzed in a manner that I achieved only in my dreams.

Gage stood up to meet her, taking my hand and pulling me with him. "Bailey, good to see you." He looked at me. "Honey, this is Bailey Norris, an old friend of mine. Bailey, this is my wife, Tessa Crawford." He stumbled over the word "wife," and I didn't think it was in my imagination that Bailey cringed when she heard it. I wondered how much they'd been in love and who'd given up first because it was obvious something still existed between them.

"So the rumors are true." Bailey walked into the kitchen with a sultry movement of long limbs. Her pants rode so low that a half-inch of her skin below her shirt was exposed as she moved.

I had to give those old ladies at the restaurant credit. They sure knew how to spread the word.

"All this time and only now you come back?" Bailey's eyes barely flickered over me, as though I were nothing more than an inconsequential piece of luggage.

"I've been back before," he said.

"Why didn't you come see me?"

"We'd already said all we had to say."

Gage was gripping my hand like a lifeline. I curled into him, telling myself that it was only to save my hand, but in reality I wanted to wipe that sneer off this woman's face. I fit myself in the crook of his shoulder, placing my arm around his body.

"Gage, darling, it's been a long day. I think I need a nice, hot bath after our long drive. Can you show me where it is?" I leaned over and kissed him. He was so tall, my mouth landed on his neck, but his other arm encircled me as I leaned toward him so it looked natural, as though I'd kissed him like that every day since last Thanksgiving.

I thought Bailey became a little pale underneath her tan. Behind her near the doorway, Mia was giving me a thumbs-up, though she couldn't have followed half the conversation from her position. Maybe she could read the set of Bailey's shoulders as well as I could.

"Please, Gage, I really need to talk to you for a moment. I promise I won't keep you long." Bailey looked regal now, and there was a hint of vulnerability in her bronze face.

"Okay." To his credit, there wasn't even a trace of long-suffering in his voice. Or maybe he was fooling himself that he wanted her gone.

Whatever his real emotion, Gage took his arm away from me, and I felt a momentary jealousy before I reminded myself that he wasn't mine, and I didn't want him to be. He leaned over and kissed my cheek near my ear. "I'll only be a minute." I felt his breath on my skin, and there was promise in his voice that sent a wave of goose bumps down my neck and arm. A little overboard even as a show for his ex, wasn't it? "I'll be right out front if you need me." He disappeared with Bailey, and I had to admit they looked good leaving together—a striking couple.

Mia was motioning me madly. "Come! Don't leave him alone with her."

"But she wants to talk privately."

"So? You're his wife. She doesn't get to be private with another woman's husband."

I followed her out onto the porch, where a heavy wave of heat greeted us. Gage and Bailey were talking by the dirt road, her urgently, leaning forward slightly, and him with his arms folded across his chest. Bailey was too close to him, and again I felt that idiotic surge of jealousy. There was a pleading in Bailey's demeanor, and I realized she probably felt much the way I had felt when I'd found out about Julian yesterday. Yes, that had to be it. Poor woman.

Their voices were low, and I couldn't hear any words, but Mia was staring at them intently, her green eyes narrowed. "She is angry that Gage didn't come for her after he got out," she said. "That he stopped answering her letters. She said he told her he'd never marry, and what changed?" She paused a moment. "Can't really see his mouth. Oh, he's saying this is different." She smiled at me, placing a small hand on my arm. "He must really love you."

I felt guilty spying on Gage this way, but I knew if I were really his wife, this whole conversation with Bailey wouldn't be happening at all without me right there. The nerve of that woman!

No. She had a prior claim. A real claim. I had none at all, and I didn't want one. Why was that so hard to remember all of a sudden?

An old pickup came flying down the road and put an end to the conversation. A little boy jumped from the truck and waved. The truck moved on as the boy started up the walk, keeping a safe distance as he skirted Gage and Bailey. He was a beautiful child, his face closely resembling Mia's. His dark hair was in need of a haircut, but the way it curled around his ears and the nape of his neck made me suspect that Mia simply couldn't bear to cut it off. He would be a heartbreaker one day, even if he never grew to his uncle's height.

"Dylan!" There was unguarded happiness in Gage's voice.

The boy stopped and studied him, his brows drawing tightly. "Uncle Gage? Is that you?"

"Of course it's me. How you been, buddy?"

"You look different."

"You've never seen me without my beard. Come on. Take a look." Gage took a few steps toward him and squatted down.

Dylan glanced across the yard at the porch and signed something to his mother, who signed back. He peered at Gage for a moment, a smile beginning on his narrow face. All reticence vanished as he dropped his backpack and threw himself into Gage's arms.

"You look young," Dylan said. "Not like yourself."

Gage laughed and tickled him, the two collapsing onto the grass in a tangle of arms and legs. "I'll show you how young," Gage threatened.

Bailey shifted to avoid being hit by a stray foot, and as I studied her, I was surprised by the naked yearning on her face as she watched the two play. Her emotion pierced me. Nothing fake about it. I wondered if Gage felt the same—if he did, they belonged together. Maybe after all this was over, I could help them figure things out. Needles pricked my heart at the idea, but the logic was undeniable. Gage was doing me a favor, and it would only be right and noble and good to return it.

Of course forty-five thousand was a pretty good return on his "favor." I tried to scowl when he glanced toward the porch, but the sight of him wrestling with his nephew was too engaging. Next year, I'd have my own niece or nephew. I couldn't wait.

"Why didn't you come and get me?" Dylan squealed

through his giggles. "It's so much cooler when you come on the bike."

"I promise I'll come as soon as my beard grows back."

"Why not today?"

"Never mind." Gage climbed to his feet and pulled Dylan up. "It's for your own good. I'll explain it when you're older."

The evasion didn't fool this smart child. "I don't care what anyone says, Uncle Gage. I know you didn't hurt that man. Mom and me both know it. And I told that to Albert Mitchard, too. I didn't care that he ripped my paper and called me a jailbird. He's stupid, and everyone knows it."

Gage suddenly looked weary. "Don't defend me, Dylan. Let them say whatever they want."

Dylan lifted his chin. "I won't."

"You will." There was iron in Gage's voice. The voice of a murderer?

"Nope, and you can't make me." The little boy reached out and slapped him on the leg without fear. "Tag, you're it. Can't catch me." He took off across the yard, heading toward the back of the house. Gage grinned as he began pursuit.

I'd never seen him so happy—of course, I hadn't seen his face without the beard until last night, so maybe he'd been happy all along and I didn't know it. Dylan was right that he did look much younger, not even as old as the thirty-one years he'd claimed on the wedding license. Definitely a far cry from the forty I'd given him back in Flagstaff.

Mia started after them, and I began to follow, but an

approaching Bailey waved me to a stop. "So," she said, her eyes riveting on my blouse where I'd spilled the strawberries that morning. Trust her to find that flaw.

"So," I repeated.

Her nostrils flared as she brought her gaze to mine. "I know something isn't right here, and I'm going to find out what. Gage loves *me* and always will." With that she turned and flounced away, her sultry movements replaced by a decided helping of pout.

"Okay, that was weird." So much for wanting to help her.

I waited until she drove away before going to find Gage and the others. They weren't in the small grassy yard when I arrived, but beyond it in a fenced patch of weeds. Dylan was sitting near the fence sprinkling something on the ground as a bunch of chickens clucked around him. In seconds the food was gone, but the chickens didn't seem in any hurry to leave. One settled on Dylan's lap and looked every bit as content as a dog while the little boy stroked her feathers.

I laughed for the sheer beauty of it all. Even better, I could see Gage bent over with his head and shoulders inside the chicken coop. He seemed to be raking straw from the floor of the small structure.

Mia drew up beside me when I entered the gate to the chicken yard. "My husband is not a big fan of chickens, but they are sweet creatures. My brother cleans out the pens a few times a year for us."

I could understand her words better now, even after the short exposure to her, but it was odd matching her uneven inflections with her lovely face—not that it detracted from the overall picture. In fact, the words added to her delicacy. That she could speak so well without being able to hear was nothing short of amazing.

"It's good for Gage," I said. "Gets him out into nature. Everyone needs a little time working outside."

"But he is always outside. He works in the field a lot." When I looked confused, Mia added, "For his job."

Oh, yeah. I should probably know a little more than I did about his work. He'd mentioned something about field visits, but didn't geologists mostly sit at their desks reading and writing reports? "Uh, yeah, but not with chickens. Speaking of which, I never saw any chickens that loving before."

Mia laughed. "Dylan raised that one from a little chick. He loves it so much."

We stood there watching the straw flying out of the pen and the hens clucking around Dylan, but my thought had returned to what Mia had said in the bedroom.

"Mia," I said.

She didn't respond, and I remembered she couldn't hear me. I touched her arm, and her face turned in my direction. "In the bedroom you said Gage went to prison to save you." I don't know what I was expecting. A confession maybe? She and young Dylan both seemed sure Gage was innocent. Was that because Mia knew something or because they wanted to believe? It could be like how Lily and I had kept expecting my mother to miraculously become a real mother to us. You blind yourself to the people you love. It hurt less that way.

"He didn't tell you?"

"He doesn't talk about it." Which was true as far as it went because he hadn't talked about the circumstances surrounding his sentence at all. I had the feeling that if I asked, he'd tell me again that it was none of my business.

Mia nodded as though she had expected as much. "I was there. A man was making trouble at the store where I worked. Gage tried to protect me, and they started fighting." She shook her head. "So much hitting. Blood. They passed out. I went for help, but when we came back—" She broke off, her green eyes pleading. "When I came back, the fireplace poker was shoved here in the man's head." One hand fluttered to the back of her neck, her finger angling up into the skull to show the placement. "Gage was still unconscious where I'd left him."

"Didn't you testify to that?"

"I told the police, but this man had . . . hurt me the week before, and they believed Gage had acted in revenge. I wasn't strong enough to use the poker, they said, and no one else had a motive."

She swallowed hard, her voice becoming softer and almost intelligible. "Sometimes, I think I did it. I was strong enough, no matter what they say. Gage knew I could have done it, and he thought I might be accused, and that's why he didn't fight the charges. But I *know* he didn't do it. My brother could have killed that monster by accident or in self-defense, but he would never murder an unconscious man. But you know that, or you wouldn't have married him."

What she'd proven was that Gage might be guilty after all. I'd seen a hint of how responsible he felt for his sister, and the fact that she called the murder victim a monster meant he'd hurt Mia deeply. "There was nothing else? No other evidence?"

"Skeet—that's the monster's name—his wallet was missing from his pocket. Never did find it. And I know he had money, a lot of money, because he showed me before Gage came." She let out a sound that was somewhere between a hiccup and a sob. "The money was gone when we found the body, but nobody believed me."

I wasn't sure what to say to that because I didn't know if I believed her.

"Maybe if I can find enough new information, they'll reopen the case," she continued. "This past year I've been volunteering at Sarah's House—a place that helps women and children leave abusive situations—and so many problems I see there are because of alcohol and drugs. I started to think maybe drugs are why Skeet was murdered. He had drugs in his system when he died. The authorities said he was just a user, but all that money had to come from somewhere. He might have been selling drugs, and maybe that was why he was killed."

"It's going to be hard proving anything after so long," I said. She had glanced away to check on Dylan, so I waited until she looked back to say, "How long ago was it?"

"Over seven years, but Kingman is a small town. Not much changes. Someone here has to know more than they are telling, and I'm going to find out what." She paused as if debating something within herself. "Look, I know I'm on the right track because someone left this in my mailbox yesterday."

She pulled a note from the pocket of her apron and

handed it to me. It was typed in big, bold letters on a folded sheet of unlined white paper that had no distinguishing marks. I opened it carefully.

Justice has been done. Don't mess with things unless you want more trouble than you got with Skeet.

A shiver of dread rolled through me. "Mia, you said Skeet hurt you. What did he do?"

She shook her head, her ponytail swinging with the force of her effort. "No," she said faintly.

I guess that meant she wasn't ready to talk about it—at least not to me. "This note proves something," I said.

"That's what I think. I've been asking everyone questions, and I must be getting close. Look, I know it's not a great time, but do you think you and Gage could stay a few more days until my husband gets home from his trip? I'm so afraid someone will come while I'm sleeping, and I won't hear them. I'm never afraid with Gage here." She took the note from my fingers and tucked it back inside her apron.

"What about the police? You need to tell them about that note."

"I will if you come with me." Mia held up a hand. "But you can't tell Gage. He says it's done and over and I should forget it. But I can't—not anymore. That record will haunt him the rest of his life. He wouldn't have been able to find a good job if one of the prison guards hadn't put in a word for him with his brother who manages the company Gage works for, and I never, ever thought Gage would marry because he said he didn't want any child of his to grow up like we had to. But you saw how he is with Dylan—he deserves to be a father to his own kids someday."

"Maybe if Gage saw the note, he'd have hope."

"No. Until there's a real chance of clearing his name, I'm not telling him anything." Tears started in Mia's eyes. "I failed my brother seven and a half years ago, but I won't fail him now. I should have taken the blame."

"No one should accept blame that doesn't belong to them. Besides, you had your husband and Dylan to think about." Since Dylan was in the first grade, that meant Mia had been expecting him about the time of the murder, or shortly after.

Mia ran her fingers under an eye to catch the moisture, glancing to make sure Gage and Dylan were still occupied. "It wasn't because of them that I didn't do it. It was the shock of everything that happened then. I—I lost myself for a bit. I'm stronger now, but the note frightens me."

"So is the note the real reason you wanted Gage to come here now?"

"Yes. I mean, of course I'd want to meet you anyway, but I was glad to have the excuse. I also hoped you might have some ideas about the murder since you can look at it with fresh eyes. You have as much stake in his future as I do."

I swallowed hard, loath to reply. I had no business delving into Gage's life, not in this way, but I didn't want to let Mia down either.

"We'll stay," I said. "At least until your husband comes home." I wasn't exactly excited about running off to Lily's where I'd have to explain that my marriage was fake and over with before she even met the groom she'd raved about. Besides, staying here would probably go a long way toward convincing my grandfather's attorney that my marriage was everything I claimed. "But we should talk to the police as soon as possible, so they can start looking for whoever put that note in your mailbox."

"We can go before dinner. I know one of the officers from school. Maybe he'll have time to talk to us." There was a relief in her voice that came clearly through the fear, and I knew insisting on going to the police was the right thing to do. I had to admit that I hoped Mia was right, that Gage really was innocent.

"Mommy, is something wrong?" Carrying a chicken, Dylan was coming toward us. I turned to see him, and that made Mia become aware of his approach. He signed something.

"No," Mia said aloud, signing at the same time. "Nothing is wrong. I am so happy to meet your new aunt. Come, meet her yourself. Her name is Tessa. She and your uncle are married."

Dylan stared at me, more in consternation than anything. "Married?"

I smiled. "It's nice to meet you, Dylan." I held out my hand, and he shook it solemnly. "Those are way cool chickens you have. Do you think they'll let me pet them? I've never touched a chicken before."

Dylan was all too eager to show me. I was holding a big white one when Gage finally emerged from the chicken coop, stooping to clear the door.

"Uncle Gage, how come you didn't tell me you were getting married?" Dylan called to him.

"I didn't know it myself." Gage's eyes met mine. Big circles of wetness stained his T-shirt, and his hair was matted with sweat. My stomach flip-flopped.

When a guy in desperate need of a bath made my stomach react like that, I was in trouble. I'd have to put some figurative space between us.

"Do you kiss her and everything?" Dylan asked.

"Sure. Why not?"

Dylan made a face. "Ooh, gross." Yet he giggled and watched us expectantly.

My stomach started to churn.

Gage reached for me, but as much as I secretly wanted to kiss him one more time to prove to myself that last night's amazing kiss had been a fluke, he was covered in straw and chicken manure.

"Yuck! You need a bath!"

"Oh, come on. Just one little kiss. It's our honeymoon, after all." He chased me to the gate, which I opened hurriedly and dived through.

Mia stood watching us, her face all smiles again. She signed at him and spoke at the same time. "You do kind of stink. Go take a nice long shower, or your wife might change her mind about marrying you."

Gage sobered almost instantly, and I felt a little sad when the light-heartedness vanished from his eyes. "She won't change her mind," he said.

Why did the words make me feel so terrible? He was an ex-con, for crying out loud, and I was paying him for his help. That's all there was between us.

We exchanged a look that did something funny to my chest, and I turned away so he couldn't see. Shrugging, he ran to the back steps and disappeared into the house. Mia watched me with a satisfaction that left me more confused.

"Thank you for staying," she said before turning to shut the gate that Dylan had left slightly ajar.

I waited until she turned back around before speaking. "I haven't told Gage about staying, yet. He might not agree."

"He'll be fine with it." She looked around for Dylan, who seemed to be heading around to the side of the house. She clapped her hands, and he stopped and began signing, making me wish I understood the language.

Mia shook her head, and he followed Gage inside the house, looking annoyed.

"What?" I asked Mia.

"He wanted to get the mail, and I can't let him do that. There might be another note."

"Oh." I shivered, though the day was still entirely too warm.

Eyes seemed to be watching us from behind the trees. Watching and waiting.

W hen I emerged from my turn in the guest bath, I was fully dressed and my hair nearly dry. Fortunately, I had brought hair gel, so I managed to coax a bit of body from the roots, but the orange heap was pretty much a straggly mess. I had a few waves, but none of the lovely curls I'd seen on some strawberry blondes. I would give a lot for the curling iron Avery had used on me yesterday.

From habit, I checked my phone and saw that Lily had called five more times. Didn't she understand the word *honeymoon*? I clicked to read the text she'd also left: *Call me. Terrible news. I'm so scared for you.*

Great. Obviously, Julian had been busy sharing Gage's name with my family. With nothing to do but surf the Internet while she was on bed rest, Lily would know more about the murder than I did. I'd been waiting for the opportunity to research it myself, and obviously I needed to get on it before I called Lily back.

I opened my laptop on the dresser where I'd left it and turned it on. What would I say if Gage walked in? Well, it wasn't as though I had to show him what I was doing. Still, I walked over and locked the door.

In the end it didn't matter because Mia's Internet was protected with a password. I tried the names of their family in different combinations, but without luck. Sighing, I shut the laptop and went to find Mia.

In the kitchen, Gage was seated at a small counter where Mia's computer was located. I could see he was checking email. Mia and Dylan were nowhere to be seen, but the beautiful smell of roasting meat and onions wafted from the oven. My mouth watered. It would definitely be a miracle if I didn't gain ten pounds on this excursion.

Gage looked up as I entered. "So, Mia tells me we're staying a few days?"

"She's nervous without her husband here."

"And you care why?"

I glowered at him. "Look, if you don't want to stay, don't. She's your sister. I can leave tomorrow. You can stay or leave—whatever you want. It was your idea to come here, not mine."

"Sorry." He stood and walked over to me. The smell of chickens had been replaced by something spicy that made me want to step closer. "I guess I just don't understand what set her off. It's been six months since she's wanted anyone to stay here while Aiden is out of town. I thought she was past that."

My anger lessened a bit at the apology, but his closeness was doing odd things to my heart. I eased away slightly. "Why did she need someone to stay?"

He frowned. "Something happened to her after high school, and it made her really scared—so scared she was almost paralyzed with it. Her deafness only complicates matters, though we've done everything we can to make her feel more secure. We put in an alarm that activates bright lights in her room, we've put in a phone she can type words into so she can easily call anyone, even if she's too upset to make herself understood. The person's verbal response appears on the screen as well." He took a single step that brought him closer to me again.

"She's still afraid." I knew it must be somehow connected with the murder or whatever Skeet had done to Mia the week before the killing, but even now Gage obviously didn't want to let me in on what exactly had happened.

"I thought it was behind her. She's been helping out some deaf kids who were abused. People from Sarah's House called her in to translate for the counselors, and she's been volunteering a lot there. It helped her recover. Aiden and I have been hopeful." There was a bleakness in his voice that told me the situation with Mia was worse than anyone was saying, which explained why he hadn't put her off when she'd begged to meet me.

"Sounds like Aiden needs a new job that'll let him stay home more." I went to the cupboard, trying to guess which ones held glasses. I was feeling much in need of a cold drink of water. With lots of ice.

"He's lucky to have any sales rep job in this economy, and unfortunately, that means traveling. She used to go with him a lot when Dylan was younger, but he's in school now. Is there some reason you keep walking away from me?" He dropped his head and sniffed his shirt. "I don't still smell, do I?"

"I need a drink, that's all. Where are the cups?" He pointed, and I filled one with ice and water from the dispenser on the fridge. "We can stay. Not a big deal."

He was coming toward me again, and my pulse started racing. I was saved by Mia sweeping into the room. "Oh, good, you're all ready. Gage, will you keep an eye on Dylan and what's in the oven? Tessa and I need to go somewhere."

"Uh, sure." He looked rather nonplussed. "I guess."

"Sorry to steal her away, but we need to . . ." Mia trailed off, looking at me helplessly.

"I need to get a few things at the store," I said. "Womanly things. We went off so fast. I didn't plan well." I'd still rather tell Gage about the note and our plan to take it to the police, but that was for Mia to decide.

Mia bobbed her head. "You know, nightgowns, nylons, makeup, fingernail pol—"

"I get it." He signed as he spoke, as though anxious for her not to say anything more personal. "I have work to do, anyway. I hadn't planned to take off, and there's a report I need to file."

I grinned. I *knew* geologists had to do reports.

"You can have a proper honeymoon later," Mia said. "Aiden will be home on Monday at the latest."

Gage's face softened at her eagerness. "Actually, that's probably for the best. I just got an email from my boss, and I really should go on site for a bit tomorrow morning to take samples that I was supposed to have completed yesterday."

"Good. Then it's settled." She turned and opened the oven to baste her roast.

"Samples?" I asked.

Gage carefully turned his back to Mia. "I work for a mining company. I thought you knew. I'm in the field a lot, taking soil samples and the like. They're going to open a new mine outside Flagstaff, and I need to recheck the soil to see if the mineral levels are where they should be before we sign the contracts." He smiled. "Want to come? It's interesting."

"Okay." I'd have nothing else to do tomorrow—the day I was to have become Mrs. Julian Willis. I crossed my hands over my stomach.

Despite my attempt to mask my feelings, something must have shown in my face, because Gage put a hand on my shoulder. "It'll be okay." The gentleness in his voice made me want to give in to my tears.

I shook my head. "I can't believe I was so blind. And the fact that I still care for him when he so obviously doesn't feel the same—it's stupid."

"Happens more than you think. It's not easy."

I wondered if he was talking about Bailey, but if she'd ever given him reason to worry, it all seemed in the past now. Should I tell him she was completely crazy for him, even though I personally thought the woman had all the appeal of a grub?

Yes, but not now. Not with Mia watching us. Not when my heart was leaping about in my chest. From stress, of course. It wasn't every day I lost a fiancé and married a near stranger with a questionable past.

"Kiss her and let us go," Mia teased.

Gage looked over at her, surprise on his face, as though he'd forgotten she was there. "Oh, yeah." He bent toward me swiftly and planted a fast peck on my cheek.

"Lame." Mia rolled her eyes. "If Aiden kissed me that way, I'd kick him out." She grabbed hold of my arm. "Tessa, maybe a little time away will make him less shy."

I'd never thought of Gage as shy, but he did seem to have a little color in his face at the moment. I laughed and winked at him. "See you later, sweetheart. Don't miss me too much."

"I always miss you," he countered. "Need any money?"

Likely a clear reminder of our deal and what I owed him. Aware of Mia's gaze, I choked back a retort and held out my hand sweetly. "Sure. You never know what wonders I'll find."

To his credit, he didn't hesitate to draw out his wallet and place a fifty-dollar bill in my hand. "Is that enough?"

I stared at it, feeling suddenly awkward. I didn't want his money—he was the employee here. But I couldn't give it back with Mia watching, so I crumpled the bill and shoved it into the pocket of my black pants. "Perfect."

He gave me a mocking grin. "Have fun." He bent down and kissed me again, this time putting his arms around me and drawing me close.

I tried to resist, but my muscles refused to obey, as if they had a mind of their own. His lips touched mine softly and then more firmly. Blood rushed through my veins, and fire tingled on my back and shoulder where his hands touched me.

When we broke away, the one thing I knew was that last night hadn't been a fluke. Either he was better at kissing than any man I'd ever kissed, or I was far more attracted to him than I was willing to admit.

Neither thought gave me much comfort.

"That's more like it." Mia gave us a thumbs-up like a judge revealing her rating. "Dylan's in his bedroom. He'll need help with his math." She grabbed my hand and pulled me toward the door. I stumbled after her like a sleepwalker.

Gage didn't move from where I left him, his veiled eyes digging into me as we went out the door.

Ha! I thought. I might be attracted to him, but at least it wasn't all one way. If questioned by the attorney, he could truthfully admit to feeling attraction for me. Maybe letting him help me hadn't been such a bad idea after all. Well, besides that little issue of murder, and with Mia proclaiming his innocence, that had become almost easy to overlook.

Before the door closed behind us, I saw a flash of something cross Gage's face that chilled me to the bone.

Fury. Loathing.

I didn't know who it was directed toward. Was he angry at me? Or the situation? I put my hand in my pocket and clutched the crumpled bill.

Mia was climbing into a small red car. I blinked a little in surprise before hurrying around to the passenger side. "You can drive?" I asked, sliding into the seat. She didn't reply so I touched her arm to get her attention and repeated the question.

She laughed. "Of course I drive. Believe me, I notice a lot more than you people who hear." She backed down the drive and onto the road, turning the car with obvious skill.

Okay, so I guess it was a dumb question. I mean, I didn't remember anything about hearing on the driving test, and there were all those mirrors to see any flashing ambulance and police lights. Mia probably did notice more than most hearing people.

"Sorry," I said, but she didn't respond. Her attention was on the road, not on my lips, and rightly so. I'd taken my hearing for granted all my life, and being with Mia was eye-opening.

We drove in silence to the police station. My hands itched to turn on the radio, but I managed to control them. Maybe if I had experienced more silence in my life, I wouldn't be here in Kingman, attracted beyond all reason to an ex-con whom I knew so little about. Of course, it didn't help that he looked the way he did and that Julian had broken my heart.

Julian. I wondered if he'd written me off, or if he was holding a powwow with my parents on how to get me back. The girlish part of me wanted him to ride in on his white horse and prove his innocence, but the woman in me knew he had never been truthful and wouldn't start now. Letting the music blot out these thoughts would have been a lot more comforting than having to rehash them.

Mia touched my hand, and I realized she'd been saying something. I broke from my reverie and saw we were already at the police station. I climbed out, and she pushed a button on her key chain to lock the door. The lights went on and off to signal her success. Nice, since she wouldn't have heard a beep.

I noticed she'd removed her apron and changed from

her jeans and T-shirt to a tan pantsuit that did little for her pale skin. She was still lovely but blended into the scenery more, like a woman trying to hide. Maybe she was.

"I need to talk to Ridge Harrison, please," she told the lady at the desk in a forced but fairly clear voice.

"I'll see if I can find him." The lady was turning away as she spoke, reaching for her phone, so Mia couldn't have read her lips.

"She's seeing if she can find him," I told Mia, making sure she was watching my lips.

Mia looked back at the lady. "He knows I'm coming. I called him."

"Okay." The woman looked between us several times before saying rather loudly, "What's your name?"

"Mia Reed."

"Have a seat. I'll let him know you're here."

I turned away, unable to stop the laughter.

"What?" Mia said, signing something at the same time, probably forgetting I didn't understand sign.

"She's talking really loud," I mouthed.

Mia grinned, and her face gained a bit of needed color. "People do that a lot. I never know, though. It really used to irritate Gage. Before he . . ." She hesitated, her smile vanishing, and I knew she meant before he went away because he wasn't around others with her much these days. If my guess was correct, he'd distanced himself to protect her and Dylan.

"Mia." I looked at the voice, and Mia followed my gaze.

A police officer in uniform emerged from a hallway.

He was of average height, clean-shaven, and nice looking. His hair, so short it was almost shaved, was that indescribable shade between dark blond and light brown. He looked as if he kept fit, probably in a gym, and not because he was vain about his appearance but because he didn't want lack of preparation to be what allowed a perp to get away. He walked with the confidence of someone you could go to in times of need, knowing he'd be ready and able to help you.

"Hi, Ridge," Mia said. "This is Tessa." She looked nervous, and I wondered why when the officer was so personable. I waited for her to add that I was her sister-in-law, but she didn't, and I felt relieved not to have to lie to yet another person. We shook hands, and I noticed his eyes were the delicious color of milk chocolate.

"So, what can I help you with, Mia?" He was talking to her but looking at me, probably deciding what color of orange to call my hair, or wondering if he'd seen me on a rap sheet somewhere. No, that was just my guilty conscience. Once I extracted myself from this marriage sham, I was never, ever going to do anything remotely wrong again.

For the first time I began to worry about what kind of legal trouble I might get into if anyone official discovered my real motive for marrying Gage. If someone contested my reasons for marriage, and I lost, did I lose everything? Go to jail? I really should plan my fiascos a little more carefully.

"Is this about the children you've been working with at Sarah's House?" Ridge asked. "The counselor says you've done a tremendous job with them."

Mia's eyes skittered over a couple who were coming into the police station. "Can we go somewhere else to talk?"

"Oh, sure." He motioned us to follow him down the hall. "So, Tessa, I haven't seen you around before. How long have you known Mia?"

"Not long." I wouldn't say we'd only met today because that would lead to questions about how long I'd known Gage and why he hadn't introduced me to Mia long before the wedding. "You?" I asked.

"Since we were little kids. We weren't close growing up, but I was best friends with her husband. Aiden was nuts about her even then. He was always dreaming about the future. He was sure they'd end up together."

"Sounds like a great guy."

"He really is." He turned his face more sharply in my direction. "There was a bit of talk when they got together after high school—you know, two misfits and everything—but it wasn't anyone's business, and the talk didn't last. They make a fine couple."

"What do you mean?" I'd seen a picture of Aiden at Mia's, and besides being very blond—even his eyebrows were white—he looked completely normal. I knew from things Gage and Mia had said that Aiden could hear just fine.

"Mia didn't tell you? Aiden's an albino. Apparently not as severe a case as some, but he's very pale, and his eyes are sensitive to light. Always wearing sunglasses. Never could be out much in the sun when we were young or his skin would burn."

"I didn't know that. He looks normal in his pictures."

"He is in everything that counts. Just like Mia. She's the best sign language translator they've ever had at Sarah's House. I recommended her when a mother showed up with three deaf kids claiming her husband was abusive. The kids opened right up to Mia. She knew just what to say. Those kids love her." Admiration filled in his voice.

"Stop talking about me." Mia slugged him on the arm.

"What?" Ridge said, looking to her.

"I can always tell. You turn your head so I can't see your lips." Her gaze switched to me. "Is he telling you about my work at Sarah's House or about Aiden being a freak of nature?"

I laughed because she was dead on. "A handsome freak of nature, if he is one," I added, remembering the picture. Aiden had the kind of smile that made you want to join in.

Mia grinned. "I know. Can't wait for you to meet him. I already called, and he's seeing if he can come home early."

"Great." That meant I could make sure Aiden knew what was going on with Mia's investigation and get on my way. If there was something funny going on here in Kingman, it probably wasn't smart to get involved. I had my own problems to deal with.

We'd finally arrived at a small room, where Ridge had to kick out two officers who were watching a training video on a small screen. They good-naturedly agreed to make a run for doughnuts.

"They have no intention of getting doughnuts," Ridge

said, rolling his eyes. "They always say that to mess with visitors' heads. You know, the whole cop and doughnut thing."

We sat down, and almost immediately Mia pulled the note from the small brown purse she carried. "I've been looking into the murder," she said in her direct way. "Asking some questions. I have proof my brother didn't kill anyone. Look."

Ridge carefully unfolded the note, and I noticed he didn't wear a wedding ring. After he'd read the paper, he let it drop onto the desk. "I'll have it dusted for prints, but how long have you had it? How many people have touched it?"

"Just me and Tessa and whoever put it in my mailbox yesterday." Mia shifted uncomfortably. "I didn't think about prints."

"Does Gage know about this?"

"No. I didn't want to get his hopes up. But don't you think it means something? If someone didn't have something to hide, they wouldn't threaten me."

Ridge leaned back in his chair and sighed. "Gage decided to change to a no contest plea months into the trial, and he was convicted. Only the skill of his attorney prevented him from being in prison a lot longer."

"He was convicted to protect me and because no one would look at any other evidence!" Mia said, her voice rising. "It was him or me, and you know Gage would never let me go to prison. This note has to prove something. I was just looking around, asking questions about that night, and then this suddenly shows up in my mailbox. Whoever killed that monster is still here. I know it!

And this time I'm going to fight for Gage. I was too young and too scared then, but not anymore. Not since I've been at Sarah's House. Those poor kids are willing to fight for each other and their mom, and that's what I'm doing for Gage, even if he doesn't want me to."

I had to struggle to understand her impassioned words, but Ridge seemed to follow every word. He folded his hands over his lean stomach, elbows on the arm rests of his chair. "But it's over, Mia. Gage is out and working. He's bought a house. He's gone on with his life."

"It is *not* over!" Mia stood, her small frame shaking, and her voice becoming high pitched with emotion. "He can't live here and watch Dylan grow up. He can't go pick up my son from school or run to the store when he's visiting unless he's grown out his beard so no one will recognize him. To everyone in Kingman, he'll always be a murderer. What about his children, if he ever has any?" Here she cast a sorrowful glance at me before rushing on. "Please help me, Ridge."

"She's scared," I added. "And after reading that note, I think she has a right to be."

"Of course, I'm going to look into it." Ridge smiled reassuringly at us. "I promise I'll do everything in my power to discover who wrote this and why. At the very least, I'll give a couple of pranksters a tour of our jail. Meanwhile, I don't want you to get your hopes up too high, Mia. A lot of time has passed, and you have to understand that while I want to help your brother, it may not be possible. Even if it is possible, it'll take a while."

"But you'll investigate?" Mia pressed.

"Yes. Of course." He grinned. "I just said I would, didn't I?"

Mia nodded, the fight seeping from her body. "Thank you."

"I'd like a list of people you were asking questions and what kind of questions. Any Internet sites you visited or mailing addresses you wrote to. That will help me figure out where to start." Ridge handed Mia a notebook and a pen, and she sat down again and began writing.

"So where are you from?" Ridge asked idly, his eyes dropping briefly to my hand on the arm rest. Ah, so guys did the ring check like women did.

I felt consternation when I looked at my own hand. I must have left the fake ring back at Mia's when I'd taken my shower. "I'm from Flagstaff," I said, "but I've been working in Phoenix."

"Where?"

"Crawford Cereals. My father's company, actually. I was a shift manager until I left a few weeks ago."

"Going to be here long?"

"A few more days. I'm staying with Mia."

He nodded several times, and his Adam's apple moved up and down twice before he said casually, "I could show you around a bit, if you'd like. That is, if you don't have someone already doing that."

I felt completely flattered. He liked me. *Take that, Julian.* Ridge was a nice, decent man who would probably ask me for a real date if I encouraged him. Of course I couldn't do that because I was supposedly married, and I'd have to say no, which was disappointing. Nothing like a little admiration to put a woman to rights.

Mia laughed, apparently catching at least part of his invitation. "No, Ridge, she's not the girl I want to set you up with. This is my new sister-in-law. She married Gage."

"Oops." Ridge made a face that only endeared him to me more. "I thought you—please forgive me, I didn't see a ring, and Mia told me last week she had a friend she wanted me to meet."

"I must have left my ring in the bathroom when I showered," I said. "Don't worry about it. I'm flattered. Honestly. You're very sweet to offer." *I wish I could say yes,* I wanted to add.

"They only got married yesterday," Mia explained. "All on the spur of the moment. They haven't even planned a honeymoon. I can't believe Gage." Her voice left no doubt as to her disgust.

"My dress was beautiful," I said for Ridge's benefit, "and we had a nice dinner, and we saw a show and went dancing. It's not as if it was a real—" Oops. My brain finally overcame my motor mouth. "A really long ceremony. We had time to get out and see the town a bit."

"That's good," Ridge said politely, but I could tell his interest had wandered.

Mia bent her head down and furiously scribbled two addresses she copied from an address book in her purse. "There. Finished."

"Is there anything you want to add?" Ridge asked me. When I shook my head, he said, "Well, if you don't mind putting down your contact information, in case I think of any questions."

"Sure." I scribbled at the bottom of the paper where Mia had written a half-dozen names, an equal number of questions, several Internet sites, and the two addresses. A few of the names had notes off to the side: angry, didn't want to talk, happy to help, knows some sign language. I noticed one of the names was Bailey Norris, Gage's ex-fiancée.

Ridge walked us to the front of the police station. "Thanks for coming in. I'll do what I can." He nodded at me a bit sheepishly. "Nice to meet you. Here's my card, if you ever need to get a hold of me."

I liked him enough that maybe after this was all over, I would look him up. He didn't have Gage's rugged, eye-catching handsomeness or Julian's aristocratic manners, but he was nice, dependable, and underneath all that, I suspected he was capable of passionate commitment, which looked pretty darn good to me these days.

Mia breathed a sigh of relief as we reached the car. "I'm glad that's over. Ridge is good at his job. I feel better already."

"I'm glad."

I thought we'd go straight back to the house, but to my surprise Mia drove to JCPenneys. "What are we doing?" I asked.

"Spending that fifty bucks Gage gave you. If we come home without anything, he'll be suspicious. Come on."

She was good—I hadn't given our excuse a second thought. As for what to spend the money on, I could use another pair of jeans and a few shirts. I might be able to make the money stretch that far, and if not I could always use my debit card. As soon as I received my trust fund, things wouldn't be so tight.

To my embarrassment, Mia headed directly to the

sleepwear department and began pulling out lacy negli-
gees. "You're a six or an eight, aren't you?"

"I don't need one of those." I told her. "That's taken
care of." My face was aflame. All I needed was to go back
to Mia's with something like that. My sweats would do
for now.

"My treat," Mia said. "You didn't even get a fun bridal
shower, and that's what I would have given you." Before
I could protest further, she turned her back and disappeared between the racks.

Sighing, I went to find a pair of jeans, which fit
remarkably well, two fitted tees on clearance, and a dressy
purple blouse I could wear with my black pants. At the
last minute I picked up a black skirt that was on sale, in
case Mia went to church on Sunday. I'd attended church
every week in Phoenix on my own, though growing up
I'd only gone at Easter and Christmas.

The lady in front of me in line offered me an extra
fifteen percent off coupon from a small stack she carried,
which I was not too proud to use, and that meant only
a few bucks ended up on my debit card. Lily would be
proud. She was constantly telling me of the bargains she
found for Mario and the girls they sheltered.

Mia was waiting for me when I finished paying. She
carried a JCPenney's sack and wore a beatific smile that
would have rivaled an angel. If I'd had even a minuscule
amount of artistic talent, I would have wanted to paint
her in that moment.

"What did you get?" I said, frowning.

"You'll see." She hurried to the car, with me lagging
behind.

The drive to Mia's was again too silent for my comfort, but I had to admit she was an excellent driver. I was pondering how I could sneak Mia's shopping bag away and hide it so Gage would never find it, when Mia began honking the horn madly. The car lurched to a stop on the dirt road in front of her house.

What was going on?

I looked around frantically as Mia jumped out and raced up the walk, waving her hands and screaming.

I hurried after her, my feet stumbling on the road as I realized what was wrong. Standing in front of her porch was a man with greasy brown hair pulled back into a short braid. He had a wispy goatee and a fuzzy little mustache, the kind that men talked themselves into being proud of when they couldn't grow anything better. He was tall, but far too thin, and he had the worn look of an alcoholic. Not much of a match for Gage, who stood on the porch looking down on the stranger.

Or wouldn't have been much of a match, except for the gun in his hand.

8

"**G**et out of here, Charlie Norris!" Mia yelled, her voice high and unnaturally shrill. "Leave my brother alone!"

I could barely understand her, the words having become garbled with emotion, and I doubted the strange man could pick out anything.

He turned from Gage, the gun not quite pointed at anyone, but wavering now in Mia's direction about knee height. "This has nothin' to do with you, Mia."

Gage leapt off the porch and placed himself in front of his sister, heedless of the wild look in the man's eyes. "Go on home, Charlie," he said. "You don't want anything to happen here. You've seen me fight before. Even if you won, the police would come after you. Believe me, prison is not a pretty place—especially for a scrawny thing like you."

Charlie lifted his chin. "I didn't come to hurt no one. I came to tell you to stay away from my sister. I won't have you breakin' her heart again. I won't let you or anyone hurt her."

"Bailey's a big girl. She can take care of herself."

"She's gone on you. Always has been. She was all broken up after you went away."

"We were over before I went to prison, no matter what she might have told you."

"Yet the minute you're back, she comes runnin' over."

Gage shook his head. "She only came here to meet my wife. That's all."

"She come home cryin' and yellin' and—did you say *wife?*" The words finally penetrated Charlie's brain.

"Yes." Gage gestured toward me, frozen on the sidewalk to Charlie's right. "This is Tessa, my wife." I could only hope Charlie didn't decide to shoot me and clear the way for his sister.

Charlie's mouth formed an O. "I didn't know you were married. But you told Bailey you would never marry, not her or anyone."

"This is different."

I thought Gage's words would anger Charlie, but the gun hand slowly fell to his side. "I didn't know you were married."

So he'd already said. Obviously, Charlie was not big in the brains department.

Charlie was shaking his head. "So that's why she was cryin'. She thought you loved her. How come you never wrote?" He was half crying himself, now.

"I did write twice, but since it was over, it seemed kind of pointless after that."

Charlie punched the air with his free hand. "That wasn't the way it was supposed to be. It was supposed to be you and Bailey, and me and Mia."

Mia shook her head. "No, Charlie. I love Aiden. I've always loved Aiden. You know that."

"You might have loved me if Skeet hadn't done what he did. I wasn't ready to be a father, and Skeet messed everything up."

"I loved Aiden," Mia repeated. "Skeet doesn't matter."

Charlie blinked. "Oh."

"Why don't you go home and rest?" Gage said, taking a step forward slowly, as though confronting a frightened animal. "Why don't you leave that gun with me?"

In a rapid motion, Charlie brought the gun to his chest, hugging it. "You can't have it. I might need it to protect myself. Besides, it's borrowed."

Gage held up his hands in a gesture of surrender. "Okay, just go on home."

Charlie nodded and started down the sidewalk, shuffling along with a slight limp. I stepped out of the way as he approached, and he nodded at me as though nothing out of the ordinary had occurred. Sweat beaded on his forehead and along his hairline. His eyes were so reddened, I couldn't tell their color.

He stopped and turned around. "You're right. Skeet don't matter. He's dead. You stay away from my sister, Gage, or you'll be dead, too. Ain't the first time I had to protect her."

We watched him hobble down the dirt road to a battered Ford sedan that had been old a decade ago, all of us guarding the silence.

"Is he always like that?" I asked finally.

"I don't know, really," Gage answered. "He and Bailey and their mother came to live with their aunt after their old man died. We were all in high school then, but Charlie dropped out of school and went into the navy. We didn't see much of him after that. They kicked him out after a year or so, and I don't know what he did then. He shows up every so often to visit Bailey."

Interesting. "Was he in town the time of the murder?" I asked.

Gage's eyes narrowed. "I don't know where you're going with this, but Charlie wasn't there that night. It was me and Skeet."

"And Mia."

"Leave her out of this," he retorted, his gaze dark.

"I'm not *in* anything. But if you are innocent, you shouldn't have taken the blame."

"I did what I had to do, and I paid for it."

Oddly enough, his insistence convinced me more than anything Mia could say that he wasn't guilty. "And if you had to do it again? Now that you're older and wiser? Would you make the same choice?"

"Yes," he growled.

"Okay then. Everyone's happy."

"Exactly."

Except that he was glowering at me, and I was glowering at him, Bailey was crying, Charlie was threatening Gage with a gun, and Mia was receiving threatening notes. Something was not right in Kingman.

"Stop, stop, stop!" Mia wedged her way between us. "This is all my fault. I should never have brought you here right now. You should be on your honeymoon."

Gage put his arm around his sister, his other hand moving rapidly. Whatever he said calmed her, despite its brevity. She signed something back and went inside the house.

"She says to tell you dinner will be ready in a while and that she's sorry."

"For what?"

He shook his head. "I don't know. None of this is her fault, but Mia's like that. She feels responsible—a lot. She's always sorry for everything. It's one of the reasons I can't live here. She'd die inside a little every day if she saw how people treat me when they know who I am."

"Not too much better in Flagstaff, I bet."

"It's a lot better. I'm more of a mysterious figure there. Besides, there's this horse I like to visit, and a pretty girl."

I laughed, wondering how we could go from wanting to strangle each other one moment to flirting the next.

"I'll go park the car," Gage started down the walk.

For a moment I watched the broad lines of his back, the graceful movements when he folded himself into the small car. If Gage hadn't murdered Skeet, would that change things between us?

No. What we had was a business deal, nothing more.

A business deal that I seemed to conveniently forget every time he kissed me. Which, if I thought about it, he really shouldn't be doing.

Inside the house, Mia was in the kitchen talking to Dylan, who was setting the table. Utter silence reigned. I wondered if it was like this all the time, or if when Aiden was home, he turned on music or something.

Then again, simply because I couldn't understand the language, didn't mean there was silence. Obviously, Mia and Dylan were communicating perfectly well. I had to begin looking at things differently, think of them differently. The mother cooking, the boy arranging the dishes on the table. Stopping to move his hands in her direction, a smile playing on his face. Warm sunlight streaming through the window onto the back of Mia's ponytail as she answered.

Not silent. Warm, happy, loving. Better yet, this little boy knew two complete languages. I'd read that multiple languages improved a child's cognitive abilities, so maybe Dylan had more advantage than most children from a single-language home.

Dylan was the first to notice me in the doorway, and I realized I'd begun humming something under my breath. Some song from my childhood, whose title eluded me. "Hi," Dylan said shyly.

"Hi. I see you're helping your mother."

"I always set the table. It's my job."

Mia looked at me. "Everything okay?"

"Fine. Except I'd like to check my email. I have a laptop, but I need to use your Internet connection. You have wireless, don't you? Would you mind giving me your password?"

"Aiden is always changing it, and I don't remember what it is. Dylan, do you know the password?"

He nodded eagerly. "Can I put it in?"

"Sure," I said. "If it's okay with your mother."

Mia made a motion with her hands that even I understood meant for us to go.

"So," I said to Dylan as we walked down the hall to the guest bedroom, "it's pretty cool that you know sign language."

"I guess."

"Was it hard to learn?"

He shrugged. "I don't remember. I just know it."

"Does your dad use sign language?"

"With my mom. Not with me. He talks to me."

Of course he did, which was why Dylan was functional in both the hearing and non-hearing worlds.

"Your mother lip reads pretty well, though." We were in the bedroom now, and I opened my laptop where I'd left it sleeping on the dresser. Dylan was a little short to reach the keys, so I unplugged it and brought it to the bed. "Do you sometimes just talk to her?"

"She doesn't let me. She wants me to learn sign. Besides, she can't really tell exactly what people are saying all the time. Sometimes she has to guess, especially if people mumble or talk really fast."

"Or if they turn their backs or something."

He nodded. "Yeah."

"Well, she does a great job. And with speaking, too. It's amazing."

"She used to hear when she was younger, but she stopped when she was my age." There was worry in his voice now, and I wondered if he feared the same thing would happen to him, a scary thought, especially for a child.

"Come sit here beside me." I patted the white coverlet on the bed.

He was so short that he had to jump up on the tall mattress, but he did it with practiced ease. I clicked on the only wireless option available and set the computer on his lap. He put a thin little hand on the computer and began to type with one finger. His black hair curled at the nape of his neck, and I had to resist the urge to smooth it. I couldn't wait for Lily's baby.

"There," Dylan said, handing me back the laptop. He slid off the bed. "Let me know if you need help again. But you shouldn't need the password because it will connect automatically. I told it to save the password."

He was so serious that I matched his attitude. "Thank you very much. I appreciate it."

He smiled, and for an instant, I clearly saw the family resemblance to Gage.

Now that I had the Internet connection, I suddenly felt uneasy about searching Gage's past. However, Lily had texted me again twice more, and I didn't want to leave her worried, not in her condition, so I swiftly typed in Gage's name and *murder* and *Kingman* in the search box. Slowly, the screen filled with listings.

I clicked on each one and read through the information. Gage Braxton arrested for murdering Skeet Thompson. The attack happened at night inside a convenience store, with no eyewitnesses, except for the defendant's sister, who had seen the two fighting earlier. There had been no working video surveillance.

Nothing was said further about Mia until the fourth site, which had been written during the trial. It was a brief reference about Skeet assaulting the defendant's sister the week before the murder. Given Mia's rumored emotional state, the reporter hinted Gage might have been out for revenge. Another article mentioned that Mia had married during the months of the trial itself, not before the murder as I'd previously thought. In the last news article, a reporter had snapped a photo of Mia, whose pregnancy was beginning to show.

So what did that mean? Did it change anything that she'd been married afterward and not before? Not really. Unless you believed the reporter who'd written about Mia's fragile emotional state. Not exactly a good time to be getting married.

Understanding hit me like something I should have known all along. Skeet's assault on Mia must have resulted in her pregnancy with Dylan. After the killing, she either hadn't come forward about the rape or someone had blocked the press from discovering the whole story. No wonder she hadn't been able to help her brother fight the murder charge. The emotional trauma of the attack, coupled with morning sickness, would likely have consumed her.

What did that say about Gage? Had he really committed the murder for revenge after all? Surely he knew about the rape—and Aiden, too. Maybe even the police, which could be why they hadn't looked for another suspect. But wouldn't the jury's knowing about the rape have helped Gage receive a shorter sentence? Perhaps it had. There was a sad dearth of information online.

Sighing, I clicked off the Internet, shut my laptop, and set it next to me onto the bed. Time to call Lily.

She answered on the second ring. "Tess, where have you been? I've been so worried!"

"Uh, honeymoon," I said.

"Yeah, but . . ." There was embarrassment in her voice that made me smile.

"What's up with all these texts anyway?" I said,

feigning innocence. "How am I in danger? Is Julian coming after me?" That might do wonders for my self-esteem, even though I knew it wasn't likely.

"This isn't about Julian. It's about your new husband. Tess, how well do you know this guy?"

"I've known him since last year. Thanksgiving. I'd see him when I'd ride Serenity."

"Yeah, but you never mentioned him. Tessa, I have to tell you, and I don't want to because I can hear how much you like him, but Julian's got Mom and Dad all riled up, saying you've married a murderer. Your husband can't be the guy I've been reading about on the Internet, right? It must be a mistake. I bet he just happens to have the same name."

I wasn't surprised. It was Murphy's Law or something. If you wanted something so badly not to be discovered, it would be.

"Slow down, Lily. All this excitement can't be good for the baby."

"I'm worried about you!"

"Don't be. Yes, Gage did serve time, but he's not a murderer."

"What? Did he go to prison for murder or not?" Her voice was high and thin, bordering on hysterical.

"Lily, don't worry. He's not going to hurt me. Look, it's not in the news articles, but Gage's sister was hurt badly by the man who was killed. She claims she was there that night and that Gage didn't kill the man, but that he went to prison to protect her."

"Why would he do that? Did she kill the guy?"

"No, but she was destroyed by the attack and ended

up expecting a child because of it. She's also deaf, which makes her more vulnerable. She's really sweet and a great mother. She didn't kill anyone."

I stopped talking because I really didn't know what I believed. It could have been Mia. Or Gage, or even Mia's husband, Aiden, for that matter. He had every bit as much reason to want the man dead as anyone else. Or more.

"Tess, you have to get out of there. Please."

"I'll come see you on Monday."

"What if you can't see what he is because you love him too much? What if you can't get away?"

Her distress worried me. If she lost this baby, it would devastate her. Maybe it was time to come clean. "Look, even if he were guilty, it doesn't matter. I didn't want to tell you, but the marriage isn't real. I discovered that Julian's been unfaithful, and when Sadie told me, I was hurt and angry, but I still wanted to get my trust fund, so I came up with this plan." A stupid plan, I knew now, but I wouldn't tell her that. "It's a business arrangement, and I'm paying him. Don't worry. It's all going to work out. Of course you can't tell Mother."

There was utter silence on the phone, and then Lily asked in a small voice, "You did this because of me, didn't you?"

Great, exactly the conversation I'd been trying to avoid. "A little bit, yeah, but I also want to be out on my own until I can find my way, without having to work for Dad's company or depend on a man. Maybe I'll go back to school and get a useful degree. I did this for me every bit as much for you." I sounded as if I believed what I was saying. Point to me.

"Tessa, it says in the will that it has to be a real marriage."

"A marriage in good faith, to be exact, and I know there's a clause that says someone can contest, but who's going to do that? Even if our parents do, they don't make the decision about my intentions. They aren't the executors. And if Julian tried, well, he is a liar and a cheat—who's going to believe him?"

"But it's fraud. You could go to jail!"

"Don't worry about it, Lily. I told you, everything's going to be fine. Grandpa's idea of waiting until we're married or thirty makes no sense, not in this day and age. He'd be the first to admit it if he were still with us. You know that."

"Marriage isn't something you fool around with— you're the one who always told me that."

"I know. Maybe it wasn't the best decision, but I've come this far, and I'm finishing it."

"You're fooling yourself. I think you really like this guy."

"He's nothing. I said not to worry."

"That's not what I hear in your voice. Have you kissed him?"

I hesitated. "Well, at the wedding, yes. But you already know that. You saw the picture."

"I meant since."

"Yeah."

"And?"

I couldn't tell her how it made me feel. That would set her off again. "Look, I'm still getting over Julian. How do you think it felt? Awkward."

"No," Lily said. "You didn't love Julian. Not like you should love someone you marry."

Her words were a slap in the face. "Then why does his betrayal hurt so much?"

"Because he's a jerk, and he let you down. But your face never glowed when you talked about him. You sound happier now."

"That's ridiculous."

"I hope so. I don't want you to love a murderer."

"Stop calling him that. You don't know him, and I'm sure he didn't do it anyway."

Another silence. "Tessa, do you hear yourself? You have to leave there. Now."

I know. My heart pounded furiously.

"If you really did marry him only for the trust fund, you can leave now. You can do the rest through an attorney." She was right—as long as my parents didn't contest anything.

Except there was the little matter of Mia. "I promised his sister I'd stay with her until her husband comes home on Monday. She's afraid to be alone."

"Then someone else is there with you?"

"Yes, his sister and her little boy. He's adorable. Speaks fluent English and sign language. You should see it."

There was disapproval in the silence that followed, so I added hurriedly, "Don't worry, Lily. I have everything under control. Think of it. You won't lose your house. Those girls are going to have somewhere to stay until they're ready to leave. I know what I'm doing. Please give me some credit. I'm the big sister, remember?"

That was when Gage walked in with the shopping

bags. He set my larger one down on the floor before looking with interest inside the smaller bag.

"I have to go, Lily. Tell everyone I'm fine. Love you." I hung up the phone without waiting for a reply.

"Your sister, huh?"

"Apparently my family has learned about your past, and she's worried."

"Thanks to Julian." He didn't sound repentant.

"Thanks to you. You practically invited him to Google you."

Gage whistled as he reached into the bag and pulled out something made with a lot of lace and short lengths of blue silk. "My sister says this is our wedding gift." He tossed it to me. "It's your color. Don't think it would look nearly as good on me."

"I don't know." I pretended to study the negligee, which was really beautiful, with exactly the right amount of lace versus material—for a real honeymoon. "But I think she should have bought you a larger size."

Gage laughed and met my gaze. "I think it's perfect."

I shivered, feeling a compelling urge to kiss him again. What if he hadn't been wearing that scruffy beard when I'd seen him all those times with Serenity? What if I hadn't been preoccupied with Julian? Maybe I would have caught a glimpse of the real man underneath as I had in the past two days. I might have wanted to get to know him better.

"Gage," I said, my voice coming out husky.

His intense stare was making me uncomfortable, and I searched for anything to distract him. Lily was right—I was getting in too deep. The last thing I needed was to imagine myself falling for Gage. I had to remember who he was and my purpose for this whole fiasco.

"Yes?" He took a step closer, his eyes fastened on my lips.

"I had a talk with Dylan. He told me Mia used to be able to hear when she was young."

"That's true. She had only partial hearing loss until she was six or seven." Another step. The silk was beginning to feel hot in my hands. *Nerves,* I told myself.

"Well, is it hereditary? He seemed to be worried about losing his own hearing."

That got Gage's attention. "It is hereditary, but the chance of passing it on is very small. Dylan's already been tested. He's fine."

"Well, somebody ought to tell him that. Or explain it again."

Gage nodded almost reluctantly. "I'll go talk to him. Maybe he didn't understand. Or maybe he thinks his parents don't want him to worry." With another look at the fabric in my hands, he turned and strode out the door.

With a sigh of relief, I put the negligee back into the sack. Inside was a matching, full-length robe, every bit as silky as the gown. Nope, I wouldn't be wearing this tonight. Or any night. I'd leave it here when I left. I didn't want to be obligated to Mia or Gage in any way.

My phone beeped, signaling another text. I checked, already knowing it was probably from my sister. Sure enough, it read: *What if he kills you and keeps all the money?*

Great. Just great. Pregnancy must be doing something to her brain. The idea that Gage would kill me to get at my money was ridiculous. Wasn't it?

I swallowed hard and dialed my grandfather's attorney. "I need to talk to Mr. Carson, please. It's important. Yeah, he can call me back."

Fifteen minutes later, I answered my phone as it began to ring. "Hello?"

"Mark Carson here. What can I do for you?"

"Thanks for calling me back. I need some information about my trust fund."

"I haven't received your documents yet."

"You should get them by tomorrow. We sent them overnight from Vegas this morning. But that's not why I'm calling. I wanted to know what happens to my funds if something were to happen to me. You know, a car accident or something, and I died. Would my money shift into a trust fund for Lily, or would it go to my heirs?"

"I'll have to check, but from what I remember, it goes to your surviving children and spouse. Only if you die without marrying and without heirs would it automatically revert to Lily and her children."

"Is there a way to change that?"

"Yes. Once you actually are cleared to receive the funds, there is a way to name a new heir—whoever you want. I can have the papers drawn up, if that's what you'd like."

"Yes, please. I want to name Lily as my heir, no matter what, and I want her to get the money right away, not to go into a trust fund or anything."

"That will work." Mark hesitated. "Uh, Tessa, is there something wrong?"

I forced a laugh. "Oh, no. But my husband doesn't need money, and Lily does, so until I have children, I want her to be my heir."

"If you're in trouble—"

"No trouble. Really."

"It's just that . . . well, a few hours ago, my secretary received the strangest call. Someone was asking about your trust fund and your heirs. The woman pretended she was calling in your behalf."

His words turned my blood to ice. "What did your secretary tell her?"

"Nothing—we don't give out confidential information without identity verification—but it's strange someone would be asking. I mean, your family has a copy of the will, and they can always talk to me if they need clarification."

"Is there any way someone outside the family could get that information?"

"Not through normal channels. Short of hacking into our server or bribing someone. No, the information is safe. But it makes me uneasy that someone was asking about it at all. If they are determined, they may be able to find out what they want to know from your family's friends or acquaintances. That sort of thing. There are a million methods of extracting information from people. In fact, I was about to call your mother and warn her not to talk to anyone about the terms, just in case. You never know what they might do with the information."

Too late. I bet my mother had already spilled everything to her friends, the neighbors, the postman, and all the relatives who'd come for the wedding.

"Thanks," I told Mark.

"I'll get everything processed as soon as possible. You go and enjoy yourself."

He could say that because he didn't know I'd married a

man convicted of murder, though he would as soon as he talked to my mother. Then he'd also know why I'd called and what I was afraid of.

I hung up and stared at my phone. It had brought me nothing but bad news in the past two days, and I was seriously considering throwing it away.

Gage returned to the bedroom. "You were right. Dylan was worried. He's okay now."

"Good. He's a sweet boy."

His eyes swept the room, and I felt satisfaction that I'd put the negligee and bag in the dresser out of sight. "Mia says it's time for dinner."

"First I'm going to change into some of my new clothes, even though I haven't washed them. My others are decidedly dirty. I think this white fluff came from those chickens." It clung to my wrinkled black pants no matter how I tried to brush it off. "Do you think Mia would mind letting me use her washing machine? I'd only need to do two small loads."

"I'll probably need some things washed, too."

I forced a grin. "So now you want me to do your laundry?"

"Isn't that a wifely thing to do? Or I could do yours instead." He winked. "It'll seem funny if we do it separately."

"I'll do it, then." No way was I letting him touch my delicates. "Or maybe we should tell Mia the truth."

He was quiet a long moment and then, "I'd rather not. Please."

"Why?"

He didn't quite meet my gaze. "This is going to be

the closest I ever get to marrying. I want her to have that much. She blames herself for that, too."

"Why wouldn't you ever get married?" It was on the tip of my tongue to tell him about Bailey's love for him, but I couldn't get out the words. "You said yourself that you've done your time. If you moved to a bigger city, no one would ever know."

His jaw tightened. "I'd know." He turned in the doorway. "Are you coming?"

I followed him out the door.

9

I was dreaming about a warm beach, a fabulous-looking man, and strawberry pancakes when Gage pulled the pillow off my head on Saturday morning. I squinted at the light. "What are you doing?"

"I'm needed on site today, remember? You said you wanted to go."

"Not this early."

"Early? It'll be nine soon."

I peered at the alarm clock on the night stand. "In an hour. Way too early to be up."

"I would have gone hours ago if I hadn't been waiting for you. Besides, if I'd slept any later, Mia would know I spent the night on the couch." He rubbed his neck as if there were a kink. "And that stupid rooster started crowing at five. How could you sleep?"

"Like this." I grabbed the pillow again and put it over my head, pressing my arm on top.

He lifted the corner. "So I guess that means you don't want the pancakes I made."

"Two days in a row?" I mumbled. "I'll get fat."

"The strawberries are fresh. So is the whipped cream."

I moaned. This man did not play fair. Last night he'd insisted on staying in the room with me until he was sure Mia was asleep, strutting around in his sweats and one of Aiden's T-shirts that was much too small for him, and now he expected me to get out of bed before ten. Totally unreasonable.

He'd looked really good in that shirt—not that I'd ever admit it to him. While he pored over one of his geology reports, I'd spent the time reading a book, staying dressed and as far away from him as possible.

"Okay, but weren't you getting married today? How would you have gotten up for that?"

"The wedding wasn't until one." I felt nauseated at the thought. Julian and me married. My mother and father happy. My trust fund available and Lily taken care of.

But Julian would have kept lying. Marriage didn't change people like that, not unless they wanted to change. Today, for some reason, the pain of that knowledge didn't hurt as much, though it did force all thoughts of sleep from my head.

"Fine!" I sat up and hurled the pillow at Gage. He ducked, grinning with satisfaction when it missed.

His eyes fell to the top of one of my new T-shirts. "I see you didn't use Mia's gift."

I threw the other pillow, and this one smacked him right in the face. I smirked. "I'm saving it for a special occasion. Like a honeymoon."

"Ah." There was regret in the word, though whether it was because he thought the gift wasted or because he wouldn't be around to see, I really didn't know. Or care.

I rolled my eyes. "I'm coming. Where are these famous pancakes?"

In the kitchen we were soon joined by Mia and Dylan. Dylan ate more pancakes than any of us. At this rate, he'd outgrow even his uncle.

Mia kept looking between me and Gage thoughtfully, as though concerned about something. "So," she said at last, "are you two okay? You're not fighting or anything, are you?"

I stared at her blankly. "If you're talking about yesterday, that's over."

"I'm talking about why Gage slept on the couch."

I exchanged a look with Gage, who was flipping pancakes. So much for his subterfuge. Gage opened his mouth, but I beat him to the explanation. "Gage snores horribly," I said with a smile. "Terrible. Like an earthquake. I'm surprised you couldn't feel the vibrations in your room."

Ignoring the outrage on Gage's face, Mia nodded. "He used to snore when we were little, but I figured he grew out of it." She laughed lightly. "Not that I could hear it now either way."

"Ha! Gage's snoring is probably the reason you went deaf," I said. Dylan choked on his milk, and Gage stared at me. "Oh, I didn't mean—" Me and my big mouth. But Mia was laughing. She laughed so hard, Gage had to pound her back to help her breathe.

"No one ever tells me deaf jokes." Tears gathered in Mia's eyes. "Except Aiden. I can't wait to tell him this one." She took the spatula from Gage and went to the stove.

I sat back, relieved. Gage cast me a sardonic look that I ignored—except for the heat that surged in my face.

"Better take some sunscreen," Gage said, not missing a thing. "You don't want to burn."

"Don't worry. I'm religious about using sunscreen." And I was. With my pale, freckled skin, sunscreen was my best friend.

"My dad has to use a lot of sunscreen," Dylan said. "He's albino."

"Cool," I said, glad Ridge had already filled me in at the police station. "I can't wait to meet him."

Dylan grinned at me, and I knew I'd said the right thing.

"You about ready?" Gage looked at my full plate.

"Give me five minutes," I said, digging in. "It's your fault. You made them."

"If I hadn't, you'd still be in dream land."

"Yeah, but I was dreaming of strawberry pancakes." Well, not just pancakes. That man walking with me on the beach had looked suspiciously like Gage. Color filled my face again.

"Why don't I believe you?"

"I never lie."

"Never?"

I knew what he was referring to. Our marriage was a complete lie.

"Well, almost never," I amended. "And never again."

Gage nodded almost too gravely. "Good." He came to his feet. "I'll go fill up the bike with gas and come back for you."

"We're going on the bike?" My legs were barely

beginning to feel halfway normal after being on it so much the past few days. If I hadn't been accustomed to riding Serenity, I might have been a lot worse off.

"Of course. That's all we've got."

"On our next honeymoon, remind me to bring a car."

"Okay." Our gazes met and held, and under his smile I saw sadness and something more I couldn't identify. I wondered if it had something to do with Bailey and the reason he'd decided never to marry.

Leaning down swiftly, he planted a warm kiss on my forehead before going out the side door.

Mia was looking at me with a bemused smile. "He loves you so much."

Now it was my turn to choke on my milk, but I couldn't tell her how wrong she was.

Dylan signed something to his mother.

"Yes," she answered, speaking for my benefit and signing at the same time, "go feed the chickens. Don't forget the water."

"Okay." Dylan shot out the door as if the pancakes contained rocket fuel.

I took another bite as Mia slid into the chair opposite me. "I've been thinking," she said. "What about hiring someone to research those people I was looking at?"

"Shouldn't we leave this to the police?"

Her head swung back and forth, her face grave. "Ridge will do everything he can, but this is only one of his cases. A hired investigator might get faster results, if we can find someone good. I'm willing to do anything for Gage—and for your future children."

My bite of pancake had somehow formed a large

lump in my throat, and it was only with effort that I could swallow it. "I hope you're right about this, but what if you aren't? Skeet was a terrible man. I know what he did to you. No, Gage didn't tell me—I guessed. What if Gage really did kill him?"

Mia's face hardened, and her eyes gouged into mine. "You don't know my brother very well if you can say that. In self-defense, yes. To protect me, yes. But never in cold blood. If you loved him as much as he loves you, you would know that." She held up her hand as I started to protest. "I think you love him enough. The rest will come. It did with me and Aiden."

I didn't know what to say. I knew Aiden had loved her a long time and that she'd told Charlie Norris when he'd come over with the gun that she'd always loved Aiden. But always didn't mean you consciously knew something. Deep down I'd always known my father and mother didn't have a relationship I wanted to emulate, though I'd never defined the idea so clearly in my youth. I'd always known proper mothers spent more time with their children. I'd always known Lily wouldn't succumb to pressure.

I'd always known Julian was hiding something.

I could see it now. Unexplained absences, unexpected gifts that were really apologies, the subtle comments from people I knew.

I'd been completely blind. If not for Sadie, I would have paid dearly for that blindness. I needed to call and talk to her, but not now. Not when I was so close to losing it.

"Aiden came to me after Skeet attacked me," Mia said

quietly. "Gage called him. He helped me that night. And later, after the murder and finding out about the baby, I was thinking of adoption, but he wanted to marry me. He promised to take care of us. I was afraid at first, but he'd always been nice to me, and I liked him. Eventually, I said yes." She smiled through her tears. "Later I realized he'd always been there for me. Always. I'd just never thought of us being together like that. We were friends, or so I thought, but it became much more. He's the only one I love more than Dylan and Gage."

"I'm glad. You and Dylan are both very lucky."

Mia glanced at her wall clock. "You'd better hurry. Gage will be back soon. I'll make you two a little picnic."

"Thanks."

Mia shook her head. "I'm glad you're here. We will get to the bottom of this."

"Yes, we will." The more I knew Gage, the more I wanted her to be right, though I probably had no business agreeing to anything she proposed since I didn't plan to be around long enough to see it through. "But I think you should have more faith in the police. Ridge seems like a good cop."

"He is. Maybe I'll wait for a bit."

Morosely, I went into the bedroom for a quick shower, remembering after to slather my body with sunscreen. The new jeans were a little snug after all those pancakes, but they'd been worth every bite.

My hair was refusing to obey, and in the end, I pulled the mass into a ponytail. Anything I tried to do to it would be ruined on the bike anyway. Good thing I wasn't trying to impress Gage. Well, forty-five thousand dollars was impressive enough. A bitter taste filled my mouth, and I had to brush my teeth three times before it left.

Gage was waiting outside, stowing the lunch Mia had given him. I was glad to see he was also wearing jeans and a T-shirt. His leather jacket was packed inside the bike's plastic compartment with the lunch. Guess it was part of the motorcycle.

I climbed on and put my arms around him. Until I did, I hadn't realized how much I was looking forward to doing just that.

I was really in trouble.

Hours later, I was glad we'd taken Gage's bike as we bumped along a makeshift road outside Flagstaff. I had no idea where we were, though I'd lived in Flagstaff most of my life. All around us was desert, calm and far more green than many people would guess. Some people preferred mountains or oceans, but I loved the desert, the mild winters, even the heat of summer. This September morning was beautiful, and the red plateau we were heading for looked like something on a postcard. The beauty caught at something in my chest and made me glad to be alive.

Gage stopped the bike, and my ears felt briefly odd without the roar. Everything was still. The day was hot and going to be hotter, but there was enough of a breeze that it felt good and not too stifling, though people from cooler climates might think differently. I jumped off the bike and stretched. The blue sky went on forever, and the marshmallow clouds were doing their best to form figures I recognized. One resembled a teddy bear with a missing ear.

"What are you doing?" I asked Gage, who was rifling through his backpack. I caught sight of a chisel, hammer, a bunch of plastic zip bags, and a marker.

"This is just a preliminary run. If these samples show what I think they will, we'll do more extended samples next week, in whatever area these indicate. Then my employers will finalize their rights to the land, and we'll start mining."

"For what, copper?"

He seemed surprised that I knew. "That's what we're here for. The land has been in private hands for a long time, but the owner is ready to sell, or at least the mineral rights. The government has to stamp its okay as well, but that's not my department. I just have to make sure the old tests done years ago still show what we expect. But I'm almost positive. Come on."

Handing me the bag with our lunch, he hefted his backpack. Soon we were heading up the incline toward a higher location on the plateau. "There's a bit of a canyon through here," he said. "That's where I need to go first."

I was already glad I'd worn tennis shoes because this was not what I'd expected.

We began a long hike through tall red rocks. Every so often, Gage would take out his chisel and hammer to chip away at the rocks, carefully documenting where he'd taken the sample with the marker directly onto the bag, using a GPS to pinpoint our exact position. Sometimes he collected some of the dirt as well. Several times, he had to do a little climbing or digging to get samples that satisfied him. Eventually, we entered a small valley and began to circle around, and I saw a pattern to his work.

The valley wasn't green, and there weren't many trees, with the exception of a few hardy pines, but the place had an austere beauty and gave me the sense that no one had ever been here before except us.

"What?" Gage asked, seeing my smile.

"Seems like we're the only people in the entire world."

He laughed. "That's what's so great about my job. I love exploring new places and knowing I'm the only human for miles."

"Must get lonely sometimes."

"Sometimes."

We were standing very close. I became aware of him—his stance, his eyes, even the smell that was uniquely his. My heart was doing strange things in my chest, banging so loudly he could probably hear it. I wasn't the only one. I could see his pulse beating in his neck. The expression on his face told me he was feeling something, too.

"We'd better get going." His words came with effort.

I was glad when he moved away.

No, I wasn't. I'd wanted him to look at me that way. It did a heck of a lot for my bruised ego. I also knew what I was doing wasn't wise. It felt a lot like falling in love.

It's just the scenery, the whole scary convict thing, Julian's betrayal, I told myself.

Blame whatever I wanted, the fact remained the same. I liked Gage Braxton. A lot.

Now that I was getting to know him better, and the tumult of events was subsiding a bit, I remembered more of our talks over the past year. I remembered him telling me how much he loved to camp. How he hated peanut butter, loved cinnamon bears, and enjoyed the smell of rain on the pavement.

He was already several yards ahead of me, so I shelved the memories and started out after him. We took five more samples before he stopped in the shade of a rock outcropping. "This looks good for lunch."

I nodded and sank onto a rock. Not exactly an ideal spot for a picnic, but it felt right. We ate sandwiches made of last night's pot roast, cut vegetables, packaged raspberry-filled donuts that were surprisingly good, and water to wash it all down.

"Look over there," Gage said.

My eyes strained in the direction he pointed, but all I saw was rock. "What?"

He moved closer. "A lizard. Over there."

"Where?"

He put his arm around me and pointed. I saw it now, staring at us with unblinking eyes, almost blending into the rock where it lay.

I turned to say something to Gage, but he was no longer looking at the lizard. His eyes were on my face, and there was something deep and compelling in his gaze. I couldn't look away.

His hand came up to stroke a bit of my hair that had come loose from the ponytail. I'm sure the humidity was not being kind to it, but he seemed fascinated and didn't withdraw his hand. The tension between us built—a wall of water behind a dam that could never hold. When at last he kissed me, I let him.

Fire ignited between us. His hand on the back of my neck urged me closer, and for a long moment I was lost in the feel of his lips and the delicious fire that heated but did not burn. His lips left mine to trail across my cheek and down to my throat. I shuddered. His breath and my own came faster as our lips met again in a burst of flame. Yet amidst the heat and passion was another emotion, one I couldn't identify. Something that made it feel right. I floated on the wave of my heartbeats. Or were they his?

When we pulled away at last, Gage said a little hoarsely, "Sorry about that."

"Me too." But I wasn't, and I didn't think he was, either. What was going on with us?

We were silent a long moment, exchanging wary, longing glances. "What I said yesterday," Gage said finally. "About doing it all again? I lied. If I had it to do over, I'd plead innocent, but at the time, I thought it was the only thing I could do to protect my sister. She was so broken, so destroyed, and I couldn't let her suffer anymore. But now I don't think they would have gone after Mia. If I'd insisted I was innocent, they might have looked to find who really did it."

"You don't sound certain. About them looking."

His green eyes were haunted. "What if she did do it?"

"What are you saying?" I knew he was trusting me with this confession, but I didn't like the idea of Mia killing an unconscious man—no matter how much he'd deserved it.

"You didn't see her that night, the night of the attack. She called me crying from the convenience store where she worked. He'd jumped her in the parking lot. She was a mess when I got there, her clothes torn and dirty. The look in her eyes . . ." He stopped a moment, struggling for control. "She wouldn't let me take her to the hospital or anything. She went crazy when I tried. She was strong— she threw me off as if I weighed nothing. I'd never seen her so wild. I called Aiden because I knew how he felt about her, and he called his friend from the police department. They came to the house. No one could do anything for her except Aiden, who kept talking to her real calm until she fell asleep in his arms. I was useless. I felt so angry." His jaw clenched and unclenched. "I went looking for Skeet that night. If I'd found him then, I would have killed him."

"Maybe. Maybe not—probably not. What happened the next time you saw him?"

"After five days Mia went back to work as if nothing had ever happened. She wasn't the same, though. She was afraid of her own shadow. Could barely ring people up when they came in to buy something. But she insisted on keeping her job, and her co-workers covered for the hours she spent crying in the bathroom. She was near the end of her shift about a week after the attack when the guy working with her that night went outside to fix the tire pump. He didn't come back. They found him later, unconscious behind the station.

"Fortunately, Aiden and I were keeping a close eye on Mia, taking turns picking her up before the end of her shift. It was my turn that night, and I arrived in time to see Skeet walk in. You can bet I ran in after him. He started waving money at her, saying he'd pay her if she'd keep her mouth shut. I slugged him. He was strong.

He was on something—I'm sure of it. He had a knife, and he knew how to fight, but I managed to get it away from him. The last thing I remember is him falling back and hitting his head on the counter. I must have collapsed."

"And the poker?"

"I was working full time at a fireplace store and going to college part time."

"Don't tell me—the poker matched one sold there."

"They couldn't tell one way or the other. It looked like pokers that are sold anywhere."

Was he telling the truth? I thought so, but I wasn't the best judge of character these days. He could be lying, and whatever my heart said, I wanted my mind to be in charge of whether or not I should trust him.

Yet wasn't I already trusting him? I was alone with him in a place where not even my cell phone worked. Then again, I wasn't the slime Skeet had been, and I was positive he wasn't the cold-blooded killer those ladies in Vegas wanted me to believe.

"Prints?" I asked. "On the poker?"

"Nothing. Not even mine. They said it was probably wiped off." He paused for several heartbeats before adding, "Maybe I did do it. People have blocked out worse. I was certainly angry enough." He gave me a smile that chilled me despite the heat lifting off the rocks around us. "And it's in my blood."

Because of his father. But I wasn't about to pursue that conversation. "Mia doesn't think you did it."

"Mia loves me." He began to put things away. "There aren't many samples left to take. Another fifteen minutes, and we'll be out of here."

I knew the discussion had ended.

By the time we returned to our original location, my legs felt a little shaky from so much unexpected exercise, but in a good way. It'd been too long since I'd experienced nature or worked out with any diligence.

"This is fun," I said, meaning it. "Makes me regret my degree even more."

"Not a lot you can do with liberal arts?"

I frowned at him, trying not to read too much into the fact that he remembered. "Yes, good old liberal arts, the degree you end up with when you degree hop too often." There was no excuse except that I wasn't really interested in any of the subjects, and I'd always known I'd end up at my father's company. Now that seemed poor foresight because the grapevine said most employers were looking for workers with more specialized skills

"It's not too late to do something new," Gage said. "You have your general education taken care of, and that's half the battle. I finished my degree in prison."

The word *prison* sat between us, as large and unwieldy as if he'd put it there on purpose to keep me away. It worked. We walked the rest of the way in silence.

"I need to stop by my house," Gage said, when we reached the bike. He hefted the pack, now rather decidedly bulky, into the container on the bike, barely fitting it in. Thankfully, the insulated lunch bag was collapsible. "That won't be a problem, will it?"

"Not unless my family is camped outside, which I doubt. If they have pinpointed where you live, they still wouldn't be looking for you there since they think we're off, uh, celebrating." I was glad I was already flushed from the physical exertion, or my embarrassment would be more obvious.

The sun was now making the day uncomfortable, and I was all too aware that we still had a long drive back to Kingman after we stopped at Gage's. I was glad when the wind began hitting me in the face and drying the sweat from the back of my neck. The closer we got to my parents, the more my heart hammered in my chest. I felt like a nervous wreck when we finally pulled into his subdivision.

"Nice," I said, looking over the front of Gage's house. I'd only seen the back of it from the path that ran between our properties, and I hadn't really been sure which house was even his. Unlike the brick on the other houses, his sported a band of narrow rocks along the bottom of the brown stucco. The windows had fake shutters, which I'd always thought were silly, but they gave the house a homey feel. I loved the cactus in the rock flowerbed.

Inside, there wasn't much to see, and I suspected he hadn't spent enough time there yet to leave his mark. The sparse blue and tan furniture appeared new and unused. Only on our way to a back bedroom that had apparently been set up as a lab did I spy a sitting room with an old maroon easy chair and a large screen TV that looked more like home.

"So what did we come here for?" I asked.

"Just the original report and some geological information I gathered about the area."

"It looks like you do actual tests here."

"Sometimes. But I'm dropping these off in town. I have an assistant who agreed to come in and start the preliminaries for me. If you don't mind, I think I'll call him to make sure he's on his way."

"Take your time. I'll wait outside. I need to stretch my legs anyway after being on that bike again." That was an excuse because what I really wanted was to look in on Serenity. Who knew when I might see her again?

I cut around to his backyard and over the lawn, which was practically the size of a postage stamp. There was a short chain-link fence separating his property from the path and a small gate—exactly like the rest of the houses. The path was shaded by the trees from my parents' place, and underneath them the temperature was decidedly lower, almost pleasant. I went through our gate and stayed in the trees in case someone in the house was looking this way.

Serenity was nowhere to be seen. The barn was the only place she could be, though that seemed unlikely since she rarely went inside unless it was storming. Had my mother given her away in revenge? Feeling anxious, I left the cover of the trees and slipped inside the barn. To my relief Serenity was shut in her stall, and she whinnied a greeting as she spied me.

"Sorry, girl. I don't have any sugar for you."

I'd been hoping my mother had remembered to call Sinclair when I disappeared so he would come in earlier than we'd planned to care for my horse. Though Serenity had plenty of grazing in the field and water in her trough, I'd still worried. Obviously someone had been here, though, or she wouldn't be in her stall in the middle of the day. But why was she locked up?

Wait. What was that on her leg? I bent down to look.

She'd cut herself on something sharp, and it looked as though it needed medical attention.

"I don't see how the animal could have hurt herself," came a voice I recognized all too well.

Mother.

I eased away from Serenity and climbed the short ladder into the small hayloft to hide. I was still on the ladder when Sinclair came through. His eyes widened in surprise, but I held my finger to my lip and heaved myself the rest of the way up. I prayed that he wouldn't say anything. I had missed my wedding, and the last thing I wanted now was to confront my mother on her own turf.

10

"I shut her in the stall so she wouldn't injure herself further," Sinclair said to my mother. "I found the damage in the fence—probably some kids. It'll need to be fixed. I can do that and call the vet for you."

"Vet? It's that bad?"

"Yes."

"I see." There was a little silence in which my mother was presumably examining the cut.

I peered through a small crack in the loft floor, curious to see my elegant mother with Serenity. To my knowledge, she hadn't been out here since the day she'd given Serenity to me when I graduated from high school. She was stroking Serenity's neck, who had her nose buried in her hand.

My mother was feeding Serenity sugar cubes? I wasn't sure what to think, but a strange lump formed in my chest.

"Sinclair, please do call the vet," my mother said. "And add the time you take fixing the fence to your hours so we can be sure to pay you. I appreciate you bringing this to my attention."

"You're welcome. She's a sweet horse."

"Yes, she is." I couldn't see my mother's face, but she sounded peaceful.

"Well, I'll get started."

Sinclair left, and I felt an urge to call out to my mother. Crazy. She wouldn't be pleased with anything I'd done. Truth was, I wasn't all that pleased myself. I'd taken the coward's way out by running away and not confronting Julian, but I still believed that if I'd talked to him, I would have made the biggest mistake in my life.

Now there was Gage. I wasn't sure what I felt about him, but I wanted to find out. Besides, there was that little matter of how he kissed me. What if a miracle happened and things worked out between us? I'd live close. Maybe my mother and I could be friends. Start over.

This daydream was shattered by another familiar voice. "Mrs. Crawford?"

"Who's there?" My mother's hand disappeared from Serenity's neck.

"Julian Willis."

"What are you doing here? I told you I don't know where she is."

"I've done a little research. Braxton has a sister in Kingman, and they might have gone there."

"On a honeymoon?"

"You know it's not real. She doesn't love that man."

"Apparently, she doesn't love you, either."

"She's just hurt."

"And whose fault is that?"

"I take full responsibility. I even understand in a way. But if I can see her, I know I can make it work out."

"That's the very thing her father told me—that you would make it work out if we could find her. Maybe she did the right thing leaving like she did." I was surprised to hear the faintest hint of approval in my mother's voice, and I wondered if she'd wished her younger self had made the same decision. Would it have made a difference in our lives? I rarely saw my father, especially when I was young, and he'd had little to do with our upbringing. If I'd had a father who had played with us, asked us about school, who'd maybe attended one of Lily's plays or my volleyball games, would it have made a difference? We were always on our best behavior on the rare occasions when he was home, and my desire to please him was one of the biggest reasons I'd gone to work for his company.

Not to mention one of the reasons I'd started dating Julian. A business merger for the company was all well and good, but a personal merger cemented the deal.

These thoughts flooded through my head, leaving as fast as they entered.

"I thought you approved of our marriage," Julian said, a pout in his voice, but also a bit of warning.

"What if she's in love with this Braxton character?"

Silence. Then Julian's voice again. "He's a convict. She doesn't love him. She's trying to make a point. Look, I love Tessa, and I won't let her throw her life away. I'll make this right."

"Then you have my blessing."

It was an odd exchange, and I didn't understand any of it—my mother's ambiguity, Julian's insistence on his love for me. That wasn't the Julian I knew. When someone hurt him, he became angry and withdrawn. When we had fought, I was always the one who had to initiate a resolution. The making up was good, but getting there took a lot of effort. Sometimes I was so tired of it. So utterly tired. Just once I would have liked to see him come after me and beg me to talk things out.

Well, I was through with that now. Maybe I'd never have to deal with Julian again. I shifted my weight, and my foot scraped against the floor of the loft, making a loud sound that echoed through the barn.

"What was that?" Julian asked. "Is someone here?"

"Probably the horse," my mother said.

"Sounds like it came from up there."

I held very still, except for the thundering of my heart. A line of sweat trickled down from my hairline. Did I have the strength to resist him?

"Well, go take a look if you like," my mother said, sounding amused. "But you'll ruin those pants."

"Not worth it. I need to see my father right away. He knows some people in Kingman."

Their voices faded as they left the barn. I slumped on the loft floor, my body going completely limp. Saved by Julian's expensive trousers. Maybe I'd send him another pair once I received my inheritance.

I lay there without moving, allowing my heart rate to return to normal. I knew I should get up and go find Gage, but I couldn't make my muscles move. It had been too close for comfort. Yet a part of me wanted to stroll up to the house, to go into my bedroom and take a nice, relaxing bath with my own bath products. Have my hair and nails done. Sleep in my own bed. To not worry about Gage and especially my reaction to him.

"Tessa?"

My muscles tensed again.

"I know you're in here somewhere."

Steps on the ladder.

"Oh, there you are."

I was lying on my back, and I lifted my chin up, tilting back my head to see Gage looming over me. "Hi," I said. He looked odd upside down, but then I guess anyone would.

"I figured you came to see Serenity. I saw your mother and Julian leaving. Guess they didn't see you."

I forced myself into a sitting position, and Gage returned to being himself instead of odd-looking. "Something like that."

"No regrets?"

I had regrets, but none of them were any of his business. "No."

He offered me a hand, and I took it. Suddenly I was in his arms, and we were kissing right there in the loft. Fire ran through my veins.

No, that was all in my mind. A delicious daydream. Gage was actually going down the ladder, completely oblivious to my fantasy. I was in big trouble. Falling fast. What if there was no one to catch me?

"Careful," Gage said, reaching out to steady me. "A broken ankle is the last thing you need right now."

The last thing I needed was him touching me. I jumped off the ladder and hurried over to Serenity. "I'll see you soon, girl. The vet is coming to take care of you." I smoothed her neck and gave her a hug.

"Vet? Is something wrong?"

"She hurt her leg, but our vet is really good, and they're fixing the fence where it gouged her."

"The things we learn when we hide in barns," he said dryly.

I laughed. "You can say that again."

"Oh? What else did you learn?" He peered out the door before giving me the all-clear signal. We hurried out and around to the cover of the trees.

"I learned that maybe my mother isn't the person I've always believed." That maybe some slight chance remained for us to develop a real relationship. But I didn't tell him that part. It was too personal.

To my surprise and relief, Gage had pulled his Jeep out of the garage instead of his bike. In the backseat I spied a large duffel bag and a laptop. "Yay! Air conditioning," I said, wiping beads of perspiration from my forehead.

He chuckled. "Since it seems we're going to be gone longer than I expected, I'm taking a few more things back. Mia will kill me if I don't go to church with her tomorrow."

I was surprised that he'd risk being recognized, but apparently Mia's wrath was more frightening. "I wish I could get some of my clothes," I said.

He frowned. "We could stop by your house."

I shook my head.

"What are you afraid of?"

The question stung because it was so accurate. "Bigamy," I retorted.

He laughed. "Not going to happen while I'm here, but have it your way. We should hurry. My assistant is probably waiting."

My anger vanished almost instantly. I wasn't angry at him, anyway, but at myself for being unable to walk into my parents' house and pack a proper suitcase. In fact, I had one nearly packed already, full of honeymoon clothes, including evening gowns for the Paris night life that I might never see now. I wasn't even going to think about the belongings I'd already moved to the apartment Julian and I were to have shared.

In downtown Flagstaff, Gage stopped at a large building with the name Trenton Mining across the front. In the parking lot around the back, a tall man lounged in a beat-up red convertible. I fell in love at first sight. With the car, not the man, though he wasn't too shabby himself. He had blond hair like Julian's, but his was curly and playful. Messy. He had nice, even features and soulful brown eyes that lit up when he saw me.

"Hey," he said, nodding at Gage, his eyes never leaving mine. Obviously, he was waiting for an introduction. I was curious if Gage would say I was his wife or if he'd keep our temporary situation to himself.

"Tessa, this is Jeff," Gage said. "Jeff, Tessa." He left it at that, and I felt a strange sadness and more than a little resentment, which I knew I had no right to feel.

"I love your car," I said, flirting with Jeff to cover my feelings.

"I'd love to give you a ride."

Gage was frowning, a deep line between his brows. Ah, so not as disconnected as he pretended. I hooked my arm around his, rubbing a hand on his arm. He tensed at my touch, like a wire humming with electricity. "I'd love too, but you know how Gage is. Rather possessive."

Jeff blinked in surprise. "I didn't know that about him. Course, I've never seen any of his dates. Didn't know he was dating, actually."

I laid my head against Gage's shoulder. "Guess he had to find the right woman."

"I'm not possessive," Gage said, but he didn't move away.

"Okay. Then I'll go for a ride with Jeff." I released Gage and started to get into the convertible.

"We have a long ride ahead," Gage grumbled. "And Jeff has samples to test." He tossed his pack at Jeff, who caught it expertly.

"Another time then," I said.

"Sure." Jeff grinned and winked at me.

Gage glowered, but we ignored him.

"Any particular instructions?" Jeff asked.

"Just run the whole gamut."

"Okay." Jeff nodded at me. "Nice to meet you. Hope to see you around."

"Me, too."

He left, and I turned to find Gage glaring at me. "What?" I said. "It's not as if I'm really your wife. You certainly didn't introduce me as such."

He relaxed, a mocking smile coming to his face. "I see. So that's why you're acting like this."

"I'm not acting. He's cute."

"You wouldn't like him."

"Why not?"

"Because he's married and very much in love. He was trying to pull my chain, that's all."

My bubble burst. "Take me home—I mean to Mia's."

He opened the Jeep door. We drove in silence for a long time, and then he said, "I'm sorry."

I didn't know what for. He hadn't done anything wrong. Just because my heart was having issues didn't mean he had to be sorry. Maybe all the girls he kissed fell for him. "I'm sorry, too."

He smiled, and my insides felt queasy. I wanted to tell him to pull over so I could throw up, but instead I sighed and closed my eyes. Exhaustion caught up to me with a vengeance. Normally, I couldn't sleep in moving cars because I was obsessed with making sure the driver didn't fall asleep, but before I knew it my eyes were drooping.

Leave it to me to feel the safest in the company of a convicted murderer.

Then again, who better to trust than a man who would sacrifice six years of his life to protect his little sister?

Hours later as we pulled into Mia's driveway, my cell phone rang. I peeked at the caller ID and saw the number of my grandfather's attorney. I climbed out of the Jeep, stretching my free arm and stifling a yawn.

"Hello?" I said.

"Tessa, it's Mark Carson."

"What's up?" I waved at Gage and started toward the backyard for a little privacy. The late afternoon sun beat mercilessly down on my head.

"Those wedding papers you sent aren't going to work. I'm sending someone over to talk to the place where the ceremony was performed. I'll have it worked out soon,

I'm sure, but there is going to be a delay of a day or two while I track everything down. I know you wanted your funds right away, but this can't be helped. And I may need more information, depending on what we find there."

"What exactly is the problem?"

"The papers you sent don't contain an official record, and that's what we need. Don't worry. I'll get it worked out."

"Thank you. I appreciate it."

"Well, you're paying for it. At least your trust fund is, since I'm authorized to deduct my services from the account if they're related to my position as executor."

A bit of unamusing lawyer humor, I supposed. "Of course. I'm glad you're rushing it through."

"I liked your grandfather. I've revisited the terms of the trust since we last talked, and the only other issue remains is the contesting clause, which, incidentally, my notes say your grandfather only put in because your parents insisted on it, presumably for your safety. If your parents plan to make an issue of it, given their attitude toward your husband, there would be a six-month waiting period as we interview everyone in your family and in your husband's to make sure the marriage is legitimate."

Six months? Guilt ate at me. Why had I been so rash? No, it was the right thing to do—for Lily's sake.

"What happens to the money if they do contest and they win? Not that they would, of course. I'm just curious." I wanted to ask about jail time, but that might be a little too obvious.

"The funds would revert to your parents, if they're living, or to Lily if they weren't."

Great. That meant my parents had more incentive to contest my marriage. "No one's contesting, are they?"

"Not so far. But your mother asked about the clause when I talked to her last, so you might prepare yourself for opposition. Though if she won, there might be jail time involved for you, so I'm not sure she'd want to risk that. Besides, I can't imagine why she'd think you'd trade one marriage for another unless you really meant it. I mean, either way, you were getting married." Mark laughed, but I didn't find it funny at all.

Jail time. *Great.* I knew my parents could use the money to help secure their business, but would they go that far? They might feel justified if I'd managed to blow their deal with Julian's father.

"Have there been more inquiries about my trust fund?" I asked.

"No."

"Good."

When we eventually hung up, I stared into the horizon above the chicken coop without seeing anything. A little hand touched mine, and I looked down to see Dylan.

"I like watching them, too," he said.

I smiled. "I never knew chickens could be such great pets."

"I wasn't talking about the chickens. I thought you were looking at those clouds over there." He pointed.

"Oh, I love clouds. That one over there looks like a cake, don't you think? Too bad they aren't close enough to give us some shade."

"That one looks like your wedding dress."

I stared at him. "What do you mean?"

"It came while you were gone. That and some pictures. Didn't you know? They're in your room."

I hurried to the house to find both the wedding dress and the blue dress I'd worn to dinner in Las Vegas hanging in the guest closet. A thin album of wedding pictures lay on the bed. I looked through them, unsure what to think. There we were, looking confident and in love. Printed, Avery's picture looked a lot better than on my laptop screen.

"I thought you might like to keep them," Gage said behind me. I turned to find him grinning at my shock. "The dresses, I mean. A keepsake. Besides, you looked lovely in them, and you can wear the blue one to church, though now I'm thinking it might be a little too dressy."

I was not going to cry at his sweetness. I was not. It was a scam, all of it. I was *paying* him to do a job, nothing more. I let anger sweep away the hurtful sweetness.

"I suppose you think this will be on my bill," I said. "But I didn't order them, so they'll come out of your payment. You can keep them, of course." I regretted the words the instant I spoke, but it was too late.

His smile vanished, and his face darkened. "Money. Is that all you ever think about?"

"You're one to talk," I retorted. "You married me for forty-five thousand dollars."

He took a step forward, hands clenched at his sides, his face as hard as granite. "Hey, you came up with that. I don't want your money—I never have. I was doing you a favor, that's all."

"But—"

"If we're talking money, you're the one who married

to get it." He snorted with disgust. "I stepped in only to make sure you didn't end up with some psycho like the one who followed you from the dance club in Vegas, which could have easily happened."

"Why'd you even bother? Huh?" I clenched my own fists and didn't back down when he took another step toward me.

"Because I'm a nice guy."

Or maybe he was the one who had someone call Mark to ask about my trust fund. "My grandfather meant that money for me. For Lily. If he were here, I know he'd give it to us."

"So what's wrong with working for what you need? Not everyone has a trust fund, you know. You think that's what your grandfather would have wanted—for you to fake a marriage to get money?"

"You don't know anything!" I stood on my toes and shouted in his face. I was so angry, I wanted to strangle him.

"I know you didn't love Julian, or you would have fought for him—or at least confronted him. And I know that Lily would never have wanted you to throw away your future to a stranger."

I hated him. I hated him more than I'd hated anyone. Because he was right. I shouldn't have run away. I shouldn't have fallen into this mockery of a marriage. I'd taken what had seemed to be the easy way out because I'd been so hurt and worried and confused, but it had been a stupid idea from the beginning. Tears started down my cheeks.

"Look, Tessa," he said, reaching out to me. His words were gentle now, the accusatory tone gone from his voice.

I slapped his hands away. "Don't touch me." Because if he took me into his arms, I didn't think I'd ever want to leave, and he was only helping me out as a friend. I was a charity case. I had to remember that. He wasn't in this for anything but to be a nice guy. He'd certainly made it clear he had no intention of ever having a real family. If I allowed myself to feel something more for him, I would only set myself up for more pain.

I stomped past him out of the room. In the kitchen, Mia was cooking again—probably dinner. To my surprise, she had the radio on, turned up high, the speakers facing down so vibrations leaked through the floor. She was swaying by the sink, in perfect rhythm. She didn't notice me as I passed through, grabbing a set of keys from the table that I recognized as Gage's. She did see me as I slipped out the door, and she called out, but whatever she said was lost in the sounds of the drums.

I didn't want to talk to her. I didn't want anything but to get away. Run.

Would Gage report the Jeep stolen? I didn't think so. Could a wife be accused of stealing a husband's vehicle?

I had no idea where I was going. I drove until the tears stopped and a layer of hardness reformed around my heart. I could think clearly again.

Why had the dresses so upset me?

I knew why. Because I wanted them. I wanted to read into them more than they represented. I wanted to remember forever the way I'd felt when Gage had kissed me that first time after the wedding. The feeling between us when we had stayed up practically the entire night playing cards. How he'd brought me breakfast.

I wanted it to be real.

I pulled over and let my head smack into the steering wheel. Lifting it, I let it bang several more times as though the action would knock some sense into my head. Was I crazy? Yes. There could be no other answer.

I was falling in love with Gage Braxton, and I had to stop.

11

Without realizing it, I'd ended up at the police station, one of the few places I recognized in the small town. My subconscious search for order in my chaotic new world. One idea that kept repeating itself in my mind was that Gage had said he'd never marry for real, never put his children through what he'd endured, never pass on the criminal legacy of shame.

Would he still feel the same if he was cleared?

That was why I'd come to the police station. Because I'd never felt this way about anyone, and if I didn't do something, we wouldn't have a chance.

Though what made me think Ridge Harrison, the police officer, would be here on a Saturday afternoon, I didn't know. Except that he didn't seem the type to be a Monday through Friday regular but rather a man who would work on a mystery until it was solved. At least that's what I was banking on. If not, I'd have someone call him for me. I could at least tell him someone was snooping into my business. Was it connected? I didn't know how it couldn't be.

Sure enough, Ridge was in and came to meet me with a big smile. "So, to what do I owe this pleasure?" I noticed he didn't ask me back but kept me standing in the lobby, glancing behind me every time someone opened the outside door.

"I've come to talk about my husband's case." The words fell off my tongue without hesitation, which made my nerves stretch even tighter. I was as bad as a schoolgirl with her first crush.

Ridge shook his head. "We've learned nothing new. Mia may have everything wrong."

"So you think she made up the note? Or maybe wrote it herself?"

"I'm not saying that, though I haven't ruled it out."

"Do you really think she's capable of that?"

He didn't answer, but I could see in his eyes that he didn't believe it either. Today his eyes were darker, the color of bitter chocolate, though it was probably a trick of the light.

"Well, I don't believe it," I said. "She's scared—enough to convince Gage and me to delay our honeymoon so we can stay here with her."

Ridge nodded once, briskly. "There were no prints on the paper except for yours and hers, but we're taking the threat seriously."

"I'm glad. But something else odd happened."

"Oh?" He looked past me at the door, though no one was entering. Then his gaze touched on the clock behind the reception desk, and I realized he was waiting for someone.

"It might be related to the case."

"The case," he repeated, a hint of a smile tugging at his lips, as though he wanted to make a joke but realized it wouldn't be appropriate. The smile made him more attractive, but I was too irritated to give it more than a passing thought.

"I have a trust fund my grandfather left me. I'm due to receive a lump sum soon and then a monthly fee for the rest of my life."

He quirked a brow, apparently interested but not exactly sure how it connected to the threatening note.

"Someone's been snooping into my finances. A woman called the trustee's office wanting to know what happens to the money if I die."

Ridge's eyes had slid briefly past mine, but now they clicked back to me. "And what does happen to the money?"

"For now it would go to Gage. But soon it'll go to my sister."

"Why the change?"

"He doesn't need it. She does."

"I see." He paused for long seconds before adding, "It seems like those fingers are pointing right back at Gage, don't you think? He could have hired someone to call."

My heart seemed to skip a beat. He was right. Gage was the most likely suspect, but he'd seemed sincere in his claim not to want my money. "No," I said, shaking my head.

"I'm not saying he did it, mind. I don't believe he did. I'm just saying it probably isn't connected with the note Mia received."

"It's connected because it's suspicious. Look, can we sit down? I've been hiking all morning, and I'm tired."

Truthfully, the confrontation with Gage had done more to exhaust me than anything. My mind was still replaying the scene, trying to study all the nuances in order to deduce what they might mean.

"Sure." He indicated the waiting chairs in the lobby where an older woman with black hair sat with a drooling toddler on her lap.

"I meant somewhere private."

"Then we'll have to make it another time because I have an appointment in a little bit." He lifted his shoulders in an apologetic shrug, an endearing gesture that lessened my irritation.

I wonder if he was waiting for a woman, perhaps the one Mia had mentioned to him yesterday.

"I need to clear Gage," I said. "If he isn't cleared, we aren't going to make it."

Ridge nodded, his eyes focusing on me as though seeing something he hadn't noticed before. "Aiden told me how Gage feels about marriage and children. That's why I was so surprised yesterday when Mia told me he'd gotten married. But perhaps if you've come this far, you'll be all right."

He didn't understand, of course, and I couldn't tell him. Even if I could, I didn't understand what I felt for Gage, and it was hard to think past that. I took a deep breath, deciding to take another tack. "I know what happened to Mia, and I understand you came to see her after the attack."

"It was bad. Really bad." Another new note in his voice now—anger, helplessness. Exactly what I'd heard from Gage. "Truth be told, in the end Skeet got exactly

what he deserved. If Gage and Mia had been willing to
come out about the rape, everything in his case might
have been different."

"Why didn't they?"

"Mia was too fragile. We were all worried she'd do
something to herself."

"But you knew. You were a police officer then. Couldn't
you have made the other officers see?"

He shook his head, a hint of tears in his eyes before
he blinked them away. "No. They were right. She had to
be protected. We had no other choice." He swallowed
hard, his words coming rough and heavy. "I've seen it
happen before. She was too emotionally fragile. She
would have—"

Whatever he was going to say was lost when the outside
door opened to reveal Bailey Norris. Today her short hair
was slightly spiky, making her look taller than ever, and
she moved with the stealth of a predator. Contrasting
perfectly with her tan, she wore loose, off-white pants and
a matching short-sleeved shirt that opened at the collar
enough to reveal a snug brown tank. Her step faltered
briefly as she recognized me.

Ridge's entire face lit up, turning from mildly attractive to fascinating. *Ah,* I thought, knowing Bailey didn't
share his admiration.

"Bailey." Ridge stepped forward, taking her hand in
his. "You look wonderful."

He was right—if you liked tanned, well-dressed, and
classy.

Bailey pulled her hand from his and faced me, more
like a mother protecting her young than a rival for a

man's attention. "Tessa," she said coolly, her eyes running deliberately over my jeans and T-shirt.

I matched her ice. "Bailey."

"I see you two have met," Ridge said.

"We've had that pleasure. So, what brings you to our illustrious police station, Tessa?" Bailey showed teeth as she smiled, which may have added a touch of politeness if she hadn't looked like a big cat ready to pounce.

"I'm trying to find out who really killed Skeet Thompson," I said, more flippantly than I would have if she hadn't rubbed me the wrong way.

She nodded, not showing surprise. "Why?"

"Because Gage didn't do it."

Again no surprise in her face, and that told me she'd believed in his innocence all along. Of course, if they'd been close, she would have known better than I did what kind of a man he was. Why hadn't she fought for his freedom then? Or encouraged him to fight? "It's been a long time," she said. "Why stir it up now?"

"Because it's eating him alive." I knew it to be true as the words left my mouth. Not knowing what had happened that night, or the role he and Mia had played, was something impossible for him to get past.

An emotion akin to sorrow moved across her face. "He'll forget eventually." It was a promise, and I knew instinctively it didn't include me but rather her own plans for Gage's future. I felt my mental claws come out. Funny how I had the urge to protect Gage from Bailey when she so obviously intended to help him. Sometimes life wasn't very fair—or fun.

Still, in my view, she and everyone in this town was a

suspect, and Mia must have felt the same because Bailey had been on her list. "How long have you known Gage?" I asked, aware that Ridge and Bailey were now giving each other looks that indicated impatience. Whatever the reason for their meeting, they wanted to get on with it.

"Since high school," Bailey said.

"You moved here then? From where?"

"California." She cast a quick glance at Ridge, who sent her a reassuring smile.

"I met your brother yesterday," I said. "We almost had to call Ridge. He was waving a gun."

The comment caused Bailey discomfort, if her frown was any indication. "Charlie wouldn't hurt anyone. He was trying to protect me."

"Charlie's back?" Ridge asked.

"That's part of what I wanted to talk to you about." Bailey's mouth tightened over the words.

Ridge's eyes darkened. "Is he drinking?"

"Seemed like it to me," I said when Bailey didn't reply.

"You know he's had a hard life," Bailey said to Ridge, acting as if I hadn't spoken, as if I weren't even there. "I have to help him. I owe him."

"I know, but that doesn't mean he can come here and do whatever he likes."

She nodded. "Will you talk to him?"

"Of course."

It was a conversation I'd bet had been played out more than once: Bailey coming to Ridge for help with her troublesome brother, and Ridge, the dedicated cop with his heart in his eyes, coming to her rescue. Apparently, he was good at rescuing people in distress—Mia, Bailey, me, and likely a host of nameless strangers. But not even he had been able to help Gage.

"Thank you." Bailey's eyes lowered, but not before I caught a glimpse of real gratitude. Whatever her feelings for Ridge, she cared about her brother as much as he apparently cared for her. I found myself liking her for that despite everything else. "I didn't know who else to go to."

"You did the right thing."

She gave Ridge a brilliant smile that had no trace of the predator she'd showed me. "Can you come now?"

"Sure."

"I'll never be able to repay you."

I knew how she could repay him, and so did he—to look at him for once as a man instead of a police officer—but neither of us would say it. I suspected Ridge was a lot better off because Bailey didn't strike me as good wife material for an officer, especially one as dedicated to his job as Ridge. She liked bending rules, or perhaps doing away with them altogether, while he would follow them rigidly or pay a heavy price in guilt.

They started to leave, but Ridge remembered I was still there before he'd finished his first step. He paused and faced me. "I appreciate you coming in, and like I said before, I am going to get to the bottom of whoever sent that note. I promise you Mia will be safe."

There was a question in Bailey's eyes, but she didn't give it voice. "Thank you," I said, and watched them go.

Bailey cast a final stare over her shoulder—a silent challenge. I met her gaze without flinching, but when they were gone, I walked slowly out to the car, limping slightly and feeling as if I'd been through a battle. The muscles in my right calf had seized up on me in apparent protest, my heart hurt, and I was feeling really dumb about how I'd handled everything—from my breakup with Julian to this interview with Ridge. And especially my blowup with Gage.

I remembered now how Gage had tried to protest about the money at the diner when I'd first mentioned it. At the time I'd thought he'd been trying to elicit more, but quite possibly he'd only agreed to because I was so insistent. Still, that didn't explain why he'd gone to such lengths to help me, even to the point of suddenly taking the day off work and endangering his job. I shivered when I remembered the man from the night club and how easily Gage had disarmed him. What if I'd been alone looking for someone to sign my insane contract?

I drove half-heartedly around town before admitting to myself that I had no place else to go but Mia's. I wondered if I'd be welcome. Maybe Gage would drive me to the nearest car rental place, and I could be out of his life.

No, I wasn't leaving. I was going to see this through. Gage had helped me, and maybe I could help him back. Mia's talk of a private investigator had given me an idea of my own.

Pulling over to the side of the road, I pushed my grandfather's attorney's number. He picked up almost instantly. "Mark Carson."

"Hi, Mark, it's Tessa Crawford again. Look, I need a big favor really quick, and I'm hoping you have the contacts. I know it's Saturday, but I need to find out everything I can on a Bailey and Charlie Norris. Siblings.

She's probably thirty or thirty-one. He's a year or two younger, I think. They moved to Kingman from California with their mother when they were in high school. She's been here ever since, but he served in the navy. I think their dad died, or something, and they had relatives here. I particularly want to know if there's any connection between them and a guy named Skeet Thompson, who was murdered in Kingman seven and a half years ago."

"Skeet Thompson—got it. Is this related to whoever tried to find out about your trust fund beneficiary?"

"I'm not sure. But this woman knows that my husband was convicted for a crime he didn't commit, and I want to know why she didn't try to help him."

"You know I have to pay the investigator—if I can find one available this late on a Saturday. Monday would be a better bet, if it can wait."

"It really can't. Is it going to cost a lot?"

"A few hours' research time at least. I'll convince him to give you a discount."

"Mark, if I ever become rich—and that's a big if since my dad is likely to disinherit me completely—I promise I'm going to move all my business to your firm."

"I'll hold you to that."

I was smiling when I hung up. I really liked that man. No wonder my grandfather had trusted him and his firm. Given Mark's age, which I knew to be in the mid-thirties, my grandfather had likely worked with Mark's father or grandfather before Mark, but helpfulness must run in the family.

Thinking of my grandfather made me remember his funeral while I was still in high school. How sad I'd been.

Despite the heat of the day, I wished I'd brought the quilt my grandmother had made me because I'd curl up into it and feel his comfort—and hers, though I couldn't remember her. "I've made a mess of everything, Grandfather," I whispered, "but I'm going to fix it. I'll try to make you proud."

I drove back to Mia's, taking a few wrong turns along the way but eventually finding the house and the green yard, which stood out like an oasis in the desert. How much of the land behind the house did they own? If Gage was cleared, maybe he would build a house there and raise a couple of children.

With Bailey? I hated the idea.

Gage was cutting the grass when I drove into Mia's driveway, parking the Jeep in front of the closed garage. I climbed out rather sheepishly. He killed the motor and strode toward me, his eyes wandering over my face and body, as though searching for signs of a wound. Tenderness filled me. He'd been good to me, and I'd been ungrateful.

"You okay?" he asked, as he saw me limping.

"Just a little sore. Sorry about earlier."

"It's okay. So where've you been? Out driving? I do that sometimes."

I started to nod but realized I didn't want to lie anymore. "I was at the police station."

"Why?"

"Because I think you're innocent."

A flush rose in his face. "You have to stop. I don't want Mia dragged into this again."

"She's already in this. Someone's threatening her." I hadn't meant to tell, but it wasn't right to keep it from him.

His face stilled, the color leaking from it as fast as it had come.

"Mia's much stronger than she was seven and half years ago," I continued. "She's been looking into the murder, researching people's backgrounds, and asking questions. Someone put a threatening note in her mailbox."

"Where is it?" His hands fisted at his side.

"I convinced her to give it to the police, but I don't know how seriously they're taking it."

"What did it say?"

I shrugged. "I don't remember the exact words, but it said something about justice already being done, and if she didn't want worse trouble than she'd gotten with Skeet, she needed to leave it alone. That's why she's been so scared."

He turned from me and headed for the front stairs, bounding up them two at a time. I knew he was going to find Mia.

"Wait!"

He turned. Everything about him was taut, power seething under tight control. How controlled I had no idea.

"There's more," I said.

"What." It was nearly a growl.

"Bailey knows you're innocent, and I think Ridge does, too—and so do I."

Something blazed in his eyes, but I couldn't tell if it was because I believed him or because Bailey did.

Just as suddenly the something was gone. "It's over," he gritted. "Over. I won't have Mia going through that again. I won't have Dylan hurt."

"So it's okay to protect them, but they can't protect you?" I hurried up the stairs. "Sorry, Gage, that's not how it works. Like it or not, you helped me, and I'm going to do everything in my power to help you. Someone else was there that night, whether you believe it or not!"

"It's none of your business!"

"So my running off to marry someone in Vegas is your business, but your taking the blame for a murder you didn't commit to save your sister, who didn't commit it either and has done nothing to be ashamed of, isn't mine?"

"There's no reason to bring it all up. It won't change the past. It won't change the six years I spent in prison."

"No, but it will change your future, and Dylan and Mia's futures. Your children's future."

His jaw clenched, and he swallowed noticeably. "I'm not having children."

"See?" We were standing close together. "You will never have a child to take camping, a wife to love and care for."

"I have Dylan and Mia."

"Only if you're in disguise. Only if no one else is around." I was angry, more angry than I had a right to be. "If it's worth having, you have to fight for it, Gage. Or someday it will be too late."

His nostrils flared, and his face flushed with emotion—anger, frustration, and something more. His pulse beat in his neck, and the pounding in my heart echoed it. I wanted to tell him to fight for us, as much as he'd fought for Mia. Or maybe I should tell him to fight for Bailey. The thought hurt more than I would ever admit.

His eyes held mine. Deep, green, endless. I was afraid
he'd see the truth there, so I dragged my eyes away,
followed the straight nose to his square jaw and up to
his left cheek and the web of tiny scars that were barely
visible under the hair that had fallen forward over his face.
I wanted to ask him how he got the scars, to trace each
one with the tip of my finger—or maybe with my lips.
He was my husband, after all, and I'd never felt this way
about any man. I hadn't known such emotion was even
possible. My parents had never given me any indication
that marriage could be so much more.

Oh, help.

"Tessa." His voice was low and hoarse. He took a step
toward me, and I could see in his eyes that he didn't know
what he was doing any more than I did, only that he felt
something strong in this moment.

With Bailey nowhere in sight.

Ha!

Before either of us could decide whether we would
cross the bridge that beckoned between us, the roar of
an expensive engine and the sound of tires on the dirt
road demanded our attention. We turned, our shoulders
coming together and sending a shock of contact through
my arm. I wanted to lean against his strength, and when I
saw who had arrived, I allowed myself the luxury. In fact,
I stepped even closer to Gage, my breath coming faster.
His arm surrounded me protectively, and for some reason,
that made me want to weep. Gage was a protector, as I'd
seen with Mia, and in this moment he was mine.

Julian climbed out of his green BMW. He wore tan
slacks, a yellow golf shirt that was open at the neck,

and shiny brown leather loafers. His skin looked bronze against the yellow shirt and blond hair. He was good-looking, there was no question about it, and his confidence radiated in the way he carried his lean body as he strode up the walk. I wondered if that was something he'd learned in school, or if, as the child of a wealthy man, he'd developed it from infancy.

He didn't speak until he stood at the bottom of the stairs. "Tess," he said finally. "I've been looking for you."

12

I swallowed and took a breath, but Gage beat me to speech. "So you've found her. What now?" His voice held an unmistakable threat.

"I just want to talk to her. Alone."

"I think it'd be better if you got back into your car and left."

Gage had only two inches on Julian, but he was a good deal broader, and his vantage of the porch made him even more menacing. Even so, Julian wasn't cowed. "What, are you speaking for Tess now? Last I knew, she could speak for herself."

Gage tensed, and I remembered how easily he'd disarmed the man from the club. "I can speak for myself just fine," I said hurriedly. "But I don't have anything to say to you."

"You walked out on me without an explanation."

"Are you denying what Sadie told me?"

"There's a woman who's been making a pest of herself. I'm sure that's what Sadie's brother saw. I've talked to Sadie and explained—she'll tell you herself if you call her."

Yes, I'd seen that—Sadie laughing with Julian at the door to her apartment. We'd joked about his power to make himself believed, so I didn't blame her for anything. I knew how convincing he could be.

"I was never unfaithful to you," Julian continued. "I promise. Tess, I love you. We belong together." The words were perfect, so smooth, and utterly believable. As he spoke, he drew out something from his pocket: our engagement ring. The difference between it and the fake band I had replaced on my ring finger was all too glaringly clear in the stark sunlight. "Please take this and come with me."

Two days ago I wouldn't have hesitated to go with Julian. He was handsome, rich, everything a woman could want.

Except that I didn't want him, and I found he no longer had power over me. My sister was right—I hadn't been myself around Julian. I'd been what he and my mother wanted me to be: Julian's fiancée and Elaine's dutiful daughter. Not me, Tessa. Though after hearing my mother in the barn, I had new hope that she and I could reach another level of interaction. Perhaps not entirely what I'd dreamt of as a child, but enough.

Next to me Gage was glowering, every muscle poised to react, the arm around me rigid. His eyes burned into mine when I looked his way, and I saw he was afraid of what I would choose.

"Julian," I said carefully, "I don't believe you."

His eyes widened with surprise. They were blue, like the sky, but icy, without warmth. "But it's true. Honey, I can prove it."

I shook my head. "Even if I did believe you, it wouldn't matter. I'm staying here." I leaned further into Gage and felt him relax marginally.

"How can you do this? After everything we've been to each other?"

My first urge was to apologize, but he was the one who'd betrayed me, and I couldn't bring myself to do it. "Wasn't it you who once told me you had to follow your heart?"

"Yeah, but that was—" He broke off.

"For you? For your heart?" An excuse to date someone else while engaged to me?

"Are you saying you love him?"

What a thin line I walked. My gaze went to Gage, who was watching me, the tiniest of smiles on his lips. He had gone from fierce to amused, though I was sure I was the only one who detected the difference in both his expression and his stance. I linked my hands together around his waist, going on tiptoes to kiss the scars on his cheek.

"Yes, I am." I felt Gage's surprise, his arm around me tightening further.

"Sorry you came all this way," I said, turning back to Julian. "Good-bye."

"Your father's going to regret this," Julian muttered. "Did you ever think of that?"

"Maybe, but fathers don't choose who we marry."

"That's what you think." His lips twisted into a sneer that marred his handsome face. "You think you're really something, don't you? Well, let me tell you—there's a lot better out there than you. If my father hadn't been breathing down my neck about this merger, we'd never have gotten this far."

I was stunned into silence. Had the merger between my father's cereal company and their frozen foods conglomerate held more importance than I'd believed? But why would Julian's family need my father's smaller company?

"Leave now while you're still breathing." Gage said, his voice low and deadly.

Julian stumbled back as though Gage had slapped him. "You'll regret this, Tess. I promise."

"If I ever see you around here again, you'll be the one who'll regret it." Gage released me and went down the stairs slowly and deliberately.

"You want to go back to prison? Huh?" Julian challenged, but he was giving ground. "You're nothing but scum."

"And you're nothing but Daddy's little boy doing anything he can to save his father's company from a takeover—no matter who it hurts."

Julian stared at him in shock.

"Oh, yes. I had a lot of time in prison to educate myself about current events, and I've kept up on things since I was released. Because of my friendship with Tessa, I've had a particular interest in reading up on your company, and I'm thinking those two huge recalls you had last year hurt your bottom line pretty badly. The rumors say you closed four of your larger factories. What's that left you with? Three? Four?" Gage took another step forward.

Julian shot a horrified glance at me, turned, and ran to

his car. The motor revved as he spun out in the dirt and drove away.

"At that rate, he's going to have to replace those tires in a month," Gage said as he returned to the porch.

I barely heard him through my shock. Julian had been marrying me for the same reason my father had wanted me to marry him—for his company's stability. Probably for my half million as well, which might go at least a little way toward the company's recovery. I'd been marrying Julian because I'd loved him and thought he'd loved me, but it was all a lie. No wonder he'd been seeing someone else. Maybe she was his real love and I his duty.

"So, that went well," Gage ventured. He hit the tip of his shoe on a clump of mud someone had tracked onto the porch.

A tear slipped from my eye. I didn't want Julian, but this new information stabbed deeply. Had any of Julian's attentions or declarations been real, or had he laughed about them behind my back?

Gage's foot stilled. "Tessa, what is it?"

"He was using me."

He was silent for a long moment. "I take it you didn't know about his dad's company going down the tubes?"

"I thought the merger would be good for my dad's company, but I didn't realize they were using me to get to my dad—not that I was marrying Julian for the merger."

"I know," he said softly but with a strength that cut through my words. "We've talked an awful lot about him these last months. I know you cared for him."

"I don't love him." Not anymore.

"Then why do his reasons matter?"

"It makes me feel so worthless." My words were scarcely a whisper.

"Tessa."

"What."

"Look at me." When I didn't comply, his fingers went to my chin. "No man would come this far to see an ex-fiancée who had already married someone else just because of his father."

"Then why did he come?"

"I bet he realized how much he did care and how much he'd be missing out on if you weren't in his life. The essence of who you are radiates from you, Tessa, and it's beautiful. Any man would be a fool to walk away voluntarily."

Warmth flooded me, sending a current of electricity through his fingers into my skin. Emboldened, I asked, "Even you?"

His jaw worked for several seconds before he leaned over and placed a gentle kiss on my lips, a kiss that left me puzzled and wanting more. "Especially me," he whispered.

For the first time I dared to hope. I couldn't tell Gage that I'd meant it when I said I loved him, but I could ask for time. "I like you a lot, Gage, and I want to get to know you better. I love Mia and Dylan. Maybe we could take a little time before we dissolve this marriage. See where things go." Things meaning the friendship we were developing, the common interests, the fire in my veins whenever he touched me.

A swift intake of his breath told me he understood what I was saying. He took a step back, his hand dropping away. Misery shone in his eyes. "It wasn't real."

I blinked. "What wasn't real?" He couldn't be talking about the kiss. I knew a real kiss when I experienced one.

"The marriage."

"What?"

"My friend Calvin isn't licensed to marry anyone. He owed me a favor, and I had him pretend to marry us."

I remembered his arguing with Calvin at the hotel, and suddenly it began to make sense. "Why would you do that?"

"I knew you'd regret it, and I didn't want you to get into trouble with the law about your inheritance."

I stared at him dumbly, both relieved and angry. Relieved because I hadn't thrown away sacred promises, but angry because I loved him and there was nothing holding him to me. My knees threatened to collapse, and I put out a hand to catch the porch railing for support. "You lied to me." If he'd lied about this, what else had he lied about?

Gage's hand touched my shoulder. "I knew from the moment I saw your face when we sent those pictures after the wedding that I'd done the right thing. You'd realized what a terrible mistake you'd made, and you were hurting because of it. That's why I stayed and played cards. I wasn't about to leave you alone looking so lost. I felt like the biggest jerk in the world."

I had been feeling lost, and if he hadn't come to me, I would have spent the entire night sobbing alone in that big bed. I hadn't considered how my reaction might make him feel. But in the end I wasn't married, and Lily hadn't missed my big day. I still had a chance to do it right the first time.

On the other hand, no wonder Mark was having problems verifying my marriage. It was a sham.

I wanted to laugh. I wanted to be grateful. Yet all I could think about was how I'd lost Gage. Now that I knew the truth, there was no point in staying on and pretending to be married, especially when he'd made it clear he didn't want me snooping in his business. There was nothing to do but go home—either to my parents or Lily's.

Lily. There was no way I would be able to help my sister now. All the tears inside me dried up, as if stopped by an invisible tap. "What will I tell Lily?"

"I'm willing to help. I have a bit saved that I can lend her."

For some reason the fact that he'd give her money, but not marry me, hurt even more. "I should have suspected it was fake," I said, forcing a lightheartedness I didn't feel. "You've told me enough in the past few days that you would never get married."

"You know why." His voice hardened slightly.

"I know why, but I still think you enjoy playing the martyr way too much." I pushed past him, heading down the walk.

"Where are you going?" he called.

"None of your business."

"Mia will have dinner soon."

"I'm not hungry." I'd reached the road and debated which way to turn. Maybe if I kept walking, I could find a rental car agency eventually and use my credit card. I could return for my things later.

"You're going to find someone someday," Gage called

after me. "Someone who loves you exactly the way you are. Your laugh, your smile, the way you walk. He won't give a fig about your father's business. He won't mind that you sleep past ten and keep him up all night. He'll love your freckles, the scent of Serenity on your skin. He'll—" The words stopped coming, but I didn't know if it was because he'd run out of breath or flaws to enumerate.

Fight. I remembered telling him that he should fight for his future, yet here I was so thrown out of kilter that I'd forgotten it myself. I cared about Gage, but more than that I believed in him. He hadn't killed Skeet, and I wasn't leaving until I either made him fight to prove his innocence or until he threw me out. Had our situations been reversed, I knew he'd do the same for me. Of course, that didn't mean I wasn't angry at how he'd faked the marriage. Angry and relieved.

I turned slowly and walked back to the porch. "You're right," I said. "I will find someone like that one day, and when I do, I'll kiss him exactly like this." Placing my arms around him, I gave him a good demonstration that left us both breathless. "And then he won't care how many pancakes I eat or how orange my hair is."

His eyes danced. "Your hair is orange?" His arms had come around me during our kiss, and he was standing as though he didn't realize he was still holding me.

"Definitely."

I was thinking about kissing him again when Mia opened the front door. We broke apart a little guiltily.

"There you two are," she said. "Dinner is ready. Dylan is setting the table."

I took out my phone. "Do you mind if I make a quick call first? It's important. It'll only take a minute." If I reached Mark, I could tell him to stop looking into the wedding so I could save myself some money and perhaps a lengthy investigation.

"There's time," Mia said. "Come and help me, Gage."

"Sure."

I was aware of Gage's eyes on me as he followed Mia inside. I was still angry at him, but the last few seconds had greatly improved my mood. As for Lily's house, maybe I could get a job as a clerk in a grocery store if my college degree couldn't land me anything with higher pay. That would help until the baby came, even if we had to move to a small apartment and have her girls sleep on the floor. Maybe they could work and pitch in more than they had in the past—though I knew most were still trying to finish high school degrees. It'd only be temporary. *I'll make it work,* I vowed. No way would I ask Gage for money.

"Hi, Tessa," Mark said. "I was about to call you."

"I can explain," I began.

"My guy found quite a bit of tasty information about your Bailey Norris." He paused. "What can you explain?"

"You first. I didn't realize you'd find anything so fast."

"Not me. My guy. Anyway, it was all a matter of public record. The Internet has just about anything you want to know, if you know how to search, and this guy has state of the art programs for searching. Bailey and Charlie Norris were born in Covina, California, to Lew and Gretta Norris. Records show numerous calls of domestic violence to the home—all made by neighbors.

Lew was often drunk, and he was apparently a loud, violent drunk."

"And the mother?"

"Mousy thing. Not much written about her, except that every professional who talked to her believed she was scared to death and lying. The children missed a lot of school, and the counselors suspected abuse, but they could never find solid proof because they moved around almost yearly to differing cities in California. The records are all piecemeal."

Thinking of Bailey growing up that way made me pity her, and I didn't want to pity her.

Mark cleared his throat and continued. "They were in Chino when the father turned up dead in the swimming pool of the house they were renting. No defensive wounds, but clear indication that he was stabbed in the back of the head and tossed into the pool unconscious. Drugs were discovered among his belongings. During the investigation, the mother received permission to take the children to Kingman to live with her sister, where the local police department kept an eye on them. Bailey was a junior in high school, the boy a year younger, though he didn't have much credit and ended up taking the GED to get into the navy. The dad's death was never solved, but there seems to be a general suspicion that the son stabbed the father with a poker while he was sleeping."

"Did you say a poker? As in a fireplace poker?"

"Yes, according to the medical examiner, but it was never recovered. The one from the rental house was missing. The family claimed it had been lost before they moved in, but Charlie had taken a drive to the beach that same day, and rumor says he had a friend with a boat."

"So they just let the family go?"

"Not exactly. The Kingman police kept an eye on them, as I mentioned, but after a few months the officer assigned recommended dropping the case, and everything was forgotten. The consensus seems to have been that if the son had killed his father, he'd done the world a favor."

"Who was the officer?" I didn't know that it mattered, but it might.

"Guy named Harrison, an older cop. That tell you anything?"

"I'm not sure. The name sounds familiar. Did this Harrison have children?"

"A son named Ridge and a daughter Chloe. That's all the information I have since Harrison wasn't part of the request."

So Ridge's father had been the police officer in charge of the case, but how that worked into Skeet's murder so many years later, I didn't know. Ridge had been in high school at the same time as the others, so his father working on the Norris case didn't really make a difference. "Anything more about the Norrises?" I asked.

"Nothing of real interest. The aunt died a few years after the Norris family came to live with her. Heart attack. Her third. The mother died of pneumonia eight years ago. Was in the hospital for weeks. Charlie came home for the funeral. Bailey went to college and now works as a loan underwriter for a mortgage company."

"No mention of Skeet Thompson in connection with the Norrises?"

"Not a one, though both Skeet and Charlie had arrests for drugs. In fact, Charlie was kicked out of the navy for substance abuse after only a year. Skeet was born in Los Angeles, but there's no record of them running into each other there. Skeet seemed to be a high roller, while the Norrises were dirt poor."

Mia had mentioned Skeet had a large sum of money before the fight, and that it was missing afterward. The money could be connected to drugs. "They ever serve time?"

"Skeet was in prison twice, less than a year both times. Charlie has been in jail overnight. That's all."

"Thanks so much. This might help a lot." Something was coming together in my mind, and I wanted to hang up so I could concentrate.

"So now it's your turn," Mark prompted.

"What?"

"You were going to explain something."

"Oh, that." Leave it to an attorney to remember gritty details. "It's about the trust fund. I want you to call off your guy in Vegas."

"Without verification I can't give you your money."

"I know, but I need to delay things for a while."

"As executor of your grandfather's will, is there something I should know?"

I remembered what Gage had said about the truth and sticking as close to it as possible. I took a breath and began. "I've learned that the man who married us may not have had the proper authority, which means I'll have to redo the ceremony before you can turn over my trust fund."

There was a silence on the phone. "Tessa, is this a matter for the police?"

I realized he thought Gage had been trying to take advantage of me, which was so far from the truth I almost laughed. "No, it's fine. We'll get it fixed."

"Maybe a bit of a delay isn't so bad. I mean, you made this decision rather fast in the first place. True love can wait a few weeks, don't you think? You know, do it up right."

"That might be a little difficult."

"Because of your parents and your ex-fiancé?"

Oops, I'd been so concerned about my problems with Gage that I hadn't even thought of them. "Something like that. Please, don't tell them. Give me a few days to work this out."

"Take all the time you'd like. It's not my place to tell them about your personal life."

I liked him more and more. "Send me a bill."

He laughed. "Oh, I will."

Hopefully, I'd have enough in savings to pay it. If not, maybe he could employ me as a secretary or something.

I hung up, feeling melancholy. Telling Mark had made the fact that I wasn't married to Gage real. Yet what if he were free to marry? I could almost see us together at a real church wedding with all the relatives there.

Impossible. Because the murder was still hanging over our heads, as well as Gage's insistence that he would never allow his children to grow up under that shadow.

So what *did* I know? I knew that Charlie Norris might have killed his father with a poker, the same type of weapon that killed Skeet Thompson. I knew that both

Skeet and Charlie had a connection to drugs. I knew that Bailey believed Gage hadn't murdered Skeet, but if she loved Gage and planned to marry him, there had to be an awfully strong reason why she hadn't fought to keep him out of prison.

The obvious answer was that she'd been protecting someone else, and the only person she might protect above Gage was her brother, Charlie—especially if Charlie's reaction to Bailey's distress was any indication of how their family guarded secrets. Years ago he might have saved Bailey's life by killing their abusive father, and yesterday he'd shown up here with a gun and threatened Gage. No doubt Charlie did anything he had to in order to protect his sister. Yet how far would she go to protect him?

Gage had claimed Charlie wasn't there the night Skeet died, and Mia hadn't mentioned him, either. But if he'd been in town, Charlie might have had drug dealings with Skeet and entered the convenience store after Mia went for help.

So had he been there or not?

The only person who could give me the answer to that question was Bailey Norris. I would go see her right after dinner.

13

It wasn't as easy to get away as I'd assumed. Apparently, Mia expected Gage and me to play the part of honeymooners, and she kept suggesting activities for the evening—movies, dancing, a romantic video, an evening walk.

Finally, I ended up pleading exhaustion. "I think I need to rest a bit," I said.

"You're tired?" Gage's disbelief was apparent. "So early?"

"Your fault. You're the one who dragged me all over Arizona today."

"But if you go to bed now, you'll actually wake up early, and that might cause a shift in the cosmos."

"Very funny. At least I'll be up in time for church."

His eyes narrowed. "What are you really planning?" I noticed he'd waited until Mia wasn't looking to ask the question.

"I was thinking of going back to Vegas to find what I was looking for the first time." I didn't know what made me say it because I had no such intention.

His gaze deepened. "And how are you going to get there?" His voice was mild, but the meaning was clear.

I didn't feel it necessary to bring up the fact that I still had the keys to his Jeep in my pocket.

"We could go see your sister," he suggested.

I stared at him flatly. "I promised Mia we'd stay until Aiden got home."

"Fine. We'll do that." He seemed surprised that I'd stay, now that I knew the truth.

Another day or two didn't leave me much time to solve the case, but I thought I was close already. I considered taking Mia into my confidence, but what if she insisted on coming with me to Bailey's and things got ugly?

No, better to ask Bailey a few subtle questions before I went to the police with what I knew. Given his fascination with Bailey, would Ridge act upon my suspicions? I thought he would—especially if Charlie was the real murderer.

"Oh, no!" Dylan jumped up from his seat, scattering my thoughts. "I forgot the afternoon eggs."

"Afternoon eggs?" I'd never heard of those.

"I get the eggs in the morning, but some of my chickens don't lay until the afternoon. I usually get them before dinner, but that's when Daddy called, so I forgot."

"Can I come?" I asked. "I've never gathered eggs before."

Dylan gave me a pleased smile. "Sure."

I smiled back. He had also given me the perfect opportunity to slip away.

Except that Gage followed us. "Shouldn't you give Mia a hand?" I hinted, but Mia was back to following the conversation and shooed us both away. It was just as well, since I hadn't yet looked up Bailey's address.

Outside, Dylan led us toward the hen house. The chickens scrambled mindlessly about our feet, seemingly unconcerned with our presence or our intent to steal their eggs. The space inside the little house was so small that it allowed only one adult inside at a time—and then only hunched over.

I peered inside, noting the fresh straw Gage had laid down the day before. "So if you keep taking the eggs, how do you get baby chicks?"

"We sometime let a few batches get by, and they hatch," Dylan said. "I love the little chicks. They're so tiny and fluffy." He went inside. "There's five eggs!" he shouted. "Five!"

"Nice," I said taking the two Dylan gave me for safekeeping.

"Breakfast," Gage added.

I laughed. "You do have one problem," I told him, as Dylan ducked back inside for the other eggs.

"What?"

"I don't think this coop is large enough."

Gage tilted his head. "It's actually a little large for the chickens they have. Aiden and I built it that way on purpose."

"I mean for you to sleep. If our ceremony wasn't legal, you can't sleep in the guest room or even pretend to. We'll have to explain it to Mia."

Gage gave me a significant look. "Nothing wrong with the couch. Besides, I'd rather not explain anything."

"Oh, that's right. You want her to think you have a life."

Why was I baiting him? "Does that go for Bailey, too? Do you want her to think you have a life?"

"It goes double for Bailey. She's a good person, and she hasn't had it easy. She needs to get on with her life."

Spoken like a man who really cared. "So maybe it wasn't me you were helping out after all," I said, stifling my jealousy.

Before he could respond, Dylan appeared in the doorway with three more eggs. He held up a brown one in front of Gage. "This was way up in the highest nest. Big Brownie always gets up there somehow. I never see her, but the egg is always there every day."

"Cool," I said. "Is that all of them then?"

"Yep."

We waited until Dylan had raced ahead of us before resuming the conversation.

"I didn't know we'd end up in Kingman," Gage said, "or that my sister would ever know about this pretend wedding. But now that she does know, I'm asking you not to tell her the truth. I'm willing to pay you for your trouble."

He was offering to pay me? I'd never been so offended. "I don't want your money," I retorted. "Don't make that offer again."

"Why not? You did—several times."

I sighed in exasperation, but he only grinned. "Now you know how it feels."

I didn't think it was the same thing. I was beginning to care for him so much it hurt to see the now-familiar lines of his face. I ached knowing that he would never allow himself the luxury of falling in love with me.

I turned and hurried after Dylan, catching up with the child as we entered the house. "Look," I said to him softly. "I need to drive somewhere to fix up a surprise for your uncle. Do you think you could distract him or something so I can sneak away without him noticing?"

Dylan grinned at me, his thin face coming alive. "Yeah. I can do that."

"Okay, but don't tell on me. I'll bring you a treat when I come back."

Dylan nodded. "Deal." I didn't know what he'd come up with, but I knew he'd think of something. The boy was bright.

Retreating to the guest bedroom, I took my laptop, went into the bathroom, and sat on the edge of the tub to look up Bailey's information. The address was unlisted, but her phone number was there.

I was about to dial when Lily called. "Hello?" I said.

"Oh, Tessa, I'm sorry to bug you, but I had to let you know what happened." To my relief, she didn't sound frantic but excited.

"What?"

"According to Mom, Julian's dad has been calling our father nonstop. He wants to go through with the merger."

"That's not a good idea. Their company might not be all Dad thinks it is."

"Exactly. That's why I'm calling. Dad had all their financial records and stuff as part of the contract disclosures, but when Julian's dad was so anxious, he started digging deeper. I mean, he'd heard about them closing some of their plants, but he found out that they're really bad off. Worse than Dad. I mean, at least Dad's company is holding its own. He could have lost everything. You're a hero now."

"You're kidding."

"Well, of course, they aren't saying so in that many words, but they're glad you dumped Julian. The fact that Mom has called me three times in the past two days when she hasn't talked to me in two years tells me a lot more than she's willing to say. I guess you're not picking up her calls, huh? Must be why she called me—so you'd hear."

"Don't get your hopes up," I warned, startled at the happiness in her voice.

"I know. But still."

"Yeah." After hearing my mother in the barn, I knew only too well how Lily felt.

"So, is everything going okay?" Lily asked me.

"Yeah. I don't want to go into details right now, but there's proof Gage is innocent, and we've talked to the police about it. They're helping to find out what really happened. It might be drug related."

"Good. Not about the drugs, but about you maybe not being with a convict. I've been so worried. I can tell how much you like him."

"You don't need to worry. I told you I'm here with his sister and nephew. Anyway, I'll be seeing you soon."

"I can't wait to meet him."

I closed my eyes, trying to block the hurt. "Sure. Hey, I gotta go." Easier than explaining that she would never meet Gage.

"Okay. Love you, Tessa."

"I love you, too."

I stared at the phone for a minute before remembering

my original purpose for hiding out in the bathroom. I dialed quickly.

"Hello?"

"Is this Bailey Norris?"

"Yes. Who's this?"

Which told me she either didn't have caller ID, or she was buying time. "Tessa Crawford, I mean, Tessa Braxton now." I felt like a liar adding Gage's last name.

"Hello, Tessa." Her voice cooled notably.

I plunged in. "When we met at the police station earlier, I got the feeling you believe Gage is innocent, too. I'd like to come over and talk to you about that, see if you have any ideas to help him."

"Help him what?"

"I don't think he did it, and he shouldn't have to suffer the rest of his life for something he didn't do."

"Why should I care?"

"I know you love him."

Silence. I could feel it wasn't going to be enough. If she was guilty of hiding something, she wasn't stupid. I needed something more, and unlike Gage, I didn't care if she went on with her life, not if it was at the expense of his.

"Look, you were right about me and Gage," I said. "Our marriage isn't real. In fact, in a few days, I'll be out of his life completely. He was just trying to help me, and now I want to help him." You and him, my tone implied. "If we can connect Skeet to drugs or something, it may be enough to clear Gage." I didn't mention her brother and had no intention of doing anything but to steer her toward talking about him long enough for me to know if he'd been in town that night. I would also remind her that clearing Gage would mean he'd be free to have a family, which might make her willing to confess what she knew. Ridge and the police would have to take it from there.

"Okay," she said, her voice warming slightly. "You can come over and—"

Whatever she'd been about to say was drowned by a banging on the bathroom door. "Tessa, are you still in there? Goodness, woman, Mia's cooking never affects *me* that way."

"Hold on," I whispered into the phone. "Go away," I called to Gage.

"Sorry, no can do. Dylan wants to play hide-and-seek, and you're supposed to play with us. He's outside hiding now, and I'm going to start counting. You get until one hundred before I come to find you. If I do, you'll be it."

He was impossible. "I'll be out in a minute," I said.

"Okay, but I'm timing you for two minutes, and then I'm starting."

Ignoring him, I reached over and flushed the toilet. I waited until I couldn't hear anything on the other side of the door before saying to Bailey, "What's the address?" I typed it onto my word processing program. "I'll be there as soon as I can."

"I'll be waiting."

We hung up without saying good-bye.

In the room, I found a pen, jotted the address on the inner side of my arm, and shut the laptop. I started for the door, but on second thought, I took the card Ridge had given me the day before and slipped it into my pocket.

I found Gage alone in the kitchen. True to his word,

he'd started counting without me. "Fifty-three, fifty-four, fifty-five." He grinned. "Better hurry. Not much time left." He looked so normal, so attractive, so much a part of me sitting there that I wanted to go up and put my arms around him and hold him. I wanted to see him smile like that every day. To play hide-and-seek with his own children—even if they weren't mine, too.

He'd stopped counting and was staring at me. I felt his gaze like a touch, and I shivered. "Tessa," he began.

I shook my head because it hurt too much. "You'll never find me."

I ran.

Out the door and to his Jeep in the driveway, hurling myself inside and praying he wouldn't hear the engine.

Halfway to Bailey's, I began to worry about Charlie. Where did he stay when he was in town? If he was at his sister's, he might be suspicious of my questions. No, I'd be careful.

I pulled up to Bailey's house—a one-story, white affair that obviously needed a new coat of paint. The yard was meticulous, though, and I suspected a lot of Bailey's tan was real and not canned.

I sat in the Jeep for a while, feeling apprehensive. Maybe this wasn't a good idea. Maybe I was getting into more trouble than I could handle. Yet I had to do something. Talking to Bailey was the right thing—I just needed a backup in case things went wrong.

Pulling out my phone, I placed a call to Ridge Harrison. His voice-mail picked up. "It's Tessa Braxton," I said. "It's about Gage. I don't know if Mia told you—I don't remember her telling you yesterday—but she said

Skeet had a large amount of money on him before the fight, but that after the murder it was gone. I think Charlie Norris was there that night, and I think he killed Skeet with a poker just like he did his own father in California. You should look up the case—no way that's a coincidence. I think Bailey Norris covered for her brother that night like she did when her father was killed. I'm parked in front of her house now. I'm going to ask her if her brother was in town that night."

I hung up. I might be wrong, and if I was, I could apologize later. However, the fact that two people connected to Charlie had died from an attack with a poker was too coincidental. Even if Ridge didn't believe me, his sense of honor would force him to look into the matter, especially if something went wrong tonight with Bailey. I forced a laugh. It's not like she'd make me disappear or anything. Still, there was nothing wrong with telling someone where you would be.

I went up her cement stairs and knocked on the door, painted a startling emerald green that contrasted with the white house but somehow didn't look hideous. Bailey opened the door, a fake smile on her lips. She'd changed her off-white outfit for a red tank, black skinny jeans that showed off her long limbs to advantage, and matching high heels with sharply pointed toes. As in the police station, her eyes ran over my jeans, which were the worse for wear after my adventures of the day, and the T-shirt that showed a blotch where once again I'd dropped a bit of my last meal.

Great. She was good at intimidation, I'd give her that. "Come in," she said.

I hesitated, wishing I could stay outside and talk, but she'd opened the door, and I didn't see her brother around, so I went inside.

The interior was lovely, with nice furniture and numerous decorations that went well together. I didn't know much about style, but I knew what I liked, and we had similar taste. Leading me into a sitting room, she indicated that I should sit on the leather couch. She took the love seat opposite. I noticed she had a fireplace, but it was a gas one and wouldn't need a poker.

"So," she said. "How can I help you?"

"It's more like how you can help Gage. As long as he has this murder hanging over him, he can't go on with his life."

"Looks like he's gone on quite nicely to me."

I snorted. "Well, he hasn't."

"You said on the phone that your marriage wasn't real." There was an eagerness in the way she asked the question, an eagerness that tore at my heart and increased my resentment.

"That's right. I was engaged to someone else, and I found out he was unfaithful, but I needed to get married for financial reasons I don't want to go into now. Gage helped me out." I couldn't bring myself to tell her the actual wedding had been fake.

"I knew there had to be something." She grinned in triumph.

"Why?" Because she couldn't imagine him loving someone like me?

"He was adamant about not marrying, of not having children who would grow up in the shadow of a murderer like he did. I thought that feeling would fade over the years, that it wouldn't matter in the end."

"But it hasn't."

She shook her head slowly. "No. He broke things off before he went to prison. He wrote at first, and I thought we'd be okay, but prison made it worse. He stopped writing. It was . . . difficult."

"You knew he was innocent," I prompted.

"I believed he was."

"Why didn't the police look further? Why didn't you say something?"

She shook her head. "I don't know. It all happened so fast."

The trial had taken months, so that wasn't exactly true.

"I was stunned," she continued, her voice growing ever more faint. "Everything was falling apart, and nothing I did helped. I expected the police to find the truth, but they didn't. Losing Gage . . . I never got over that."

I could sympathize. All those months he'd hidden behind that beard, and I hadn't cared enough to really get to know him. I had only myself to blame for the emptiness I'd feel when I had to leave him for good.

"It must have been really hard for you," I said. "Your brother must have been a big support to you during that time."

She froze, her eyes digging into mine before she made an obvious attempt to relax. "My brother wasn't here. He was in the navy."

A lie. Charlie had only been in the navy for a year before they kicked him out.

"He didn't come home to help you once he heard?"

"I didn't tell him."

Yet Charlie had told us outside Mia's how devastated Bailey had been after Gage had broken things off. "Oh, I'm sorry. I got the impression you were close."

"We are. I know my brother has some substance abuse issues, but he's a good person, and he always takes care of me." She crossed her arms in front of her, and I was wondering if she was thinking of the torment she'd suffered from her father.

I switched tactics. "Why do you think Gage is innocent?"

"Because he wouldn't kill someone in cold blood."

"Not even a man who raped his sister?"

She showed no surprise. "No."

"Then it has to be someone else. Mia said Skeet had a lot of money on him before the fight, but afterward it disappeared. Someone took that money. If the police start an investigation into anyone who received a chunk of money at that time, we might find some answers. It might be related to drugs."

Bailey stood and paced to the fireplace. "It's been too long to track that sort of thing. Besides, anyone taking the money wouldn't be that stupid, I wouldn't think."

"Then what can we do?" I arose and went to stand beside her. "You know as well as I do that Gage's future is gone unless we can prove his innocence. Someone else was there that night. I know it. If you care about him, you'll help me find the real killer."

She turned toward me. "There's nothing either of us can do. He'll have to get over it." Her voice was bitter and desolate, and that's when I knew for certain I was right.

She might not be happy about it, but she was covering for Charlie. "There's no evidence anyone else was there."

Nothing for it but to confront her straight on. "Skeet was killed with a poker, just like your father."

Her eyes narrowed. "So? I told you—Charlie wasn't in town."

"Wasn't he?" I looked at her pleadingly. "A poker is a pretty odd coincidence, don't you think? Look, I know Charlie protected you from your father, but you can't let Gage suffer like this. You love him. How long are you going to trade his life for Charlie's?"

She didn't reply, but I saw the answer in her face. She would do it forever.

"Never mind," I said. "I'll see myself out."

As I started for the door, she came alive, her hand reaching out to grab a statue of two children from the coffee table. She came at me fast.

The last thing I knew was a terrible pain slicing through my skull.

14

"What have you done?" The male voice penetrated my unconsciousness, forcing me awake. I was lying on the floor in Bailey's sitting room, my cheek pressed against the tan carpet. Something was wrapped around my head.

"Me? It's all your fault! You're the one who got me into this mess!" It was Bailey's voice, weepy and desperate. "If you hadn't killed Skeet, Gage would never have gone to prison!"

"What are you talkin' about? I didn't kill anyone."

I knew the other voice now. Bailey's brother, Charlie, but without the alcohol slurring his speech. Ridge must have worked miracles in the hours since I'd seen him and Bailey at the police station.

"Yes, you did. You killed him, and you took Gage away from me! I had to sacrifice him for you, and I'll never, ever forgive you for that."

I opened one eye and saw Bailey in her brother's arms, hitting his chest. He was barely taller than she was and slight of build, but he was holding his own.

"Is that what you've been thinkin' all these years?"

"You had the money—I saw it!" She hit him again.

"Yes, I went there and took the money back. Why shouldn't I? It was ours. That jerk had drained us long enough."

"But he had the poker! What if he'd given it to the cops?"

"After all these years, I doubt it was even the same poker. There certainly wouldn't be prints on it after so much time. It'd be our word against his. Anyway, I didn't kill him. I wouldn't do that to you. I wouldn't."

"It wasn't your decision to make!"

I was testing my body as they argued. Everything seemed to work, though the side of my head pounded horribly, and my hands were secured behind my back.

"Mine every bit as much as it was yours," Charlie said. "I took care of it all, didn't I? And whatever happened with Gage, you owed me."

"You really didn't kill Skeet?" Bailey stepped away from him and sank to the couch.

"I told you already that I didn't. Is that why you wanted me to get out of town so fast that night? I knew I shoulda stayed. When I heard about the poker, I thought *you'd* killed him."

Bailey's body shook, and her chest heaved. Sobs came between each breath. "All these years. All for nothing."

"Not all for nothing. We're safe. No one knows about our old man."

"What are we going to do?"

Both were silent, and I shut my eyes to think. I'd learned three things: Skeet had been blackmailing the

Norrises in connection with their father's death, Bailey suspected her brother had killed Skeet, and Charlie had thought she'd done it. One of them had to be lying, because whoever had killed Skeet had used the same kind of weapon that had killed their father.

Or had it been a coincidence after all?

Impossible.

At any rate, if neither of the siblings had committed the murder, that left only Gage and Mia—or a drug deal gone bad.

I hadn't learned very much at all.

Bailey's heaving subsided, and she spoke in a much calmer voice. "They'll never believe us now that we took her."

"What do you mean?" Charlie sat beside her. I peered at them through my lashes, my eyes open only a crack. Both were staring at me. Charlie was fingering his sparse goatee. His long hair was greasier than I remembered, a few strands escaping his ponytail and lying limply over his ears.

"I mean, once she tells the police what I did to her, they'll never believe that one of us didn't kill Skeet. They'll find out you took the money, and that he was blackmailing us. They'll find out what happened with Father."

"What about that cop? He got his dad to drop the case back then."

"That was because I told him what that monster did to us. He never knew about the poker—I didn't tell him. I don't know if he'd help us now."

"He's gone on you. I think he would."

"What could he do?"

They were silent for a long moment, or maybe I lost consciousness. My head ached worse than during overnight inventory at my father's factory. A dribble of blood leaked from the bandage into my left eye. At least it wasn't gushing.

"The way I see it," Bailey said finally, "the only problem is her. If she's gone, everything stays the same."

"Not everything. Gage would inherit all that money that investigator you hired said she was going to get, and once you and Gage get married, it'll be ours. Think of it—half a million and monthly payments, too. We wouldn't have to worry again."

"It would make life a lot easier, that's for sure. Maybe I could quit work and go into the field with him."

Charlie snorted. "Like you could stand living out of a tent."

"I wouldn't mind if I was with Gage."

"Lie to yourself if you want. I don't believe you."

"I don't care what you think."

My mind took time deciphering the shocking meaning that seemed to have no relationship to the actual words. The two fed off each other, co-enablers with a distorted sense of right. Knowing about my trust fund only made things worse. Money justified a lot of malicious deeds, as I'd learned from my father and Julian.

"He belongs to me," Bailey said. "She stole him."

More silence for the space of several heartbeats, and then Charlie said, "I'll get rid of the Jeep."

"Use gloves. Don't let anyone see you."

Something had been decided between them, and though exactly what remained unspoken, I knew it meant trouble for me. Charlie disappeared briefly, returning to slip his hand into my back pocket for Gage's keys. I waited until he was gone before opening my eyes and struggling to a sitting position. Bailey watched me from the couch, her brown eyes placid instead of troubled. That scared me more than anything. Her mind was made up.

I had to try anyway. "Bailey, please let me go. Look, you won't get the money. The marriage wasn't valid. Gage was worried I'd have regrets, so he paid a friend to fake it."

She barked a hoarse laugh. "Sounds like him. Stupid sense of chivalry cost him half a million bucks. Well, the money isn't as important as getting him. I'm *glad* you aren't really married."

"You have to help me prove he's innocent. Otherwise he won't marry you, either."

"I don't need you. I'll find my own way."

"By giving up Charlie to the police? Because the only way Gage will ever be free to live his life is to find the real murderer."

"Charlie didn't do it," she told me, but I could see by the deepening furrow between her eye that I'd made a dent in her armor.

"Maybe he just doesn't want you to know. Gage didn't do it, and Charlie's the one who turned up with the money, so he must have killed Skeet. It's the only explanation that fits. Look, I called Ridge before I came here, and I told him I thought you were covering for Charlie and that I was coming to see you. It's only a matter of time before he begins asking questions—especially if I'm missing."

I conveniently left out the fact that I hadn't actually

talked to him. For all I knew, he'd gone out of town for the night and wouldn't check those messages for days.

"Doesn't matter. I'll deny it. Anyway, he'll do anything for me."

"Not cover up a murder. He's dedicated to his job."

"Your coming here isn't my fault. He'll see that."

"I doubt it. Besides, he let Gage rot in prison, and he was innocent. Why not you?"

"Ridge wasn't on duty that night. He wasn't the one who arrested Gage."

"No, that was your fault."

She didn't reply.

"You were worried once Mia started asking questions, weren't you? Is that why you sent her that threatening note?"

"I don't know what you're talking about. I didn't send any note."

"Sure," I said. "But Gage knows about the note now. He'll never forgive you if you hurt Mia or me. He may not love me"—it wounded me to say this—"but he is my friend."

She jumped to her feet and began pacing. "Shut up, would you? I need to think!"

I'd been testing the tie on my hands and determined it was some kind of tape. No way was I getting out of it easily. "Just let me go, and I won't tell anyone," I lied.

She barked a laugh. "Yeah, right, and I'm supposed to believe you?"

"I know about your father. Charlie killed him, right? To protect you from his abuse. I know that makes you feel obligated to him, but what you did to Gage—that's not love. Tell me, does losing him atone for the six years he spent in prison for a crime he didn't commit?"

"Shut up, shut up, shut up!" she screamed, lashing out at me with the toe of her pump. Pain needled through my thigh where the sharp point hit. "Charlie said he didn't kill that creep. I believe him."

She sounded absolutely sure. A chill ran through me. Was it possible she had been the one responsible for Skeet's death? Had she sacrificed Gage for her own protection?

Yet she'd been so upset with Charlie. I wasn't sure what to believe.

Bailey began pacing the small room again, and I felt precious time ticking away. Once Charlie returned, my chances of escaping unscathed would plunge considerably.

"Please call Ridge," I urged. "He'll know what to do. He really likes you—I saw that right away."

A hint of a smile flashed over her face. "He's a kind man. But he isn't what you think, either. He's not perfect."

"Of course not. Neither is Gage. Or me."

She gave me a flat stare. "You shouldn't have gotten mixed up with Gage."

"I'm not mixed up with him."

She stopped pacing abruptly, her hands curling at her sides. "You think I can't see how you feel about him? I'm not stupid or blind. You care about him a lot more than you're saying. You may even love him, and what's worse, I think he believes he feels something for you." Venom laced these last words, and her eyes stabbed into mine as though by glaring at me I would either admit to her intelligence or disappear entirely.

Maybe she was right about Gage. I hadn't imagined the way he'd kissed me and how I'd felt—how we'd felt.

"You've got it all wrong," I said, before hope had a chance to grow any larger than a seed. "Gage will never let himself love anyone."

Someone slammed through a back door. We both turned at the clatter—me praying for rescue and Bailey with an animal readiness in every line of her slender body. She brought her hands forward, her fingers hooked like claws, though her fingernails were short and blunt, probably from her work in the yard.

"Look what I found." Charlie came around the corner and into the room, half-dragging, half-carrying a struggling Dylan. I glimpsed shock on Bailey's face before her features hardened to stone. "He was in the Jeep," Charlie said. "Hiding in the back seat."

He released Dylan, who immediately shot toward me, going to his knees and pushing his thin frame into my side. I could feel him shaking. "It's okay," I whispered to him before whipping around to face Bailey. "Let him go. He doesn't know anything. He's only a kid."

"Take them to your bedroom," Bailey said, ignoring me. "I have to think."

"Bailey!" I shouted as Charlie yanked me to my feet. "Don't do this!" Next to me Dylan let out a terrified sob.

"Wait," Bailey said, and Charlie froze. She crossed the three steps between us. Her hand drew back, and she slapped me hard. "Gage is mine. Remember that."

She nodded tersely at Charlie, who gave her a crooked smile that made him somehow resemble a scrawny rat.

His fingers dug into my skin, and his other hand closed around Dylan's narrow arm.

"I'll get some rope," Bailey said, "and meet you there."

Dylan's eyes were huge and frightened as Charlie pushed us down the hall. He looked more like Mia than ever, especially when she'd shown me the note. For his sake, I had to do something.

I twisted from Charlie's grasp and stepped away from him, hitting into the wall of the hallway with more force than I'd intended, and my breath whooshed out of me. Without stopping to see if anything was seriously damaged, I pushed off, slamming into Charlie's slight frame. He stumbled and hit his head against the wall. It didn't stop him. Roaring with anger, he came at me.

"Run!" I shouted at Dylan. "Run!" The boy's eyes opened even wider, but he hesitated only a second before obeying.

Charlie's fist jabbed my right eye, bringing a slicing, hot pain. Another shot landed in my stomach. I collapsed to the floor on my back, fighting for breath. He came at me again. I lashed out with my feet, taking him by surprise. He fell, but it was a short-lived victory. Uttering a curse, he jumped on me, pinning me with his weight, his fingers biting into my shoulders. "Don't," he said close to my face, "do that again."

I gagged on the rancid smell of his unwashed body and the tobacco on his breath. This close, the rot in his teeth was apparent. I might have felt sorry for him if he weren't trying to kill me. I wished I could crack my head into his and knock him unconscious, but I suspected that the way things were going, it'd only be me who'd suffer. Besides, my bruised and aching body rebelled at the idea.

"Okay," I surrendered. I moved my head a bit to see if Dylan had made his escape. If he had, would he know how to get help? We were too far from his house for him to know the way home, and he'd probably been taught to stay away from strangers.

Dylan wasn't in the hallway, and I allowed myself a sliver of satisfaction as Charlie yanked me to my feet, sending pain echoing through my head and torso. Charlie hesitated then, looking dazed, as though wondering what he should do next. Or maybe pondering the best way to make me pay. Heels clicked on the kitchen tile, coming our way. Bailey.

"Lose something?" she asked, stepping into the carpeted hallway. One hand rested on Dylan's shoulder. The other held a gun.

I'm sorry, Dylan's eyes said. A tear rolled down his cheek. I wanted to take him in my arms and hold him. I started forward, but the world wavered, dark patches appearing in my vision.

Dylan let out a cry as I stumbled and fell into blackness.

15

A soft, persistent touch like butterfly wings on my cheek cut through the pain in my body and my head, drawing me back to a consciousness I really didn't want. I forced my eyes open and jerked slightly when I saw Dylan's face close to mine. With a small intake of air, he drew his tied hands back from my cheek, the relief in his eyes evident. I wondered how long I'd been out. For some time, apparently. It was dark outside, the room lit only by a small lamp on the night stand.

I was lying on a bed on my left side, my head on a worn towel that was obviously meant to catch any blood escaping the cloth bandage around my skull. It didn't feel wet, so that was encouraging. My right eye was swollen, but I could see through it fine. My hands were still tied behind my back. Moving to a sitting position was harder than I expected, and I gave it up halfway through, sinking back to the bed.

"What happened?" I asked.

I meant after I'd passed out in the hall, but Dylan began back at Mia's. "I knew you were leaving, so I hid in the Jeep. Uncle Gage always finds me, so I thought if I hid in the Jeep he wouldn't for at least a little while." He paused before adding, "I'm really sorry."

I could see he felt bad and that he was worried I'd be angry or that he might have been the reason I was hurt. But though I wished he weren't here with me, it wasn't his fault Bailey and her brother were psycho.

"It's okay," I said. "We're going to be okay."

"Why's Bailey doing this? Why did that man hurt you?"

This time his anxiety forced me to sit up all the way. Too late I realized my hands had also been secured to the frame of the bed, and my arms wrenched painfully. I slid closer to the edge of the bed until the pressure eased. "It's about your uncle. You know why he went to prison, right?" I didn't know how much they had told him, either about Gage's situation or about his own conception.

"He killed someone?"

I nodded. "Only he didn't really."

"That's what my mom says, but she doesn't know who really did it. Do you?"

His terminology told me he had no idea Skeet had played any part in his life, and I was glad for that. I hoped it was something he wouldn't have to deal with for a long, long time. "I don't know for sure. That's why I came here. I thought Bailey could help." I didn't want to tell him too much because I still hoped Bailey's obsession with Gage wouldn't allow her to hurt his nephew. They might get away in the short term with making me disappear, but Dylan's disappearance would be noted quickly. His family would scour the entire city looking for him.

Unless they thought I'd taken him away from the city.

Great. With the Jeep missing, that was exactly the conclusion they would draw. Panic made my breath come faster as I imagined my face and Dylan's flashed over the TV news, the searchers focusing on Flagstaff and Phoenix, my sister and parents being questioned.

Wait. Wouldn't I have taken my clothes and my laptop before running off? And the rest of my money and credit cards? Clothes for Dylan, a favorite toy? The police would have to realize we hadn't left voluntarily, despite the missing Jeep.

The only thing I knew for certain was that eventually Dylan's involvement would add urgency to the search. Good for me. Bad for him. If I'd been the one choosing, I'd opt to have him safe at home, hiding in the chicken coop or under Mia's bed.

"Okay, look," I said. "If there's ever a chance, you need to run away. Far away. Get to some neighbor's house and tell them to call the police and your mother."

"I just knock on their door?"

"Yes. Tell them you were kidnapped and that Bailey Norris has your aunt tied up. Don't stop for anything. Don't worry about me. Got it?"

He nodded solemnly. "Uncle Gage will find us. He always finds me."

I had to smile at his faith. "Sure he will." I wished I could share his belief, but I knew I had to depend on myself. Even if Gage noticed right away that the Jeep was missing, some time would pass before they found us. The Norrises would have to act tonight while it was dark. By tomorrow, getting us—or our bodies—out of this small town would be next to impossible. That meant I had to somehow free us both and call the police.

Holding back tears, I ran one foot along the bed, following the rope to the middle of the bed frame where I'd been tied.

"I can't untie that," Dylan said, lifting his hands, which unlike mine had been secured in front instead of behind his back. "There's too much tape on my fingers."

What I needed was to free my hands so I could untie the rope connected to the bed, but I couldn't do anything with my hands taped behind my back. "Watch this." Sitting, I pulled my knees to my chest and hunched my back, working my tied hands under me. Pain reverberated through my body as I tugged and pulled myself through the circle of my arms.

"Nice." Dylan said when I'd finished, sounding so much like Gage, I smiled as I began tearing the tape off with my teeth.

"Family talent," I said, silently blessing the limberness my father always bragged about at my mother's parties. It was one of the few things I knew about his early life.

We froze as steps came down the hall. With a startled sound, I reversed my hands again. Something popped in my shoulder, but the pain lasted only an instant. I threw myself down on the bed with my head on the towel.

Dylan climbed onto the bed next to me, his thin body pressed against my stomach.

"You'll have to carry her if she's not awake," Bailey said as they entered the room.

I certainly didn't want to be carried by the odorous Charlie, so I opened my eyes. "Please, Bailey," I said.

"Shut up." Her voice was so tight it was a wonder any sound came out at all.

Charlie bent down to untie the rope from the bed frame. After several minutes of struggling, he swore and pulled out a pocket knife to cut the rope. He did the same with the rope holding Dylan. Then he held the ends like dog leashes. "Come on."

"Where are we going?"

"You don't need to know." He was standing so close that I gagged at the strong smell of cheap whisky on his breath. He'd been drinking again while I was unconscious and was jumpy and nervous as though yearning for a fix. He carried himself like a man on the verge of losing control.

I looked at Bailey, whose face was pale gray. "Bailey, you don't want to do this."

"You're right. I don't. But I'll do what I have to." To protect her brother, I inferred. To win Gage.

At my side Dylan whimpered, and my frustration grew. With my tied hands, I couldn't even comfort him.

Cloaked in darkness, they dragged us out to Charlie's old Ford and shoved us none too gently into the backseat, which smelled like stale hamburgers. Charlie drove, which made me more nervous than being tied up.

"Stop swerving," Bailey ordered. "Can't you be sober for anything?"

"Excuse me," he snapped. "Maybe I'd stay sober if I didn't always have to clean up after your messes."

"My mess? None of this would have happened if you hadn't come back."

"You think Mia would have left it alone?"

"I mean, if you hadn't tried to get the money back that night."

"Well, I only had to get the money because you killed dear old dad." His voice slurred the words. "Who cleaned up what mess then? Do you really wonder why I drink? It's the only thing that stops me from seeing his face and you with that poker. I got rid of it then, but I'm not a murderer, Bailey. Whatever you do to them, you'll have to do it yourself."

"Shut up. You always did have too big a mouth."

I stared from one to the other, finally understanding. Charlie hadn't murdered their father. Bailey had. That meant she might love her brother, but she had been primarily protecting herself when she'd allowed Gage to go to prison for Skeet's murder. If Charlie had gone to prison, no doubt the trial would have dredged up his past—and Bailey's guilt.

"I ain't gonna do it," he insisted. "I'll get them to the house. That's all."

"That's all you need to do. For now."

I'd wasted my breath appealing to Bailey. Charlie was the one with remorse, if it could be called such.

Tears leaked from Dylan's eyes. Frantically, I looked around for something to help—anything—but the road was completely deserted. Bailey half turned in her seat, watching me, the gun in her hand.

"Where are we going?" I tried again, forcing a calmness I didn't feel into my voice.

"An old house on my aunt's property. Very ancient and very dangerous. Accidents have happened there to people who break in and investigate."

So that's how it was. I hoped Dylan didn't understand the implication. If only I'd told Gage I'd intended to go see Bailey. He'd surely know about her aunt's property. Thank heaven I'd left that message with Ridge. If we could stay alive long enough, he'd be able to find us.

"House" was a loose term for the place they took us. The tiny, dilapidated, two-story wooden structure was missing half its shingles, most of the long porch had fallen off, and the windows were boarded from the outside. Everywhere, the paint had curled up to reveal gray wood.

"It's changed," Charlie said, killing the engine.

"No one's lived in it in eight years, and it was bad before Mother died. If anyone would have been willing to buy the place, I'd have practically given it away."

"I don't remember it being this bad."

"You don't remember having to go outside for water? The outhouse? What about sleeping on that flea-bitten mattress in that poor excuse for a second floor? Wasn't anything but a glorified loft. Worse than an attic." The sourness in her voice jabbed at us all.

"That, I remember. You couldn't get out of here fast enough."

"And now we're back." Bailey tossed him a flashlight and looked at me. "Don't try anything."

Bailey had to drag a piece of broken stair over to reach the doorway from the fallen porch. She opened the door with a key, and Charlie half-pushed, half-lifted us into the small living room.

"Did you leave that here?" Charlie asked, as Bailey lit an old-fashioned kerosene lamp sitting on a broken chair by the window, the only furniture in the room.

Bailey shook her head. "It was here the last time I had to kick a bum out. I thought it might still be here, if no one else had broken in."

Light danced on the ripped and faded chintz curtains and pieces of broken glass that still clung to the frame. I couldn't see the room well in the dim light, but one entire wall had oak paneling that looked remarkably intact. Another wall near the corner held a built-in bookcase with cupboards on the bottom, one of the doors drooping on its hinge.

Charlie motioned us through the living room to an even tinier bedroom. He laughed. "Our aunt's old log bed is still here, good as ever."

From the meager illumination of their flashlights, I could see flowery paper peeling from the walls, which were also darkened with water damage. In one corner someone had made a fire at one time. A hobo, maybe? One of the boards attached to the outside of the window had been partially removed. Not big enough a hole for a person, but plenty big for smoke to escape. A tattered quilt covered the bed, thick with dust and grime, but there weren't any other pieces of furniture or belongings. Bailey must have taken everything of value when her aunt and mother died.

Charlie tied our ropes around the thick log running horizontally along the bottom of the bed below the thin mattress. "What are you going to do to them?" he asked, sounding nervous.

"I don't know. I have to think." She strode to the door and into the living room without a backward glance.

I sat on the bed, and Dylan buried his face in my lap.

"Please, Charlie," I whispered. When he didn't respond, I added, "This is only going to make things worse. Please let us go."

"I can't." His body language told me he was uncertain, scared. He didn't want to be here.

"I know you aren't responsible for this. Bailey is. You can't let her hurt us. She won't get away this time."

His head jerked back and forth, like a man in a mild seizure. "She's my sister."

"She's a murderer."

"He deserved to die. He hurt her bad. He hurt all of us. My mother cried every night."

"That doesn't give Bailey the right to hurt me. Or Dylan."

"You shouldn't have come. You shouldn't have messed with Gage. He belongs to Bailey."

The set of his shoulders was changing, becoming decided. I hurried with more words. "Bailey had her chance with Gage, but she let him go to prison. Besides, you're the one who told him to stay away from her. And what about Dylan? He's just a boy. He didn't choose any of this. He's been a victim from the beginning, starting with Skeet."

Even in his diminished capacity, Charlie knew what I was saying, but Bailey's control over him was too absolute. "I can't." He set down his flashlight on the edge of the mattress and scuttled to the door, pulling it shut behind him.

"That went well," I said to myself, hoping the sarcasm would make me feel better. It didn't. At least Charlie had left us the flashlight.

Dylan lifted his head and stared at me. "What do we do now? Are they going to hurt us?"

I didn't know the answer to the second question, so I dealt with the first. "First we're going to get out of here. Let me up, okay?"

He moved off me, and I left the bed and sat down beside it, pulling my body through my linked hands as I had at the house. The tape was tighter at my wrists in the new position in front, but I was much more comfortable. As I used my teeth on the tape around my wrists, Dylan started biting on his own tape.

In minutes, my tape dropped clear. Unfortunately, the knot on the rope around my wrists proved more difficult. The knot secured to the log frame was even tighter. I'd never get it off in time, but maybe I could free Dylan. I moved closer to him, helping him with his tape. His knot was also tight, but without the tape he was able to pull first one hand free and then the other.

"Ow," he said. "That hurt."

"Yeah, but you're free." I held out my wrists. "Can you get this knot?"

He tried, but his little fingers weren't strong enough. "I'm sorry."

"Don't be. Look, the windows are boarded up from the outside. I think I can lie on the bed and bang them out with my feet. Maybe they won't hear us, and you can get out."

I heard him swallow in the silence. "Without you?"

"Once you're out, just keep following that little road until you find a house. Don't go on the road itself in case Bailey's car comes. Stay to the side and get ready to hit the ground if you see a car coming from this direction. It's going to be a long, long way, but you can do it."

"It's dark. I'm afraid." His voice wobbled.

Of course he was afraid. I was forgetting he wasn't yet seven. Maybe there was another way. "You can take the flashlight." It would make him easier to find if they searched for him, but it was all I could think of.

His shook his head, his eyes huge in the darkness. "I can't go alone."

So that was out. "Okay, how about we play hide-and-seek? We'll find a place to hide you and make them think you left. Meanwhile, I'll keep trying to get free. If I can't, then in the morning when it's light, you can really sneak out and find a house to ask someone for help. Okay? You can keep the flashlight with you and turn it on when you need to. How's that sound?"

"Are you going to be here?"

I held up my tied hands. "Where am I going to go?"

"Oh, yeah. Where am I gonna hide?"

We both looked around the room, but we could see nothing except the big bed. "It's really low," I said, my hopes falling. "Besides, they'd look there. You'll have to try to get outside."

"Maybe in the closet."

I went with him as far as my rope allowed. Several dusty, old-fashioned dresses still hung in the closet, and others had fallen onto the floor. But it was too small. No way to hide even a scrawny child in that narrow space.

"You'll have to get out the window," I insisted, desperation seeping into my words. "You can hide near the house, can't you?"

"Wait." Dylan went to the corner where the fire had been built. As he moved closer, I could see the lower wall behind the wallpaper had completely burned away, forming a two-foot-high hole in the wall. The wall was ancient enough that it didn't contain plasterboard or insulation, so the hole couldn't be very deep, yet Dylan squatted down and disappeared, returning within a few seconds.

"Well?" I asked. I was working on my rope as I waited for him, but so far my teeth had about as much success as Dylan's fingers. Maybe if I got the rope wet, it might stretch. Of course if it didn't, the knot would be that much more difficult to untie. Besides, I was already thirsty, and I didn't know if I could wet it enough with my tongue.

"It goes into a cupboard in the other room," he said, his face and hands darkened with soot. "It's open a little. I can see them talking."

Ah, the bookcase I'd seen in the living room. I stopped working on my rope. "Okay, you go inside, and I'm going to make a lot of noise trying to get that board off the window. When they come to see what I'm doing, I'm going to tell them you jumped out the window, but really you need to get out of that cupboard and find someplace better to hide. Got it? A really great place, maybe in the kitchen. Or a closet somewhere." I didn't say up the stairs because I was too afraid they were rotted out. "I'll come get you when I can."

He thought about it for a moment. "So I turn off the flashlight, wait until I can't see them, then I sneak out of the cupboard and hide somewhere else?"

"Yes. I'll keep them here as long as I can. Shut the

cupboard the way it was after you leave it, though, so they won't suspect."

"Shut the cupboard. Got it." He was still scared, but there was excitement in his eyes, too. Some part of him was enjoying this. Unlike me.

"You can use the flashlight to find a hiding place while they're in here, if you need to, but don't turn it on once you're hidden unless you're sure they aren't around."

He nodded. "Do I go now?"

"Yes."

Instead, he threw his arms around my legs.

Squatting down, I hooked my tied hands over him, returning his hug. "Look, Dylan, I'm going to do everything I can possibly do to get us out of here," I told him. "I won't leave you, no matter what."

"What if they take you away?"

"They won't, but if they do, I'll come back. I promise. You need to be brave."

"I will." He released me, ducked under my hands, and disappeared into the sooty hole. Without the flashlight, the room went dark.

I lay on my back on the bed, taking my time so he'd have a few minutes to grow accustomed to the small space and what he had to do. With my back balanced on the edge of the bed, I could reach the window well enough with my feet.

Show time.

There wasn't much glass left in the window, but it was completely covered with boards, except for a small opening someone had made, presumably to let out smoke. That opening was where I'd begin. I brought both feet up, glad that I was still wearing my tennis shoes, and gave it all I had. I hit it once, twice, and a third time. The impacts hurt all the way up my legs, but I knew I wouldn't have a lot of time before Bailey and Charlie came in.

On the third kick, I felt a board give. Was it enough to fool them? Probably not. I slammed my feet at it again. This time a piece of glass in the top corner of the window came loose, bounced off my calf, and sailed over my head onto the floor. Pain radiated from my leg where the wickedly sharp point had hit, but I didn't have the luxury of indulging in the torment. I slammed my feet against the boards twice more. The lowest one fell off completely.

Yes! My leg throbbed from the cut, and my muscles were sore from the repeated impacts, but that was nothing compared to saving Dylan.

Wait a minute. The glass! If it was sharp enough to cut my leg, maybe it could sever my rope.

I rolled off the bed in my eagerness, barely finding my feet, but I was too late. Bailey and Charlie ran into the room, Bailey holding the lantern and looking furious.

"No one's going to hear you," she spat, once she was satisfied that I was still tied. "Besides, in a few minutes it won't make a difference. An accidental fire is not only going to get the city off my back as to the condition of this house, but it will also take care of you."

"You're insane," I retorted. If she really torched the house, I wouldn't be able to keep any of my promises to Dylan.

She shrugged. "Don't worry. I'll take good care of Gage. He won't—"

"Where's the kid?" Charlie interrupted.

Bailey's eyes narrowed, her fingers clawed at my shoulder. "Where is he?"

"Gone." I motioned to the window. "I told him to run. He's resourceful. You'd better give it up. The police will be here soon."

"Let's get out of here." Charlie took two steps toward his sister. "I know a place we can go."

"No." Bailey's voice was ice. "I'm not running again. Ever. Go find the brat and bring him to me. He can't have gone far."

Charlie limped toward the door.

"Wait." Bailey released me and held up a hand. "That opening isn't all that big. What if he didn't get outside? Check the room first."

As they searched the closet and under the bed, I prayed that Dylan had left the cupboard. *Go, Dylan,* I thought at him. All too soon, they headed toward the corner where the fire had been, and I held my breath. This was it.

Charlie knelt down and stuck his whole head inside. Was Dylan still there, shivering in a corner? Could Charlie see his tracks in the soot?

Please, I prayed.

The glass that had fallen from the window reflected a bit of stray light from its new place on the floor. With the exception of one large piece, it had shattered. I nudged the piece under the bed.

"Nothing," Charlie said. "But this wall here is burned clear through."

Bailey snorted. "It'll all be burned in a few minutes. Go outside and find him!"

I was too busy hiding my relief to dodge the blow

Bailey aimed at me. Her slap stung, but I refused to flinch. Besides, despite her height and fit body, she hit like a girl. A man would have used his fist. I would, too, if I ever got the chance. I opened my mouth to comment, when I remembered the gun. No sense in antagonizing her and dying sooner than she already planned. While I lived, there was still hope for both me and Dylan.

If she started a fire, would Dylan have the sense to run outside? Or would he do as so many children did and stay in hiding, believing they would be safe?

I chewed on my lip, deciding I probably knew the answer. I had to get free.

Bailey paced as we waited for Charlie. After an indeterminable length of time, he returned alone, shaking his head. "I can't find him. We need to get out of here."

"We'll torch the house and go look for him. There are only two houses remotely close enough for him to walk to, and he hasn't had enough time. We'll find him."

"That's not all," Charlie said. "There's a car coming up the road."

"Who is it?"

"I don't know."

I experienced a flood of hope. Maybe Ridge had finally received my message and put two and two together, perhaps after Gage reported us missing.

"Just someone out for a joyride," Bailey said. "Let's get started."

Ignoring her, Charlie went back into the living room. We heard him open the front door. "It's stopping," he called.

Bailey shoved her gun into her pocket before

smoothing her pants and following her brother. "I'll get rid of them." The lantern in her hand cast shadows on the wall as she left the room.

Were they so far gone they didn't realize they'd been caught? I sat down on the bed to wait. Ready to scream, if I had to, but sure it wouldn't be necessary.

"Bailey?" came a voice from outside. I heard the remains of the porch squeaking as someone climbed the ruined steps.

Bailey swore under her breath but loud enough to carry to where I sat.

The front door banged open.

"Gage," Bailey said, her voice curiously dull.

"What have you done?" Gage said. "Where are they?"

"Would you believe me if I said I didn't know what you're talking about?"

"No."

Silence.

I came to my feet and walked as far as my rope would allow, but all I could see of the other room was the chair by the window with the kerosene lamp burning.

Then Bailey shifted briefly into my view, her hand going to her pocket.

"Run!" I yelled to Gage. "She has a gun!"

16

Gage didn't run. I should have known he wouldn't. Maybe in his view he didn't have much to lose, but I didn't want to lose him. Not like that.

"Easy, Bailey," he said. "Don't do anything you're going to regret."

"I regret everything!" For the first time, she sounded ready to cry. Maybe Gage had that effect on women, because I was close to tears myself.

"Where do you have Tessa?" He spoke the words slowly and carefully, as though not wanting to startle Bailey. "Is she through that door?"

"I know she's not your wife."

"Then you know she's not a part of this. You have to let her go."

"It's too late."

"We can still leave before the police get here." This from Charlie.

"Will you shut up!" Bailey cried.

"Don't point that gun at me!" Charlie shouted.

"Easy!" Gage said.

I hated not seeing what was going on. I pulled at my bonds, trying to move the bed. The rope dug into the soft flesh of my wrist, sending pain up my arm. I pulled harder, worry giving me strength, and managed to move the heavy bed almost a foot.

Gage stood near the front door, though I could see only half of him, and also Bailey, who stood in front of him with the gun pointed at his chest. I couldn't see Charlie at all. Gage's eyes flickered past Bailey in my direction, and then back again. The tautness in his body relaxed marginally, and I was glad the light wasn't bright enough for him to see the black eye Charlie had given me.

"This is all your fault!" Bailey shrieked at her brother, her head turning to Gage's right.

Charlie snorted. "Me? You were the one with the bright idea of—"

"I mean Skeet." Her voice became pleading, as her face shifted back to Gage, but the hand with the gun didn't shake. "It was Charlie who killed Skeet, and I let you take the blame. I'm sorry."

"I didn't kill him!" Charlie insisted. "He was already dead. I just stole the money, and that's all. I swear it!"

"I believe you," Gage said. The calmness in his voice cut through whatever Bailey had been going to say and sent a shiver through me. Because I could tell his calm was only on the surface. I felt it in the way he stood, in the carefulness of his speech, the bland expression on his face. Over the past few days I'd learned this was how he hid emotion. Except the emotion he felt now wasn't frustration or attraction but plain and simple fury. Good thing he didn't know Bailey had been planning to burn the house down with Dylan and me inside, or he might not be able to hide it from her, either. "Bailey, please put down the gun."

"I didn't want you to go to prison, but I couldn't tell them about Charlie," Bailey said.

Charlie snorted. "For the last time, I didn't—"

"Charlie, be quiet." Gage's voice was a command, and to my surprise, Charlie shut up. "It's okay," Gage told Bailey. He took a slow step toward her.

"It's not okay! You'll never forgive me."

"I forgave you a long time ago. I know you suffered because of your father, and that Charlie was your only support growing up. I understand why you protected him."

"You know about my father? I never told you."

"You were afraid every time his name was mentioned— how could I not know something was wrong? I don't know how Skeet fits into all of that, but I saw how loyal you and Charlie were to each other." As he said it, I understood Bailey was another reason Gage had accepted his prison term. He'd suspected Charlie or Bailey, or both, and even though Bailey's allegiance had been clear in the way she'd deserted him, he'd wanted to protect her from further injury. Did he still love her beneath his anger, despite everything she had done?

"You really forgive me?" Bailey asked in a small voice.

"It's not your fault I went to prison. I should have fought more. The police should have looked harder for evidence."

She sighed and took a step forward, practically collapsing in his arms. "I didn't mean any of it to happen."

He took the gun from her, set the safety, and put it into the pocket of his jeans. "I know. It did happen, though, and there will be consequences. But you'll be okay." He set her gently, but firmly, away from him, and I saw one of Charlie's arms go around her. "I'm going to free Tessa, and then we're going to get out of here and go talk."

"We didn't hurt her." Bailey's petulant voice told me clearly that she wished she had, but with her collapse, the tough exterior she'd shown to me was completely gone.

The question was for how long?

Because Gage didn't know the whole truth—that she'd been protecting herself that night even more than her brother.

Gage turned his back on them, though every nerve in my body wanted to scream at him not to.

Yet neither Charlie nor Bailey moved as Gage strode into the bedroom toward me. He took the switchblade I recognized as belonging to our attacker in Vegas and put the tip under my rope, slicing it through.

He rubbed my wrists with his thumbs. It felt so good to be free, to have him touching me, though I could feel the slickness there too, from the cuts I'd sustained trying to move the bed.

"I'm sorry," he whispered.

That was much better than the expected, "Why didn't you leave it alone like I told you to?" The tension in my body cranked down a notch.

"Dylan's here," I said, keeping my voice low. "Hiding. We may have to look for him if he doesn't realize it's safe to come out. He stowed away in the Jeep. I didn't know until Charlie found him."

"I figured it was something like that." He traced the contours of my face with a finger, frowning at the swelling around my right eye.

"How'd you find us?" I wanted to throw myself in his arms, but I didn't know how that would be taken. Besides, Bailey and Charlie were watching us, though they weren't close enough to hear what we were saying.

"I started to worry when I found the car gone. I thought you'd gone back to Flagstaff or Phoenix. But when I couldn't find Dylan, either, I knew something was up. That's when I remembered you'd been in the bathroom when I went into the bedroom. At the time your laptop was missing from the dresser, so I figured you must have been doing something on it in secret."

"Observant, aren't you?"

His smile came easily. "I found Bailey's address where you'd typed it, and I broke every traffic law to get there. When she wasn't home and didn't answer her cell phone, I broke in. I saw blood on the towel in the bedroom and the rope tied to the bed frame." Here his calm cracked noticeably, and his grip on my arms tightened. Was that because he cared about me or because he believed Dylan was with me?

I was feeling dizzy, but I didn't know if that was from relief or from the fact that my pant leg was soaked in blood from the wound caused by the glass. "So what now? We both know you didn't kill Skeet."

Something flared in his eyes. Hope. "Then who did?"

I kept my voice low. "Could be Charlie, but I'm betting on Bailey. You guessed that her father was abusive, but what you don't know is that she's the one who killed him.

Charlie tried to hide the evidence, and that's why the police suspected him. Skeet claimed to have the poker that Charlie tried to hide from the police after their father's death, and he'd been blackmailing them for years. Might even be the same poker that ended up killing him."

I waited until the information sank in. I didn't blame Bailey as much for what she'd done to her father as I did for the years she'd stolen from Gage. The future she'd stolen. To me, at least, her actions were unforgivable.

"But she seems to think Charlie killed Skeet."

I shrugged. "Probably covering up. If it came down to her or Charlie, I bet she'd throw him to the wolves."

Gage gave a quick nod, as though coming to a decision. Turning, he started across the small room, keeping one hand around mine as though he was never letting go. Bailey and Charlie were waiting, fear and defiance in their eyes. Bailey had regained some of her backbone, and her eyes met mine without flinching.

"You both claim to have nothing to do with Skeet's murder," Gage said, "yet your father was killed with the same weapon."

"The same *kind* of weapon," Bailey corrected. "Charlie says he didn't do it."

"I thought Bailey did it," Charlie added.

Bailey flinched. "I wasn't even there." A shudder went through her as she stared at Gage. "You did it after all— didn't you?"

My flesh broke out in goose bumps, and I felt like screaming. Gage couldn't be guilty, could he? Yet Bailey and Charlie seemed sincere.

Gage regarded Bailey for several long seconds without

speaking. "I did not kill Skeet. If neither of you did it, and Mia didn't, who did?"

"Maybe Mia did," Charlie said. "She's fierce enough."

Gage's growl caused Charlie to jerk back several paces. "Not after what happened, she wasn't."

"Stop," I said to Charlie, encompassing Bailey in my glare as well. "Let's look at this from another direction. I don't believe in coincidences, so the question should be, if you two didn't do it, who else knew about your dad being killed with a poker?"

Silence fell as the two siblings stared at one another. I couldn't tell if they were about to burst into another round of blaming each other or finally say something useful.

When neither ended up speaking, I turned to Gage. "I should go find Dylan. He might not be hiding where he can hear us. He'll be scared, and Mia's probably out of her mind about him. The sooner we find him and call her, the better. This can wait."

Gage nodded. "I'll help." Was that because he didn't want to let me out of his sight? That was how I felt about him.

"I suppose anyone could have read the newspaper account if they wanted," Bailey said before we could leave. "But no one here ever mentioned it to me. Charlie and I never advertised the fact that our father was dead."

"We ain't stupid," Charlie muttered.

Bailey went on as if he hadn't spoken. "There was only one person I ever told about what happened to our father, but I didn't tell him about the poker or about the blackmail. Anyway, he wouldn't have killed Skeet. He's not like that." Her face blanched. "Wait a minute,

I think I know how he could have found out about the poker."

Gage stopped moving and faced her. "Who was it?"

"It was after his sister died. She was raped, you know—a few years before we moved here. She never was the same after. They took her to a lot of doctors, but she was mentally unstable and ended up taking her own life. Pills, I think. He was devastated. I was a mess, too, back then, and one day I told him about my dad. What he did. What I did. He didn't blame me. Not after what happened to his sister. He understood that my father was a monster."

The sound of a car drew my attention. I wondered who it was now. Ridge finally catching up with us? Mia? Or maybe even Aiden? Mia had said he was trying to come home early. What if he was somehow involved? He'd been around at the time of the murder, too.

Charlie peered out the window. "Police car," he announced.

"Must be Ridge." I was relieved that it wasn't Aiden or Mia. "I called him before I went to Bailey's." He was too late to do much good, but there was no time like the present to start pressing kidnapping charges against the Norrises.

"I called him, too," Gage said. "After I found the blood and the rope at Bailey's."

Bailey gasped. "We need to leave." Her fingers grasped at the sleeve of her brother's shirt.

Gage reached out and took her arm. "No more running, Bailey. I told you there'd be consequences. You need to face up to what you did."

"But it was him," she hissed. "He's the one I told about my father."

She'd told Ridge. Ridge, whose father had been the officer who closed the investigation into the death of Bailey's father, deciding the Norrises weren't guilty after all. Or maybe, influenced by his daughter's suicide, he'd decided they'd been justified. He would have known about the poker, and he could have told Ridge.

"Not Ridge." Gage was shaking his head. "I've known him forever. He's our friend, and he helped more than you can imagine with Mia that night."

"Then who else?" I demanded from them all. No one had an answer. I wanted to disappear and hide like Dylan, but I didn't want to leave Gage.

Ridge opened the door, the moonlight reflecting off the skin I could see through his cropped hair. "What's going on?" A worry line creased his brow.

"Nothing," Bailey said quickly. Even I could see her smile was forced.

"She kidnapped me," I countered. "I want to file charges."

Bailey glared at me, but Gage nodded agreement. "You have to face it before you can put it behind you, Bailey."

"Kidnapping? Surely, that's a mistake." Ridge stepped into the house, using the door frame to pull himself up from the broken step. His voice was casual, but as with Gage, I sensed something beneath the calm. I didn't know him well enough to decipher what.

"No mistake. She was planning to set fire to this house with me and Dylan in it." I held up my bloody wrists. "We were tied up in the bedroom here."

Bailey stepped closer to Ridge. "She was going to blame Skeet's death on Charlie! You know what reopening that investigation will mean." She looked pleadingly at Ridge, who seemed to melt under her gaze. He put an arm around her, and she sagged against him. But it was all an act. I couldn't miss the brief look of fear she gave him when he glanced away.

"It's all over now," Gage soothed. "Look, we're about to get Dylan and leave. Why don't you escort Bailey and Charlie to the police station, and we'll meet you there?"

"I didn't kill him," Charlie said. "Skeet or my father. And I've only been doing what Bailey told me to tonight. I don't want to go to the police station. They'll give me a drug test."

I rolled my eyes. Leave it to Charlie to worry about his drugs.

"No one thinks you killed Skeet," Ridge said. "I believe it was because of the drug money he was carrying. If I'd had more experience then, I would have been able to convince the lead detective of that. Many people would kill for a lot less than five thousand dollars."

"It was ours," retorted Charlie. "That's why I took it back." He paused a minute before adding, "How'd you know it was five thousand, anyway? Did Bailey tell you?"

"Shut up, you idiot!" Bailey ordered.

Everyone else had gone perfectly still.

"Mia told us Skeet had money," Ridge said. "And Tessa reminded me tonight when she left her message."

Gage took a step toward Ridge. "Mia never knew how much money. Skeet just waved it under her nose. There's only one way you could have known—you were there."

He reached for the gun in his pocket, but Ridge beat him to it, drawing out his police revolver.

"Don't," Ridge warned.

"It was you," Gage said. "You killed him. Why?"

Ridge didn't answer. "Slowly take out your gun and set it on the floor. Push it to me with your foot." When Gage didn't comply, he shifted the gun to my head, keeping his eyes on Gage. "Do it."

I began trembling. I'd never had a loaded gun pointed directly at me before. It was probably twice the size of Bailey's smaller pistol.

Gage did as he was told, the awkward movement of his body advertising his reluctance. Ridge bent down to retrieve the gun and tucked it into his pocket.

"I couldn't let Skeet get away with what he did to Mia," Ridge said. "I saw how much pain my sister endured after she was raped. Even with Aiden around, I knew Mia's life would be hell. I had to do something for them—and for Bailey, too. She'd suffered enough without that creep blackmailing her anymore."

"You sent Gage to prison." This from Bailey, who had taken a step away from him. "You took him away from me!"

"I didn't see *you* fighting for him," Ridge retorted.

"I had to protect Charlie."

Ridge shook his head. "You mean yourself."

Ah, so he'd reached the same conclusion I had.

"When I confronted Skeet about Mia," Ridge continued, "he accused me of being a hypocrite, of protecting a murderer. You, Bailey. But I knew you were the victim. I didn't mean to actually kill Skeet, not at first.

I just wanted to teach him a lesson before taking him in and booking him, but I realized he'd end up walking like too many others, and I got angry. Especially when he boasted about what he'd done to Mia. I hit him with that poker, the one I'd found earlier in his car. I did it for you, Bailey. For Mia and Aiden and my sister, Chloe. Even for Dylan. It was justice."

He smiled, shifting his eyes to Gage. "I thought you'd wake up and run away, and that because of the money his death would be attributed to drugs. I didn't know Charlie would take the money or that you'd stay and call the police."

"Baloney," I scoffed. "You *wanted* Gage to go to prison. You wanted Bailey for yourself." As his eyes narrowed, I mentally slapped myself. Scoffing at a man who was pointing a gun at you is not exactly the wisest course of action. I needed to control myself, no matter how angry I was in Gage's behalf.

"Maybe," Ridge said a little sadly. "Not that I ever had a chance with her. But tell me this, how can a lifetime of doing good, of helping those who are too weak to help themselves, be destroyed in a single moment, especially by scum like Skeet? I know what I did was wrong, but I also know he deserved what he got."

"Did Gage deserve to spend six years in prison for something he didn't do?" I asked, my tone slightly subdued.

Gage gave me a look that clearly ordered me to shut up. "You can make this right," he told Ridge, taking a step and diverting Ridge's attention from me. The gun now aimed at Gage's chest.

"The one and only thing I did in my entire life that was wrong," Ridge continued as if we hadn't spoken. "Back in high school I got my dad to back off Bailey and Charlie. Since becoming an officer, I've caught every rapist who ever committed a reported rape in my city. I made sure their arrests were solid. I've risked my life on too many drug cases to count. I've helped dozens of women free themselves from domestic violence. I've tracked drunk drivers to make sure they stay sober while they drive. I've gotten stupid cats down from trees, and once a child. All that has to say something about me, about who I really am. It can't all mean nothing because of one stupid mistake."

I expected him to become emotional with this outburst, but all the words were calm. Premeditated. He'd planned what he'd say, perhaps for years.

Gage took another step away from me. "Of course not, Ridge. You've done a lifetime of good. Don't let that end tonight."

"I won't." Ridge gave us a smile that didn't quite reach his eyes. "I want to continue to help people. That's why I have to do this. I tried to warn Mia with the note, but she didn't listen. This is her fault, really, if you want to blame someone." He glanced at Charlie. "Take us to where you had Tessa tied up. Everyone, go in front of me, or I *will* start shooting."

He would kill us so he could continue doing good? He was insane—that was the only explanation for his behavior. Perhaps instability that had prevented his sister from recovering from her attack was genetic.

Gage and I had no choice but to follow Charlie and

Bailey back to the tiny bedroom. At least I hadn't found Dylan. For now, he was still safe. Somewhere.

"Charlie, tie up Tessa and Bailey."

"No," Bailey whimpered. "Please, Ridge."

"I'm sorry, Bailey, but you're the price I have to pay for my sins. Losing you will atone for it, and it will end your suffering. He will never love you like I do." There was the slightest crack in Ridge's voice, but beyond that, he remained calm.

"He forgave me!" Bailey said, tears sliding down her cheeks.

Ridge shook his head. "It doesn't matter. You're a murderer, and you aren't capable of loving anyone but yourself. I should have understood that years ago. Fortunately, we will right that wrong tonight. You and Charlie will both pay."

"Whatcha talkin' about?" Charlie growled. "I didn't do nothin'."

"Shut up and tie them."

The cuts on my wrists burned as Charlie retied my rope. I felt more than saw Gage start to move, but the gun shifted to me again and stopped him in mid stride. Ridge checked my rope and was satisfied, but he made Charlie retie Bailey's.

"You shouldn't have done that, Charlie. I can't have her getting away before the fire, can I? And now it seems we have a problem. What to do about you and Gage? After all, there are no more ropes." In a rapid movement, Ridge slammed his gun down on Charlie's head with a sickening crack.

Charlie crumpled without a sound. Bailey let out a sob.

With a guttural roar, Gage launched himself at Ridge. They stumbled back, grappling for the gun. Gage was stronger, but Ridge was police trained. Plus, he was insane, which seemed not only to make him oblivious to pain but to give him additional strength. He brought up his knee, aiming for Gage's groin. Gage punched him hard in the face. They slammed into the wall near the door, and the flimsy structure collapsed under the impact. The gun fell from Ridge's hand and clattered out of reach.

I prayed. There was nothing else I could do, as the men rolled around on the ground, fists pounding. I went to the end of the rope, almost able to see the entire living room now that much of the wall was missing.

Ridge was on top, one fist aiming a blow. Gage arched and twisted, slithering out from under him and leaping to his feet. Ridge met him halfway, the two appearing locked in a strangely graceful dance as they exchanged powerful blows. Ridge stumbled back toward the outside door, breathing hard. Gage stepped toward him, every movement full of rage. Ridge took another step back. Was he going to run? Gage would never let him go.

I started to breathe again.

"You've learned a thing or two since we wrestled in high school," Ridge said, a note of admiration in his voice.

"You learn a lot in prison," Gage spat.

"Not enough, apparently." Ridge brought out Bailey's gun that he'd taken from Gage earlier.

My heart sank.

Gage lunged, and Ridge fired. Gage's body jerked.

"No!" I cried.

I couldn't see where the bullet had entered or how

much damage had been done, but Gage was still in motion, hammering into Ridge with his fists and body. Ridge fell to the ground, his head making a solid popping sound as it collided with the old hardwood floor. The gun skittered away from them. Gage fell on top of Ridge, and I couldn't tell if it was on purpose or if he'd collapsed. The light was too dim for me see if there was much blood.

Gage raised his fist and slammed it again into Ridge's face.

"You'll all go with me!" Ridge reached up his hand and jerked the chair holding the kerosene lamp. It fell to the ground. For a second nothing happened, and then flames burst out on the old curtains. I heard a light whooshing sound as the fire eagerly rushed up the ready tinder. Just the beginning. The whole place would be devoured within minutes.

Gage punched Ridge again, and his body went slack.

The fire crackled as Gage pushed himself to his feet. He took two steps toward me and stopped. With effort, he lifted his foot again, teetering.

He fell.

"Gage!" I screamed.

No answer.

Fire licked across the ceiling.

I had to do something or we would all die. I looked around me, searching for an answer. Bailey was kneeling next to Charlie, patting his cheek. "Charlie, Charlie. Wake up." She repeated the pitiful request like a litany.

I thought about helping her. If we could get him up, he might free us.

Or he might free Bailey and leave the rest of us to feed the fire.

Better to find another plan, though what I could do in my tied-up, wounded condition escaped me.

Wounded.

That's when I remembered the glass falling from the window and cutting my leg. Collapsing to my knees, I dived under the bed where I'd shoved it with my foot, cutting my fingers as I lifted it. Apparently sharp enough. I wedged it under the rope on my wrist, and something warm dripped down into my left hand. My brain registered pain, but I had to keep pushing.

Beside me, Bailey was sobbing. *Not so fun when you're*

the captive, is it? I wanted to taunt, but my wrist hurt too much, and I was too worried about Gage. And Dylan. If he'd hidden upstairs, I might not free myself in time.

Besides, if I said anything to Bailey, I might lose all my nerve and collapse in a shivering lump of fear.

The rope parted at last, and I dropped the glass before I did more damage. My entire hand was running with blood, but I wrapped it in the bottom of my T-shirt and pressed it against my stomach.

"Don't leave me here," Bailey whined. "Please."

I had no choice but to pick up the glass again and work on her ropes. No choice because I wasn't a monster, and I didn't want to be the cause of her death. I sliced her ropes more cleanly than I had my own, not even scratching her with the glass.

"You have to help me with Gage," I told her. "I've hurt my wrist, and I don't know if I can carry him alone. Once we get him out, you come back for Charlie while I search for Dylan. He's hiding in the house somewhere."

I didn't wait for her reply but hurried to where Gage had fallen. The sound of the fire was louder here, crackling merrily as if happy to be freed from its long prison. My face grew instantly hot. Near the window, only feet away from Gage, Ridge's body was aflame. My stomach twisted at the terrible sight, but there was nothing I could do for him.

I knelt beside Gage, feeling for a pulse. Relief spread through me as I detected a steady beating. He was alive— for now. But the bullet had hit him in the upper chest, and he was losing blood fast.

I glanced behind me at Bailey, who hovered uncertainly

over her brother's body. "Help me!" I shouted. "He's bleeding. I need your help!"

Bailey took a step toward me, her face frozen as she stared at Gage. Only one step, and she stopped, her face a mask of indecision. Then she turned and grabbed her brother's arm, dragging him out of the little bedroom and past me to the outside door.

I wasn't surprised. Not really. She'd chosen her brother once before, and nothing had changed in all these years. She loved Gage, but she cared more for Charlie—and herself. Maybe she was hoping we'd all die in the fire and her secret would remain safe.

Bailey stumbled at the door and fell. Coughing, she wrenched it open and reached for Charlie again.

"Gage!" I yelled in his face. "I need you! Wake up!"

No reply. I slapped his face hard with my good right hand. Once. Twice. His arm came up to stop the third blow. He tried to speak, but I talked over him, yelling to be heard over the greedy fire. "We need to get you outside."

He shook his head. "Dylan."

"I'll come back for him as soon as you're out."

"We'll get him together."

The whole ceiling was aflame. There wasn't time to argue. "Where would he go?"

"Kitchen. He always hides in the kitchen when we play inside."

I prayed he was right. I helped him to a crouch as best I could. He was a big man, but I had no idea he was so heavy. We stumbled together toward the open kitchen door. Several times I didn't think either of us would make it. We should have crawled, but I couldn't have helped him then.

I dared a look behind me and saw that Bailey had succeeded in getting outside. The oxygen from the open door only fueled the fire more. It was too much to hope that she'd come back to help me with Gage.

Once in the kitchen, Gage shut the door behind us and immediately the roar of the fire dimmed, but I knew it was only an illusion of safety. Smoke still poured around the door, and the air was so hot that sweat dripped from our bodies.

"To the floor," I said, dropping flat. Gage followed my example, grimacing at the pain.

The kitchen was brighter than the bedroom had been before the fire, illuminated by the moonlight streaming through an intact, unboarded window. Unlike the rest of the house, it seemed to have much of its original furniture and other contents. Dishes and pans sat in piles along the short countertop and had obviously been used without washing. More transients, I supposed. The table was metal with a Formica top and matching chairs. Ugly and out-of-date, but sturdy and unbroken. Cupboards and closets filled the better part of two walls. I crawled toward them. Gage started for the other side, but he was moving slowly.

"Dylan!" I called. "Come out now."

"Dylan!" Gage echoed. "I'm here."

He wasn't in any of the closets, cupboards, or under the sink, and a feeling of horror crept into my mind. If I hadn't sent him away to hide, he would have been safe with us now.

"Look for something you'd never guess was big

enough." Gage had slumped up against a cupboard, apparently unable to move. He looked terrible and sounded even worse. "Something that couldn't possibly hold his size. He's good at pulling stuff over him. Lying down. Making himself small."

Impossible. The only thing in any of the cupboards besides loose trash was a wooden box that I was sure had once held potatoes because it resembled a box my grandmother had used. A burlap bag lined the bottom. Surely there hadn't been enough room inside to hide even a tiny little boy.

I backtracked toward the pantry where I'd seen the box, tears running down my face. "Dylan," I shouted. "It's okay, you can come out now. Please."

I reached the pantry and shook my head at the box in the corner, which stood about eighteen inches tall. No way. Too small. I felt the burlap anyway, finding the box inside was far shallower than its sides indicated. Beneath the burlap was hard wood, not a soft body, and I cried out with disappointment. Behind me, I heard Gage coughing.

Would there still be enough time to go upstairs to search for Dylan? Was anything even there? Bailey had referred to it as a glorified loft.

A pinpoint of light came from the bottom of the box through the hard surface under the burlap. My imagination? I grabbed at the box and pulled. It resisted slightly, and then Dylan was blinking at me from the space under the box, holding his flashlight to his chest. At once I understood. Small holes had been drilled in the bottom to allow the air to circulate under the potatoes to keep them fresher. Dylan had turned the box over to have enough space to squeeze into, and what I'd thought was the inside was actually the underside.

The frightened look on his face subsided when he saw me. "It's okay," I said, gathering him into my arms. "Your uncle's here, and we're safe."

"Did you call for me?" he asked.

"Yes."

"I thought Bailey was trying to trick me. Or my mind was doing the tricks." He hiccupped the last words.

I wiped his tears with my undamaged hand. "You're just fine. But your uncle's hurt, and I need your help to get him outside. There's a fire. That's why there's all this smoke."

"We have to crawl," he said. "And get out quick. They said that in school."

"They're right." I'd been edging out of the panty as we talked and at that moment, Dylan saw Gage. Forgetting everything he'd been taught in school, the little boy flew through the smoky air toward Gage. I followed as fast as I could.

"A good hiding place, huh?" Gage said.

Dylan nodded. "Tessa's as good as you are at finding. Maybe better."

"Go open that back door over there, okay?" Gage said. "Crawl."

Dylan scrabbled across the floor like a crab, coughing now. I reached Gage and nudged him. "Ow," he said.

"Get going."

"Anyone ever tell you you're bossy?" He started the painful journey across the peeling linoleum floor.

"My sister."

How such a tiny kitchen could have such a long floor was beyond my understanding. It was like some kind of optical illusion. I crawled one-handed, dragging my hurt leg behind me, goading Gage on with my head or shoulder or whatever was available. Dylan waited at the door, urging us to hurry with encouragement and coughs. We fell on top of him as we rolled out of the house and as far away as we could from the fire, but he didn't seem to mind.

"Better call an ambulance." Gage lay on his back, pressing his hand to his wound.

"She took my phone."

"Mine's in my pocket."

I reached into his back pocket, wanting more than anything to run my hands over him to make sure he had no other serious wounds. The way he and Ridge had gone at each other, he might have internal bleeding as well as the chest wound from the gunshot.

"Here, take this. " Dylan stripped off his shirt and pressed it to his uncle's chest.

Gage smiled. "Thanks. Keep pushing on it hard while Tessa calls, okay?" He looked at me. "What about Bailey?"

"I cut her loose. She got out. Charlie, too."

"Good."

I wondered how he'd feel if he knew she'd chosen her brother over him—again. Did forgiving her mean he still loved her? Now that he'd been cleared of the death, the only thing standing between Gage and Bailey was her past.

And me.

I made the call to 911 and returned Gage's phone to his

pocket, shrinking a little at the intimacy of it all. I wasn't his wife, and yet I felt like I was.

"Tessa." Gage was staring at me.

"What?" I knelt by him and used my good hand to take over from Dylan, my cut wrist pressed once more against my stomach.

Gage winced as I pushed on his chest. Blood had soaked Dylan's shirt, but I thought the flow was easing. I hoped that was because of the pressure and not because he'd lost too much blood.

Dylan turned Charlie's flashlight onto the dirt. "Hey, there are bugs out here." He moved away, following something only he could see.

Gage pulled me down to the weed-stubbled ground next to him, and my hand slipped from Dylan's shirt.

"Stop," I ordered, replacing my hand. "We need to keep pressure on your wound."

His grip didn't ease. "The last thing you said to me in Mia's kitchen was that I'd never find you. Thinking you went to your sister's was bad enough, but after seeing the blood at Bailey's, those words kept playing over and over in my head until I thought I'd go crazy. I knew I'd been the stupidest man alive."

The stars overhead seemed to reverse their course. "What do you mean?"

His face was tight with the pain of his wound, and something else as well. "I mean that I've loved you for a very long time, even when all you could think of was him. Even when I knew there was no possibility of a future or of you looking at me like a man wants to be looked at by a woman."

"You love me?" I felt a little giddy, but that could have been because the stars were dancing above us.

He pulled me closer. "Remember what I said about finding someone someday? Well, it was me all along, and I knew it. I love your laugh, the softness of your skin, the shape of all those freckles, the way your hair turns gold in the sunlight."

Orange, he meant, of course, but I wouldn't correct him now.

"I don't care who your parents are, or that you're a grumpy monster in the mornings, or that you cheat at cards." Between the words he gently pulled me down to kiss my cheeks, my nose, my chin, my eyes. "I love the way you love Serenity and take care of your sister. I can't imagine my life without you in it. I want to spend the rest of my life loving you." He buried his face in my neck, and I could feel the heat of his breath against my skin as he added, "More than anything, I wish that wedding had been real."

"We can remedy that," I murmured. "The first chance we get. We still have the dress." And the silly little ring, which I would never throw away no matter how many diamonds he might buy me to replace it.

"Good." He was breathing heavily at the effort he'd expended, so I leaned over him and pressed my cheek against his, urging him to be still. His hand caressed my neck. Despite the uncomfortable ground and the ache of my own cuts, his touch was all I could think about for a long while.

Take that, Bailey.

Sirens cut through the night, and several feet away,

Dylan jumped up from the ground. "They're coming! They're coming! I'll go out front and wait for them."

"No. Stay here." I didn't know if Bailey and Charlie were out front or if they might hurt him. "I told them where to find us."

Minutes later, two ambulances, a fire truck, and a half-dozen police cars arrived. Soon, they were bandaging Gage and giving him blood right there in the dirt and weeds.

"Was there anyone else out front?" I asked.

"No," said the female EMT.

"How many cars? Two or three?"

"Two."

I looked at Gage. "They got away. After all they did."

He shrugged. "It doesn't matter. I meant what I said when I forgave Bailey. Everything I endured, those six long years—they mean nothing now. They brought me you."

That made my eyes sting with tears, but I was worried about expunging Gage's record. Without Bailey and Charlie's testimony, would there be enough to clear him?

The EMT touched my shoulder. "If it helps, I heard the police say they pulled over a car a few minutes from here. Driving erratically. The man and woman inside smelled like smoke from a fire. They're holding them for questioning."

I sighed with relief. Bailey might not talk right away, but Charlie would.

"If you'll come with me," the EMT said, "I'd like to look at that wrist before we take you both to the hospital."

"Don't forget her leg," Gage grunted.

He was stable enough, but I was afraid to take my eyes off him. I leaned over and kissed him. "I love you," I whispered. "I wish I'd known that last Thanksgiving." Known how I'd feel about him, what we'd mean to each other. Known to look past the exterior mask he'd shown to the world.

"No looking back." His thumb traced my bottom lip. "Only forward."

I nodded and thumped him on the arm. "Okay. But for the record, I do *not* cheat at cards." I waited several heartbeats to add, "Much."

He laughed. "You're still bleeding. Go with the nice lady and get patched up. Please."

Because he asked so nicely, I went.

❤❤ EPILOGUE ❤❤

I'd thought the day would never come, and I'd wondered a million times if waiting so long had been a mistake.

On the night we escaped the burning house, I'd wanted to marry Gage for real right away, but reality soon set in. I needed to be sure our feelings didn't stem from the passion of the moment. Okay, I wanted to make sure *his* feelings didn't stem from the moment, because I knew my feelings were real.

Gage wasn't worried about that so much as making sure the world knew of his innocence. He didn't want people pointing fingers at me behind my back every time we visited his sister in Kingman. He didn't want Dylan to be teased. I couldn't blame him for that.

There were other reasons for the delay—Lily wanted to have her baby so she could dance at my wedding, I decided to go back to school to study psychology, and my parents wanted . . . well, I wasn't sure what they wanted. I didn't ask. I told them I loved Gage and if they wanted to be a part of my life, they'd have to accept my choice.

I tried not to be disappointed when they kept their distance, rejecting Gage and all the notoriety, despite the fact that I'd saved their business. Despite the fact that he'd never hurt anyone. Maybe it was all those wedding gifts my mother had to return.

When our story hit the newspapers, it was big in Arizona, especially in Kingman, but it wasn't until Gage appeared on a national talk show that people in Kingman began stopping him on the street or in the stores to say they'd known that he was innocent all along.

Right.

Gage hated the attention, but he did it for me and his family. Our future family. I hoped the ladies I'd met in the Las Vegas restaurant learned about his false conviction and spread the word. The whole country would know within weeks.

The television appearance also had a huge effect on my parents. My mother backtracked graciously, inviting five hundred of her dearest friends to my wedding reception. Since my father had to foot the dinner bill for all their attendees, I knew his business was doing well.

Dylan was the kid of the hour. For weeks the students crowded around him at school asking for details of his capture and his uncle's miraculous rescue. With each telling, his story grew a bit more wild, though none of us objected. Besides, I liked the new version of my involvement, how I grappled hand-to-hand with Bailey to free us from her evil clutches and then walked through a wall of fire. Gage, of course, fought both Charlie and Ridge—at the same time, wounded, with one arm, in the dark. He was the true hero in Dylan's eyes, exactly the way he should be.

Charlie pleaded guilty and was sentenced to three years in prison. Bailey's case was still pending, but the prosecutor was sure she'd be put away at least ten years. It was less, perhaps, than she deserved, but when I testified against her, she didn't look up from the table where she was sitting, and I felt nothing for her but pity. She was all alone, while I had Gage.

In Flagstaff, I'd been staying with Sadie, who was still my best friend. Taking advantage of my sudden jump to fame, she found me a job as a receptionist for a local psychologist. When I wasn't at school or work, I was with Gage or Serenity. Weekends we spent with either Lily in Phoenix or with Mia in Kingman.

Finally the end of April arrived, seven months after our near fiery death. School was over for the semester, and I was getting married.

"Does it look okay?" I asked Lily, staring into the mirror at the church. Sadie and Lily had swept my hair up on my head, copying the style from the photographs we'd taken in Las Vegas.

"Gorgeous." Lily hugged me. "Beautiful. He won't be able to take his eyes off you. *I* can't take my eyes off you!"

My mother walked into the room. I turned toward her, the hard little ball of nervousness in my stomach doubling in that instant. Then I saw baby Jonny in her arms, and the incongruity of my elegant mother cradling him dissolved the nervousness and made me want to laugh. Her navy dress was glittering and expensive, and

Lily's two-month old son hadn't spit up on her yet, but he was bound to before the hour was out.

I couldn't wait.

"Look who I found hanging out with his daddy," she said in high falsetto, caressing his little cheek with her finger. "Isn't that right, sweetie? Isn't it? Isn't it? But he wanted his grandma. Yes, he did. Yes, he did."

Lily's jaw dropped at my mother's baby talk, but she recovered quickly. "We're ready here. Where's Gage and Mario? And Dad?"

"Outside the door," Sadie answered, peeking out. "Looks like Gage is chomping at the bit to see Tessa. He's pacing."

I smoothed my wedding dress, the same one I'd worn in Vegas, though it didn't need smoothing. The odd feeling in my stomach was back, but now it stemmed more from excitement than nervousness.

Lily hugged me again. "I love you, sis," she whispered. "I just want to say thanks. You've always been there for me. Without you, we would have lost everything."

"Not me. Gage."

He'd paid her mortgage for four months until my parents—and their business—had come around. Next week when I received my funds, we'd pay off the house completely. We had big plans when I finished my degree to buy the land next to her house and turn her small halfway house into a larger operation to help more girls.

"It was both of you." Lily pushed me toward the door. "Hurry, he's waiting."

I stopped only to slip the handle of a small gift bag over my wrist.

Gage's eyes snapped to me as I emerged from the room. I was vaguely aware of my father and Mario, Lily's husband, standing nearby.

"You look . . . incredible," Gage said, drawing me away from the others.

I thought he looked even better in his black tuxedo. "Aren't you supposed to be waiting for me in there?" I motioned to the doors leading into the main room.

"I wanted to see you first. I wanted to tell you—" He broke off and looked back at our small audience before placing his cheek against mine, angling his face toward my neck, his voice lowering. "Tessa, I know we needed to do this for real and for our families, but I have to confess that a big part of me is missing that day in Vegas when it was just us."

I knew exactly what he meant. At that moment, I wanted to get behind him on his motorcycle and drive off into the sunset, just the two of us. It would be easy since Calvin was expecting us at the Lover's Lane Hotel and Chapel, where we were spending our honeymoon.

"Since that day, it's always been you," Gage continued. "Well, actually long before that, but that's when I finally admitted it to myself. And it will always be you. Always."

Tears started in my eyes, and I blinked to stop them from falling and ruining Lily's makeup job. He smiled at me, and I knew I didn't have to say a word, that it was all there in my eyes.

Gage leaned in tighter and kissed my neck, his thumb teasing the new ring on my finger. Not the one from Lover's Lane Hotel, though I was wearing that one, too, on my right hand. He took a breath. "Okay, we can go."

"Wait." I removed a short length of blue silk from the gift bag on my wrist, letting the bag fall to the ground. "Look what I brought for you."

He gave a low chuckle, his hand running over the silk and lace. "Mia's present. I've been wondering where that got to."

I winked at him and pushed the nighty into the pocket of his tuxedo. With a low growl in his throat, he kissed me again.

Behind him I could see my father looking at my mother, baby Jonny still in her arms. He took her hand in his. I doubted things would ever really change between them, but they had forgiven Lily enough to talk to her, and they were at my wedding behaving like normal grandparents.

For today, my day, it was enough.

Rachel Branton has worked in publishing for over twenty years. She loves writing women's fiction and traveling, and she hopes to write and travel a lot more. As a mother of seven, it's not easy to find time to write, but the semi-ordered chaos gives her a constant source of writing material. She's been known to wear pajamas all day when working on a deadline, and is often distracted enough to burn dinner. (Okay, pretty much 90% of the time.) A sign on her office door reads: Danger. Enter at Your Own Risk. Writer at Work. Under the name Rachel Branton, she writes romance, romantic suspense, and women's fiction. Rachel also writes urban fantasy, paranormal romance, and science fiction under the name Teyla Branton. For more information or to sign up to hear about new releases, please visit www.RachelBranton.com.

Made in the USA
Monee, IL
11 May 2022

96223098R00157